"Don't play with me, lass," Devlin growled, his words harsh. "It could lead to serious business."

"But I'm entirely serious," Alyssa countered. Her inviting smile transformed her into the most desirable woman Devlin had ever encountered. She ran splayed fingers along his broad shoulders and was satisfied with the shudder she felt beneath her touch.

"I'll not steal anything that should, by rights, belong to your husband," Devlin ground out, the cords of his neck bulging and prominent as he fought for self-restraint.

"You cannot steal what is freely given, Devlin Fitzhugh." The words were a whisper on the wind.

"But there can be no future for us, Alyssa. Surely you understand that."

"All the more reason to enjoy the present," she murmured, her lips seeking his once more.

At the firm pressure of her mouth, Devlin's resolve began to crumble....

D1449031

Dear Reader,

The team of authors who write as Erin Yorke returns to one of their most popular settings this month with *Devlin*, an emotional tale set in Ireland and England. It's the story of an Irish rebel who saves the life of an Englishwoman and is captured by the English for his efforts. The young woman rescues him from prison, but the two of them must battle distrust and betrayal before finding the happiness they deserve.

Deborah Simmons also returns this month with *The de Burgh Bride*, the sequel to her steamy adventure, *Taming the Wolf*. This book is the story of the scholarly de Burgh brother, Geoffrey, who has drawn the short straw and must marry the "wicked" daughter of a vanquished enemy, a woman who reportedly murdered her first husband in the marriage bed!

A city banker forced to spend a year recuperating in the country goes head-to-head with a practical country widow and learns that some of life's greatest pleasures are the simple ones, in Theresa Michaels's next book in her new Western series, *The Merry Widows—Catherine*. And corruption, jealousy and the shadow of barrenness threaten the love of a beautiful Saxon woman who has a year to produce an heir, or be separated forever from the knight who holds her heart, in Shari Anton's stirring medieval tale, *By King's Decree*.

Whatever your tastes in reading, we hope you enjoy all four books this month. Keep an eye out for them, wherever Harlequin Historicals® are sold.

Sincerely,

Tracy Farrell
Senior Editor

DEVLIN

Erin
Yorke

Harlequin Books

TORONTO • NEW YORK • LONDON
AMSTERDAM • PARIS • SYDNEY • HAMBURG
STOCKHOLM • ATHENS • TOKYO • MILAN
MADRID • WARSAW • BUDAPEST • AUCKLAND

ISBN 0-373-29002-0

DEVLIN

Copyright © 1998 by Susan McGovern Yansick and Christine Healy

Books by Erin Yorke

Harlequin Historicals

An American Beauty #58
Forever Defiant #94
Heaven's Gate #124
Dangerous Deceptions #152
Bound by Love #176
Counterfeit Laird #202
The Honor Price #239
Desert Rogue #285
Devlin #402

ERIN YORKE

is the pseudonym used by the writing team of Susan Yansick and Christine Healy. One half of the team is married, the mother of two sons and suburban, and the other is single, fancy-free and countryfied. They find that their differing lives and styles enrich their writing with a broader perspective.

For Gary—
You were really patient with this one

And for Chris and Dave, who learned to fend for
themselves

Thanks for understanding. You're the heroes in my life.

And

For Natasha Antonova Smith

Who went from "a wonderful life" to "pretty woman" in
three weeks. May the happiness you found here follow
you home to Russia.

Chapter One

Ireland, 1593

Lying in the belly of a trench near Dublin Castle, Devlin Fitzhugh felt a chill travel along his spine that had nothing to do with the briskness of the mist-shrouded night. The sensation was so odd and unfamiliar that he was bewildered for an instant until he recognized it for what it was. He swore softly in the darkness. He hadn't been plagued by fear before a skirmish since he was a stripling lad.

Slowly, he released his pent-up breath while he awaited the signal that would begin the raid. Yet try as he might, Devlin couldn't shake the sense of foreboding that tingled along the base of his skull. He didn't have to ask himself why a man who had charged recklessly into battle innumerable times before should suddenly feel trepidation. He knew the source. It was the child the Macguires had recently brought to camp. The one they maintained he had fathered. The one they insisted was now his responsibility.

There was no reason to dispute their claim. Muirne's coppery hair and the single dimple she sported in her left cheek echoed his own, loudly bespeaking her bloodlines. But what was he to do with a motherless mite no more than three years of age? He had never had ties other than those he owed his lord, yet here was an obligation of a different sort, one that prevented him from tendering unconditional allegiance to any chieftain, even Eamon MacMahon. The idea perplexed him and filled him with guilt. He was at a loss as to how to deal with it, but he would have no choice other than to do so once he rescued young Niall and returned him to his father's camp.

His determination to sort out his life, however, did nothing to bring Devlin peace. The lethal calm he always experienced before battle continued to elude him. Somewhere in the back of his mind, worry still ate at his warrior's resolve. Muirne had but lately lost her mother. What if she lost her father as well? What if he didn't return from the impending fray? Devlin pushed the possibility from his mind. Surely thinking such a thing would make it so. Quickly, he crossed himself, as though to ward off evil.

"Your prayers won't help Niall or any of us," came a derisive voice at Devlin's side.

"Perhaps, but they won't bring about any harm, either," Devlin responded gruffly. He stared straight ahead into the darkness, resisting the urge to throttle Cashel MacMahon, Eamon's nephew and foster son.

No other man would dare speak to him in such a manner.

"That remains to be seen, Fitzhugh. It's beyond me why the MacMahon, wounded though he is, would entrust *you* with the task of seeing to my cousin's deliverance. Wasn't it your fault the boy was taken in the first place? He was riding with you when the attack took place."

"You don't have to understand anything other than you're to remain silent and await the sign that the North Gate is open. And when it does come, you'll do as I tell you," Devlin replied through gritted teeth. His voice held a deadly calm that would have quieted most men. Yet Cashel pressed on.

"And if I don't?"

"Then you put the rest of us and our success at risk. Should that be the case, I will have to kill you." Devlin stated his intent matter-of-factly, ignoring the attention his whispered words had earned from the others. His hand snaked back to rest lightly on the hilt of his dagger. He'd not permit Cashel's unfounded pride to bring more disaster down upon their heads.

"Aye—allow the MacMahon's son to be captured and then slay the foster son. Mayhap you want both Niall and me out of the way so Eamon will consider naming you his heir," Cashel spit. His brown eyes glittered in the darkness as he looked to the rest of the rescue party for support. Receiving none, he became angrier. "I've never trusted you, Fitzhugh."

"'Tis wise to distrust a man who dislikes you,"

Devlin said casually, though a lethal note attended his words all the same. "And at the moment, I find I dislike you intensely."

"Hold your tongue, Cashel," urged Sean. "Your grudge sounds as if it is founded in naught but your own jealousy."

"Founded in my rightful anger, you mean, an anger derived from Fitzhugh's failure to safeguard my foster brother. The gallowglass is an outsider—a hired sword—no blood kin to us. It was bad enough that Eamon trusted him with teaching Niall the ways of warfare, allowing such a one to usurp a task that by rights should have been mine. Fitzhugh couldn't keep the boy safe within our own territory. What makes the MacMahon, or any of you, think he can snatch Niall from the clutches of the English now that they have imprisoned the lad?"

"Because I vow by all that's holy, I'll move heaven and earth to return Eamon's son to him," Devlin growled as his fingers itched to unsheathe the dagger they clutched.

"Promises! You're good with those, but with little else. Your newfound brat is testimony to that. What promises did you make to her mother when you lay with her?"

"Silence, man!" warned Dugal as Devlin's fury blazed across his face. But Cashel ignored the caution, bent on his attempt to belittle Devlin in front of the MacMahon's men.

"I know I would have lain down my life to protect Niall, yet it was no great surprise to me, Fitzhugh, that you returned to camp alive to tell your tale of ambush. I should slay you now for your cowardice. But I am a rational man and will leave justice to the clan. At present, I will do no more than relieve you of your command, and assume leadership for this raid."

Devlin could control himself no longer. Quickly, his knife sliced through the night air, a muted flash of reflected moonlight. The weapon's point lightly grazed Cashel's neck in warning, leaving a scratch that could as easily have been a mortal slash.

"If my words fail to make an impression, then perhaps my blade shall," Devlin hissed. "Understand once and for all, Cashel MacMahon, that I am in charge here. I'll tolerate your insubordination and insults no longer. Now, will I have to spill Irish blood before I take on the English, or have I your word you'll do as I bid in order to rescue Niall?"

"Aye, you have it," came Cashel's sullen and begrudging reply. "But may God have mercy on you if you don't succeed, because I will show you none."

Then the signal for which they had been waiting sounded, and there was no more to be said.

"I'm no less a prisoner than the Irish he has been sent to convey to England," fumed Alyssa. She tossed back her long blond hair as she paced her temporary apartment within the walls of Dublin Castle, her violet eyes flashing in anger.

Just recently torn from the only home she'd ever known by a father she couldn't even remember,

Alyssa Howett found being answerable to the capricious whims of this stranger quite difficult, especially when she despised the man who sought to tame her.

Shortly after Alyssa's birth, Cecil Howett had nonchalantly assigned her care to his sister-in-law in Ireland. For the seventeen years since then, he had furthered his career in England without giving her a thought. Now, on her aunt's death, he had arrived to move his daughter to London. Well, if he expected her to go willingly, to leave the country she considered her home for the one that had seen her birth, he was a fool, in Alyssa's opinion. He had already curtailed her liberty, going so far as to decree that she was not to leave the room assigned to her in Dublin Castle without his permission. What sort of life would she have with him in London? The thought terrified her. The devil take the man! She owed him no obedience.

Perhaps he had sired her as he claimed, but he'd never raised her, had never loved her. In truth, Alyssa suspected, he had only come at this juncture because her aunt's death had coincided with an order from Queen Elizabeth to transport prisoners from Dublin to London. Turning abruptly toward the high windows, Alyssa yanked their coverings aside and stared up at the dark sky overhead.

"Without the Irish moon and the dreams my heart spawned here, I will never survive in England," she moaned, her words a soft echo in the nearly silent room. "But what more can I do to convince him not to take me to England? He ignores my arguments and hasn't responded to either my pleas or my tears.''

Only the crackle of the fire and the whisper of the rushes underfoot broke the hush, a quiet Alyssa found mournful rather than comforting. She had lost her aunt but days before and still the Englishman who called her daughter showed Alyssa no mercy, expecting her to do his bidding without question. The monster had to be stopped!

Again Alyssa began to move, her dainty slippers making barely a sound as her feet wove irregular patterns back and forth across the floor of her private rooms in Dublin Castle. Her tread was so light the scent of the herb-strewn grass was barely noticeable as she recrossed the aromatic straw. The candles threw her shadow on one barren wall and then the next.

"Just because he suddenly considers me his parental responsibility I must be uprooted and taken to rot in that cold, dank country he calls home? Truly I warrant, the only thing Cecil Howett cares about is his duty to the queen. Family is clearly secondary or this father of mine would have come for me years ago,'' she mused, chewing her lower lip.

"Still, if I were as rebellious as the Irish he has been ordered to transport to English prisons, how long would he wish to keep me in his company? Wouldn't he prefer to see such a disobedient daughter banished from the public eye to waste away in exile—in Ireland perhaps?''

The thought of it made Alyssa smile, girlish hope

bursting forth to light her delicate features like a bea-
con of sunlight escaping a cloud-filled sky. There was
no certainty that her scheme would work, but at least
it was better than simply waiting for the ship to England to sail with her as an undocumented prisoner.

What would make the man truly, irrevocably furious with her? So furious he would leave her behind
as punishment.

Inspiration struck. She would openly defy him before the whole of Dublin Castle.

Not only would she leave her rooms, but tonight
she would visit the Irish prisoners in their cells, bringing them warm blankets. Then, tomorrow morning
when the royal jail was adither with questions of who
was helping the rebels, she'd boldly cross the bailey
to bring them extra food. She would do whatever was
necessary to thwart her father's will, and keep on doing so no matter how many lectures she received on
being dutiful. He would be forced to renounce her,
forced to leave her behind. Having a daughter who
was sympathetic to the Irish rebels wouldn't further
his career in the service of the queen. It would end
it.

Glancing around the simple apartment, the girl
spied the bed drapings and grinned. Closely woven to
keep out the night drafts, they would surely keep in
a body's warmth. And they'd be more practical to cart
across the courtyard than the feather mattress that
covered her bed.

The way the men on guard duty had stared at her
when she and her father had arrived at the castle left

Alyssa no doubt that a winsome smile and an inch or two of exposed ankle would get her exactly where she wanted. And, after all, when she was found out, her excuse was simple. As a softhearted country lass, she was merely making the prisoners more comfortable. What was the crime in that?

Quickly Alyssa unfastened the draperies and bundled them tightly. They weighed more than she had anticipated, but perhaps one of the guards would carry them for her once she got to the tower where the cells were located. She opened the door and slipped into the dimly lit hallway.

"Cecil Howett," she murmured, "before I'm through, you'll pray to leave me in Ireland."

The inky black sky barely acknowledged the pale slip of moon as Devlin and his party moved silently through the obsidian shadows toward Dublin Castle. For a moment, the Irishman fretted, wondering if the English might have secured Niall elsewhere. However, he quickly discarded the idea. The English wouldn't expect the MacMahon to know of his son's capture yet, much less mount an effort to free him. No, Niall would be secured in the South Tower where Irish rebels were always imprisoned, Devlin assured himself.

When he and the others reached the small side gate standing open as promised, he and Cashel moved as one, flying across the open courtyard to the door where the English stood watch, unsuspecting of their enemy's approach.

As contrary as Cashel might be, he was a skilled fighter, Devlin had to admit as they dragged the fallen guards from their station and, moments later, waved the others forward to join them.

Crossing the threshold of the tower, Devlin again blessed himself, still feeling the need of extra protection. The strange uneasiness continued to ride his shoulders. The gallowglass glanced behind him, his eyes missing no detail, but the MacMahon forces were doing just as ordered. Yet his senses remained heightened, his nerves stretched taut beyond all reason.

Niall could not be freed without taking a risk though, and Devlin would be the last man in Ireland to willingly avoid his duty for some superstitious chill. Castles were always drafty, he told himself, disregarding the fact that he'd felt the qualms outside as well. With a shake of his coppery head, he signaled the others to follow as he inched up the stone stairs to the cells at the top.

Given its sixteen-foot-thick walls, no one could burn the tower down, let alone undermine its massive plinth. Would that stealth and subterfuge could succeed where force might not, Devlin prayed.

With his sweetly voiced offer of warm drink, Dugal's girlish tones and slight figure disguised in borrowed skirts ought to distract the guards stationed on the upper level. Once that was done, the worst would be over.

"Thirsty, men?" asked Dugal from the shadows as the guards leaped to their feet, knives ready.

"Where's Hawkins? He always comes up with our drinks at night," protested the watchman. "We're not expecting any visitors."

"I'm not a visitor. I'm just delivering th-this warm cider," stammered Dugal, his soft tones slipping.

"So you claim. Take off that shawl and let us see your face," ordered the Englishman. "Then we'll decide if we're thirsty."

Without hesitation Devlin sprang forward from the dusky stairs. The ruse had worked long enough for his men to join him. Now was the time for skilled fighters to take over.

"Why, you—"

As the Englishman grabbed Dugal, a flash of silver flew through the air, unnoticed in the poor light. Cashel's knife easily found its mark, burying itself in the speaker's neck and leaving him gasping for air, his arms freeing Dugal to clutch at the embedded blade. Instantly Cashel was on his victim, stabbing him once more until the guard fell to the floor, the first man dead in the raid.

"Take the keys, free whomever you want," the second jailor cried.

"Check the cells for Niall," ordered Devlin, catching the ring and tossing it to Sean as Cashel approached the other guard with murder in his eyes.

"Cashel, leave him. Niall is more important—"

"Here I am, Devlin," called a weak voice.

Devlin turned and relaxed for the first time in three days. Niall was alive—filthy, clearly frightened but thankfully upright and moving under his own power.

"Are you all right then, lad?" As the boy emerged from the darkness, Devlin wrapped Eamon's son in a warm embrace.

"I'll do."

"Thanks be to God," Devlin murmured. "Let's go home."

"We must take those fellows along," Niall explained, gesturing to the other prisoners already fleeing the jail.

"As you say," agreed Devlin, "at least until we're outside the castle. No matter what his crimes, no Irishman deserves to stay in this English hellhole."

Suddenly a bell tolled, echoing in the yard as Cashel and Devlin exchanged glances.

"They must have found the guards at the gate. We've no time to waste," urged Devlin. "Down the stairs to the passage in the north wall. Niall, don't stop for anyone or anything."

Going first in order to protect Niall, Devlin descended the steps with his sword and dagger drawn. In all his life, he'd never had a presentiment of disaster as strong as this. Every nerve in his body was alert, every sense working to anticipate what might lie at the foot of the circular stair.

"Hurry," he called over his shoulder. As shouts in the bailey resounded off the stone walls, he increased his already quick pace. "Tell the others it's each man for himself, but all of us for the MacMahon's son. I'll try to distract pursuit."

Then, unbelievably, he had reached the ground. Taking a deep breath, Devlin opened the door to the outer corridor, only to be nearly bowled over by a mound of moving fabric that hit him like a heavy blue cloud.

"Ho! What?" His breath knocked from him, he could only motion the men to go without him while he disentangled himself from the folds of material and the squirming form beneath them.

"Devlin?" questioned Niall anxiously.

"Go quickly now. I'll join you later," Devlin ordered, pleased the boy hesitated only briefly before obeying.

"Get your hands off me, sir, or I'll have you jailed," warned a feminine voice from beneath the unwieldy draperies as she attempted to free herself from them.

It had taken Alyssa longer than she expected to leave the main part of the castle. Then there had been that loud clanging noise erupting out of nowhere that startled her and made her drop the cloth earlier—where there had been no guards about to assist her. It had seemed like ages until she had been able to pick up the bed hangings, and here they were all over the floor again, no thanks to the dolt towering above her, an Irishman from the sound of him.

Raising her eyes so she could give him a piece of her mind, Alyssa stopped short. A man, a tall giant of a man, with red hair and angry blue eyes glared down at her, weapons in both of his hands.

"Sir, you might have killed me—" She gulped, her eyes wide with trepidation. Could these be escaping prisoners? Her father would turn murderer himself if she got involved with them—and she would be his victim!

Then another figure darted forward, yanked her to her feet and shoved her in front of him toward the door.

"She can be a hostage for us—just as they took Niall," rejoiced Cashel. He needed to escape the castle immediately, before his part in the crime was discovered. No Englishman would be able to identify just which Irishman had placed the woman in jeopardy, and if he were taken, he'd say it had been Devlin's idea.

"No, let her go. She's hardly more than a child," protested Devlin. He grabbed for the man, but Cashel was already through the door with the girl, leaving Devlin no choice but to follow.

"My daughter! My God, they have my daughter," cried an anguished voice as they headed across the bailey. "Tell your men to be careful."

"My men will do what they must in order to recapture the prisoners," said the governor of the prison. No one, English or Irish, had ever escaped his jail alive and he'd be damned before one did tonight. "Get MacMahon, lads! There's a healthy bounty on the boy, and there'll be more for every Irishman you take, whatever his name."

They swarmed from nowhere, swore Devlin, dodging right and left to avoid the onslaught until he could catch Cashel and the female. Then, they fought their way nearly across the compound, while steel clanging loudly upon steel shattered the night. Every moment brought more English soldiers to the skirmish. But Devlin knew he and the others couldn't yield and live.

Methodically, the gallowglass worked his way toward his goal, the escape route in the north wall, engaging one after the other of Her Majesty's troops, relishing the victory of each step that brought him closer to freedom. Hard put to follow the movements of all under his command, he was nonetheless aware of several Irishmen making their way through the gate into the safety beyond Dublin Castle.

"Please, God, let Niall be among them," he whispered.

Cashel, however, was still within the bailey, having a difficult time of it. Maintaining his hold upon the girl, the fool was keeping her all too close to the fighting for Devlin's taste. If she were killed, they'd have an innocent child's murder on their heads.

"Release the lass!" Devlin roared above the din. Once she had scurried away, he and Cashel could no doubt slash their way out of the English stronghold.

"Devil the girl! I won't give up my life for hers," Cashel balked. "She's our only hope of getting out."

"I'm ordering you to let her go," Devlin roared, fending off one attacking English sword after another as he moved forward, still monitoring Cashel's progress.

All at once Cashel, near the open gate, obeyed, roughly casting his hostage away from him and flying toward safety.

Yet Devlin cursed him as Eamon's foster son, in his haste to turn tail and run, sent the girl tumbling to the ground, directly into the path of numerous English soldiers, swords drawn to slash anyone between them and their quarry.

"Keep down, lass," he ordered, eyeing his own tenuous path to freedom as the guards circled nearer.

But the trembling girl ignored his warning and scrambled to her feet, ready to flee, only to put herself directly in the way of a descending English blade.

Instinctively, and without a thought as to the consequences, Devlin moved to block the brainless female from the English weapon rather than continue in the direction of the gate. Swiftly, his muscle-laden arm reached out to thrust her behind him before the point of a sword could inadvertently end her life.

His protective action took no more than an instant, but it was an instant that Devlin did not possess. Suddenly the gallowglass found himself encircled by the enemy, and all hope of escape vanished. The girl was pulled out of range and half a dozen blades took aim.

"Take him alive," commanded an authoritative voice. "I want to know who is responsible for this outrage."

Devlin fought like a man possessed, hacking wildly, striking out in futile desperation, welcoming the heavy thud of his sword against others. But his feverish assault was to no avail. His route to freedom had been sealed off, Cashel the last man through. The gate was forever beyond him.

Still, the Irishman would not concede the inevitability of his capture. Eight men surrounded him, their swords slashing freely at his arms and face. Blood dripping, he defended himself more valiantly than ever. Yet even his great strength could do no more than stave off for a few moments a fate that could not be altered.

Eventually he was subdued, though it took near a score of men to hold Devlin while the shackles were clamped around his wrists and ankles. Once he was securely fettered and yanked to his feet, the soft clinking of his chains echoed desolately in the night air as he looked around him in frenzied disbelief.

The ground was littered with five fallen English and only one of the men under his command. The girl he had saved stood enfolded within the arms of a middle-aged Englishman, who gave rein to freely flowing tears. She regarded the man with a baffled look before she slowly rested her head upon his chest, allowing the fellow to clasp her more tightly.

Devlin wanted to bellow his rage. Now that he had been taken as punishment for his good deed, who would be there to comfort *his* daughter as the English wench was being comforted? The answer was stark and grim: no one!

He had consigned Muirne to existence as an orphan. There were none to protect her as her father would have done, nor would any love her as intensely. Devlin agonized at the inequity of it. But whom did he have to blame for his predicament? No one other than himself. And that galled him all the more.

Groaning, he reviled his soft heart and even softer head, having traded his daughter's future for that of a witless Englishwoman too stupid to get out of harm's way. Cursing himself for being the greatest fool God had ever fashioned, Devlin saw the girl turn in his direction. When her shy glance traveled across the crowd to meet his, he spit in disgust. Resentment rose like bile in his throat, so that coldly, without a hint of compunction, Devlin Fitzhugh damned her and then damned himself as well.

Chapter Two

The morning was young, and remnants of last night's struggle were still visible in the bailey below Alyssa's window. Though the inhabitants of the castle sought to return things to normal, a sense of upset hung heavily in the air. Nowhere was it more pervasive than in Alyssa's bedchamber, where the distraught girl fought to blink back tears.

Though she had troubles aplenty of her own the fate of the Irishman who had saved her life touched her heart. And now, because of her, the brave, comely gallowglass was confined in the tower. Devlin Fitzhugh was his name...or so the charges read.

Remorse plagued the girl's heart. Who knew what awaited him? 'Twas not meet that so fine a man should have to endure suffering as a result of her defiance against her father, a defiance that now appeared childish and shallow when she considered the consequences it had wrought.

The point had been brought home when she had seen her Irish savior dragged away. His thick, coppery hair and his proud, sullen face had captured the early light of dawn so that he was aglow with fierceness, despite the wounds he had sustained. The sight of him had caused Alyssa's breath to catch in her throat. He appeared a magnificent rebel, a man who should be free roaming the green hills of his homeland, not destined for an English jail or worse.

Alyssa shuddered. By comparison, her own future suddenly seemed not so bleak. The look of horror on her father's face when she had been in danger, the tears of joy he had shed when he had clasped her to him after she had reached safety, surely indicated that he felt at least some fondness for her, that he was not the complete ogre she had imagined him to be. Still, how could such a sentiment be reconciled with the unalterable fact that he had abandoned her following her mother's death in childbirth? That he had sent her off to Ireland with his sister and never once come to see her?

The relationship with her father, life in England, the fate of the man in the tower—there were so many emotions swirling around in Alyssa's troubled heart. Mindlessly brushing back a blond tendril that had escaped to nestle in the hollow of her cheek, she began to pace her quarters, but dozens of repetitions did nothing to soothe her. Instead, her upset and bafflement only increased with each step.

Finally, a frustrated Alyssa threw herself down onto a straight-backed wooden chair beside a small table. Wearily, she propped her elbows on its worn surface, closed her eyes and leaned her head against her folded hands. Life had been so simple a few months ago. Nay, even last night, before she had visited the cells, her situation had not been as complex. How could it have worsened so much within so little time? Things had been bad enough without more trouble finding her. Once again, the image of shackles on the strong arms that had defended her wrenched Alyssa's heart. Oh, trouble hadn't found her, she thought with self-disgust, she had gone looking for it. If only she could do something to gain the Irishman's liberty, or at the very least ease his plight. Perhaps if she spoke to her father...

Alyssa's thoughts were interrupted by the squeak of a hinge and the sound of her door slowly swinging inward. A masculine footfall stopped beside her, and then warm, compassionate fingers swept a strand of hair back from her forehead before coming to rest atop the crown of her head.

"Your mother had hair as beautiful yet unruly as yours," her father said quietly. Heartened that the girl had not batted his hand away as she would have a few days ago, Cecil patted her shoulder awkwardly before settling himself in the chair on the opposite side of the table. He was finding it exceedingly difficult to shoulder the day-to-day responsibilities of fatherhood so late in life.

When she raised her head and regarded him somberly, Cecil was concerned that Alyssa's arresting violet eyes were made more vivid by the pale lavender smudges staining the delicate skin beneath them. Like her mother, she had the look of a fragile female, he mused, and the girl had endured much of late. Then he reminded himself that there was a fire beneath Alyssa's surface with which he had become all too well acquainted these past few days. It was a blaze that tempered her spirit and gave her a strength her mother, God have mercy on her, had never possessed. Even now, there was the look of protest etched upon the lass's pretty features, and Cecil chided himself for thinking that the comfort she had accepted from him immediately after her near tragedy had forever changed things between them.

"Do not compare me to my mother, sirrah. You've sworn to me how very precious she was to you. Speaking of the two of us in the same breath only emphasizes my own inconsequential standing in your eyes."

"Daughter, what must I do to make you believe that you are just as dear to me?" Howett asked, reaching out to capture one of Alyssa's restless hands in his own.

"If that were true, Father, then you reward those who preserve my life quite oddly."

"The Irishman..." Cecil muttered with a sigh. "Try to understand, Alyssa."

"What is there for me to comprehend other than that you have helped punish the man who saved me from falling victim to a sword?"

"I have spoken to Governor Newcomb and done all I can for Fitzhugh. Isn't it enough that he's alive at the moment?" Cecil demanded. "In truth, the rebel should have been immediately beheaded, if not garroted, for his crimes against the queen.''

"The queen! Your duty to Elizabeth always provides you with an adequate excuse whenever your actions are questionable," Alyssa shot back heatedly, withdrawing her hand from her father's grasp.

"Her Majesty is not a sovereign to be thwarted, Alyssa. 'Tis a lesson you should commit to heart before you set foot in England. To fail to do so is to court disaster," Cecil replied, his voice stern.

"Is that why you always put your loyalty to the queen above all else? Above my mother? Above me?"

"I've told you I had no choice! When our sovereign commanded me to accompany her envoy to the Lowlands as his secretary, what could I do but go? Had I refused, I could have been thrown in the Tower, and both you and your mother left to live in poverty. As it is, your dam did not live to see my return home. But you were waiting for me," Cecil said. His words were drenched in wistful nostalgia, as though he truly did wish that things might have been different.

"A scant two months later, I was informed that my service had pleased Her Majesty, and I was to be sent abroad again. I knew that such an order precipitated a career to be spent in foreign lands. Was I to take you, an infant, with me? Expose your tender, young life to the hazards of constant travel? I had just lost my wife, I would not lose you as well. Nor did I want to see you grow to womanhood among the intrigues of various royal courts. No, as much as I wanted you beside me, I could not be that selfish. Instead, I consigned you to the care of my sister, a loving woman whose own two children had died. Even though she was slated to settle in Ireland, it seemed to be in your best interests at the time. You must believe me, Alyssa. It was because I loved you that I gave you away. If I was in error, I apologize.''

''But why didn't you visit me? Why didn't you write?'' Alyssa asked.

''What excuse can I possibly offer, my dear? Elizabeth kept me too busy to travel on my own behalf. And by the time you were old enough to read, I had hardened my heart to the pain of our separation. Perhaps I was simply too cowardly to open myself to the anguish again. But now, my years of service have been rewarded. I have been given a post in England, and after I see these Irish rebels safely in English jails, I can once more establish a home. I wish to have you there with me.''

Alyssa wanted to believe him. In fact, she yearned to do so. But the sense of rejection she had known as a child would not permit it until her father had proved himself to her.

''If you care for me as you say you do, Father, then how can you stand by and watch the Irishman who saved me be condemned to imprisonment?'' Alyssa asked stubbornly.

''Don't you think I wanted to thank your impulsive rescuer, to send him on his way laden with gold and jewels? I did. But I have neither the authority nor riches to do so, regardless of what is in my heart. The rogue led an assault on Dublin Castle, Alyssa! Soldiers of the crown were slain. Political prisoners were released, some of whom I was charged with transporting to England. And because the chaos your Irishman caused began at the cell of Eamon MacMahon's son, we have to assume he's in league with the MacMahon himself.''

"The MacMahon?''

"Aye, a right troublesome rebel, a traitorous Irish nobleman who has been stripped of his lands and wealth by the queen. The MacMahon and his band live as outlaws. To have kept his son in captivity would have been to curtail his lawless behavior and acts of aggression against the crown. But your gallowglass saw to that, didn't he? Why, his association with Eamon MacMahon is, in itself, reason for execution. I had it within my power to keep him from immediate death but little else. It was beyond me to gain his liberty. As it was, it took more than an hour of heated words with Governor Newcomb to convince him to march Fitzhugh to the tower rather than the block.''

"What did you say?'' Alyssa asked, curiosity overcoming her reluctance to prolong any conversation with the man who was her sire. Though Fitzhugh's execution had been a dim possibility, it had not been one she had considered seriously. Who would take the life of so heroic a man?

"I asserted that Fitzhugh was due some clemency for saving the daughter of Her Majesty's representative.''

"And Newcomb agreed?"

"No…not entirely. I'm afraid we arrived at a stalemate. But I managed to convince him it was unwise to act hastily. Since I am not scheduled to leave Ireland until the end of the month, when the prisoners from the outlying districts have been brought to Dublin and placed in my care, we have decided to lay the matter before the queen. A missive has been sent detailing events. The Irishman will be safe from Newcomb's wrath at least until we receive Her Majesty's reply."

"But what if…if…" Alyssa faltered in her question, her eyes growing round with horror.

"There, there, daughter, you're not to worry. The queen will show mercy. The rebel will most likely be imprisoned in England for a time, but at least he will be alive," Cecil assured her, silently praying his words contained some truth.

"How can you be so certain?"

"Do you have to ask? My dealings with Elizabeth over the years have given me some insight into her character. I promise, the Irishman's life will be spared," Cecil contended. Receiving the queen's decision in the matter was a few weeks away, but the moment to soothe his daughter was now, to make her see he was not the monster she had painted him and that life with him would not be so unhappy as she anticipated.

"And if your recommendation holds no sway with the queen, what will we do?" Alyssa whispered, her fair face paler than usual.

"I beg that you trust me, daughter," Cecil Howett implored with an intensity that oddly enough tugged at Alyssa's heart. "Your Irishman will be spared. I give you my word."

"Then I thank you, Father," Alyssa said stiffly, still uncertain as to whether or not she could believe his promises.

"Your gratitude may be misplaced, sweetling," Cecil Howett said with a weary shake of his gray head, glad the discussion seemed to be drawing to an end. "With conditions being what they are in English jails, it could well have been more merciful to have permitted your Irishman's execution."

"Nay, Father! You did the right thing, and I pray you will continue to do all within your power to keep him safe," Alyssa replied fervently. She thought about placing a tentative kiss on Cecil's cheek to seal their bargain, but hastily decided against it. She was not yet willing to chance allowing this stranger into her heart. It was a further complication she didn't need when she had more pressing things to tend to. While her father saw to it that Fitzhugh remained alive, it would be up to her to bring Devlin solace as best she could. Surely she owed him that much, and never had debt seemed such a light burden.

Though Devlin had been confined for nearly eighteen hours, his violent rage at his predicament had yet to leave him, and he savagely yanked at his confining chains. Strong as he was, his efforts were to no avail. But he could not stop himself from trying to pull the

links free of the large iron ring embedded in the wall
through which his shackles had been laced. He knew
he would not cease his attempts until he fell victim
to exhaustion. Then, perhaps, sleep would overcome
him and in sweet oblivion he would find peace of
sorts, transitory though it would be.

Once more he tugged at his chains, gritting his
teeth and silently cursing the impulsiveness that had
landed him where he was. A score of thoughts raced
through his head. He wondered whether Niall had escaped safely, and pondered his own fate, but mostly
he thought of Muirne and what would become of her
in his absence. Oh, he knew the MacMahon would
see the child fed and sheltered as best he could. But
food was not always plentiful in the rebel camp and
starvation was certainly no stranger to Ireland since a
handful of English had stolen lands that had once fed
thousands. Besides, a girl could not grow up rough-
and-tumble in a camp as he had done, without proper
guardians to see to her welfare. If she managed to
survive at all, she would likely end up as her mother
had, bearing someone's bastard and succumbing to an
early death.

The idea of it ate at Devlin's very soul, though he
barely knew his daughter, and he almost groaned his
grief aloud when he considered the life the child
would be forced to live.

He had been nothing more than a softhearted fool
not to have turned Maeve away when she had crept
beneath his blanket one dark, moonlit night. He had
never decided whether it had been the frost on the

ground or the ice surrounding his own heart that had
seen him shivering with cold that evening. The only
thing of which he was certain was that it had seemed
natural to accept the warmth Maeve had offered. But
he should have resisted temptation. Then there would
have been no child to suffer because he had been
captured.

More enraged with himself than before, Devlin had
never looked so fierce. He was about to begin his
futile pulling at the iron ring once again when he
heard a scurrying in the darkness, much too loud to
be that of one of the rats with whom he shared the
tower. Quickly, he got to his feet. He'd not appear
cowed before his English captors.

Taking a proud stance, Devlin wondered what fresh
torture was about to befall him. So far, he had not
answered any of the questions he had been asked
about the MacMahon or the location of his camp.
Would the English employ the lash or the hot iron to
bend him to their will? The method mattered not. He
would fight submission until he lost consciousness, or
at least, he prayed he would.

Suddenly, out of the darkness, stepped a willowy
female form. Devlin muttered a curse. The sight of
the girl he had saved was more painful to him than
any physical punishment. He could not bear to look
at her without silently railing against his unfathomable behavior in the courtyard of Dublin Castle, the
behavior that had cost him his freedom and decreed
Muirne would not have the life he wished for her.

''Hello.'' The voice was soft and delicate as the

English lass dropped her hand away from the candle she had been shielding.

Looking at her, Devlin could see now that she was not the child he had at first supposed her to be. Her soft curves proclaimed that she was more woman than girl, but the youthful beauty of her face hinted that childhood was not all that far behind her. Why, she was probably no more than sixteen, Devlin thought, until he realized what he was doing and began to silently berate himself. What difference did it make? What was the wench to him, anyway?

Devlin shot her a fierce look meant to send her scampering on her way in terror. But she stood her ground, overlooking the fury on his face just as she ignored her malodorous surroundings. Instead, she saw only a magnificent warrior, one with a heart so big that he had risked his life for hers though the world had declared her his enemy.

Alyssa gave a tiny sigh as she studied Devlin Fitzhugh. Her aunt and uncle might have pampered her, but no one had ever been willing to hazard his life for her before this rugged gallowglass had done so. She was as much impressed by his gallantry as she was by his physique. Surely the world had never known such a hero.

"My name is Alyssa Howett," she began. "I am the…woman you saved last night."

"As if I could forget you!" Devlin growled. "But it matters not to me what you are called, girl. Get you hence before I do you harm."

"Oh, I know you're angry, and I can find no fault

with that, but I also know that you would never hurt me,'' Alyssa continued. ''Such evil could never be in your nature.''

''Step a few inches closer so that I can wrap my chains about your slender young neck, and I'll show you how very wicked a desperate man can be.''

''I had to speak with you, to tell you how badly I feel that I played a part in your capture.''

A part? This whole thing is your fault, Devlin wanted to bellow. But he held his tongue because he knew such an outburst would be a lie. From his viewpoint, no one but he was responsible for his dilemma, and that grated on him more than if someone else had actually been to blame. Still, the sight of the girl was almost more than he could bear, reminding him as it did of his foolish gallantry during Niall's rescue.

''Please, you must believe me,'' Alyssa persisted in the face of Devlin's stony silence. ''I truly am sorry.''

''No sorrier than I am,'' Devlin ground out bitterly. If the girl felt guilty, it was an emotion that might be used to his advantage. ''What were you doing flitting about the cells in the middle of the night? Can't your father control you, or is it a habit of yours to visit imprisoned men under cover of darkness?''

''No!'' she exclaimed, her face blazing crimson. ''No to both questions. I don't know my father very well. We've just been reunited after many years apart, and when we first became reacquainted, I hated him and refused to obey him in even the smallest matters. He had abandoned me, you see.''

The simple, innocent confession tore at Devlin's being. How long would it be before he saw Muirne again—if ever he did? And, how would she feel about him if he came back into her life? Would she, too, feel her father had deserted her?

"I want you to know that I begged my father to arrange your release, but it was futile."

"A man of great honor, your sire," Devlin commented in derision, "and I suppose you are much like him."

"Don't you think I would help you if I could?"

"Prove it," he demanded. "Get me the key that will unlock my chains."

"I can't," the girl admitted shamefully. "The guard carries them."

"Then what good are you? Leave me in peace."

Despite the fact that she would have granted the Irishman his freedom if it were within her power, the thought of never seeing him again filled Alyssa with melancholy. She attributed the feeling to silly, girlish fancies and tried to concentrate on the matter at hand, easing Devlin Fitzhugh's plight in whatever small way she could.

"I've brought you something," she said, fishing in a deep side pocket of her gown.

"A weapon, a chisel?" Devlin asked anxiously.

"Nay, 'tis but an apple," Alyssa replied apologetically. "But I thought it might give you some comfort."

"Think you I have any stomach for food?" Devlin

asked in disgust. "Go away and don't return unless you want to place your life in jeopardy."

The only response he received was the dull thump of the apple as it dropped to the floor inside his cell and rolled towards him. Then there was silence followed by the sound of light, hurried footsteps marking the girl's retreat.

The quiet did not last long. It was interrupted by the gravelly voice of one of the guards. Carrying a bucket and a stack of trenchers, he was walking in the company of two of his fellows. It was obvious they were delivering the day's meal.

"We got here in time to hear that softhearted wench offer you an apple," the Englishman said derisively. Unlocking Devlin's door, he padded forward, followed by the other two, who stood with pikes pointed in Devlin's direction. "Sort of makes this your own private Eden, doesn't it?" The guard laughed cruelly, retrieving the fruit and holding it aloft before he crunched it between his few remaining teeth.

"I didn't know the serpent ate the apple as well," Devlin drawled, his voice drenched with condescension in spite of his circumstances.

"Seems to me we should give you something other than your supper, laddie. You need instruction in how to talk to your betters... the girl and me." The jailer took a small club dangling from his waist and began to wield it. Sickening thuds echoed in the darkness as the weapon found its target again and again. That Devlin bore the cruelty without pleading for clemency incensed the Englishman further, increasing his efforts. Finally, however, he tired of his sport.

"A few more such lessons, Irishman, and you'll no longer be so pretty. Then there will be no lass come to visit you and make your lot easier."

It was perhaps the most merciful thing he had heard since his capture, Devlin thought as consciousness made ready to flee and the Englishman's harangue began to fade in the distance.

"Niall, praise be Mary and all the saints," yelled Eamon MacMahon two days later as he saw the small band of men approach his campfire. Hampered as he was by his crutch and broken leg, he hobbled to his feet and embraced his son warmly. "By all that's holy, I feared I'd never see you again. But the scouts said Devlin wasn't with you. Where's the man to whom I owe my son's life?"

"Right here, Uncle," Cashel said gruffly. "Devlin was taken early on and I had to take charge and lead the fight out of the castle to save Niall. I'm proud to say we lost only one man, Kieran."

"And Devlin." Niall's voice was strident, his youthful indignation barely held in check. Initially he'd refused to even accompany Cashel, arguing about not leaving Devlin behind until the older man had tied him to his horse for the journey home. "Father, we must return at once for Devlin. I can't abandon him. In fact, if Cashel hadn't knocked me out when I tried to head back into Dublin, I wouldn't be here at all—"

"Then God bless the man, you young fool. If you were taken again, there would surely be no talk of ransom," the Irish chieftain said. "Cashel, I appreciate your putting Niall first, but was there no way to help Devlin?"

"Would you have had me risk the lives of all of these for the sake of one?" Cashel demanded. "The English were swarming like bees in a flowering meadow, their weapons ready and no mercy in their eyes. I thought it meet to escape while we could."

"Devlin told us he would try to distract pursuit from Niall," reminded Dugal. "Perhaps he did get away. He may still come along under his own power."

"But he'd never leave one of his men behind. We shouldn't have left if there was any chance that he'd show," argued Niall, repeating the words he'd echoed since escaping Dublin.

"There wasn't any!" snapped Eamon's nephew. Annoyed that concern for Fitzhugh overrode his own part in the heroic rescue, Cashel revealed more than he'd intended. "I was the last one through the gate. I saw him taken."

"And you didn't turn back to help him?" Niall was the spokesman but the murmur from the others of the clan left Cashel no doubt that the lad spoke for all. "You betrayed not only Devlin but all the Mac-Mahons when you deserted him—"

"The devil take such nonsense. It was our lives or his and I'd do the same again if need be."

"And what of your quarrel over who was in

charge?'' challenged Sean. ''You didn't like being his second.''

''I'll not deny I've questioned the MacMahon's judgment regarding Fitzhugh's ability, but I admit when I'm wrong and I was about this. Devlin Fitzhugh planned the raid on the Castle and executed it perfectly. He fought like ten men to get us free of there, but he'd be the first to agree that Niall's life must come before his own. Niall, lad, he told you in the tower, 'don't stop for anyone or anything.' Have you forgotten?''

''No, but—''

''And Dugal, didn't Fitzhugh insist on leading us out of the castle, knowing full well that the odds were against us once the alarm sounded? The man knew the risks and willingly accepted them.''

''You're glad he was taken,'' accused Eamon's son.

''Use your head. Would I choose to anger your father by abandoning a man he so values if I could avoid it? My main responsibility was seeing you out of the pale and back here before the soldiers found us. Now that you're safe, we can tend to Devlin.'' Though it galled him to say it, Cashel could see he had no choice but make it appear this had been his plan all along. Of course, by the time they returned to Dublin, Fitzhugh's rotting head on a pike might be the only part of him left. The English didn't take kindly to Irishmen who raided their jails.

''Then we'll ready the horses for you to leave at first light,'' agreed the MacMahon. He didn't know if he trusted Cashel's story, but he was kin, and one didn't forsake the clan when ordered to perform a duty. "I won't feel Niall is truly safe until you bring Fitzhugh home—and I know you're the one man who can do it."

"I'll go, too, Father," volunteered Niall.

"No. You're too inexperienced to be helpful," countered Eamon. "Cashel will pick the men he wants and when he returns, we'll feast like never before. Now, Cashel, get some rest before you head out again."

"Aye, Eamon, and you, enjoy your son. I'm thankful I could bring him home to you." The words grated in Cashel's ears, his hero's welcome evaporated for worry over Devlin. Damn the blasted gallowglass! Even absent his presence was still felt. Cashel MacMahon would never risk his life for one such as he.

Chapter Three

Devlin finally stopped his measured pacing, steps sorely restricted by the chains that still bound him to the wall. Overcome by exhaustion, he hunkered down in his dark, dank cell. With his elbows propped on his muscular thighs, he allowed his head to fall wearily forward and rest against his hands as morbid anxiety gnawed at his soul, and the iron around his wrists and ankles bit into flesh rubbed raw.

He'd been confined here only three days and already he felt a growing sense of desperation so strong that it took all of his rapidly diminishing resources to deal with it. He was a freeborn man, who had always moved about his homeland whenever and wherever his inclinations had dictated. How many of his nights had been spent sleeping under star-studded skies, how many days had seen him roaming the rugged Irish landscape as unconfined as the winds that blew in from the sea?

Yet it made no difference what his lot had been, he thought bitterly, his fingers digging into his flesh in frustration and raking down his stubble-covered cheeks and chin. Whatever had been was past. This was his fate now—at least for the time being—until either Eamon arranged his rescue or he succumbed to madness or death. Did the English plan to torture him by keeping him confined for the rest of his natural life, or did they intend to execute him for his part in Niall's escape? He still didn't know.

If not for Muirne, death would be vastly preferable to facing years of imprisonment. Yet the little one was his responsibility and it was his duty to fight for survival for her sake, Devlin reminded himself, lifting his coppery head and allowing it to fall back and make contact with a damp, stone wall.

But to be reduced to this! It was almost beyond endurance to be caged like some dangerous animal. It made him feel ferocious, ready to pounce and kill whatever living being happened into his wretched new domain.

Suddenly, a flicker of light broke through the blackness and Devlin steeled himself to his full height, even as his well-muscled body tensed in wary anticipation.

The soft, whispered rustle of material should have warned him what was about to happen, but it was not until she held the candle aloft, allowing it to illuminate the soft contours of her face, that Devlin knew who this intruder upon his dark thoughts actually was. The girl, Alyssa, stood before him again, a tentative smile brightening her face almost as much as the flame she carried.

Sweet Jesu! Would she give him no peace? Devlin stood there, wishing she would disappear, that the darkness would suddenly devour her and leave no trace behind to remind him she had ever existed.

"I want you to know I've begged to have your chains removed," Alyssa began uneasily, her slim white hand fluttering to indicate Devlin's fetters. "My father has promised me he will have it done today. At least you'll be able to move a bit more freely, even though you are still confined to a cell. I have a small cache of coins left me by an aunt, and I've used some of them to see to it that you'll have two meals a day instead of one. And tonight, there will be some fresh straw to replace that vermin-infested heap in the corner," she said, her nose wrinkling for an instant in distaste until the presence of the man whose bravery had captured her girlish heart made her begin to forget where they were.

As she concentrated on his dangerous good looks, the surrounding squalor faded away completely and Alyssa saw only Devlin Fitzhugh. His well-honed body, his stubborn stance, his arrogant bearing all exuded a masculine beauty. And his face, with its finely chiseled features, was inordinately handsome, or at least it would be, Alyssa amended, if only he would stop scowling at her so blackly. Why didn't he say something?

"Besides that, I'll continue coming to visit you every day just as I have for the past two, to see how you are faring," Alyssa finally stated, as much to break the silence as to inform the rugged Irishman of her intentions.

"Go away, girl. I've told you repeatedly I have no desire for your company," Devlin growled.

"I'm certain you don't mean that," Alyssa protested, unwilling to believe the warrior who had begun to haunt her dreams would treat her so unceremoniously. She was growing tired of his telling her to leave him alone. Wasn't it about now he should be exhibiting some degree of gratitude?

"I do," Devlin warned harshly.

"'Tis naught but your manly pride talking," Alyssa stated insistently, her violet eyes flashing. It appeared that seeing to the welfare of her Irish gallowglass was going to be difficult. But Alyssa had not earned her reputation for willfulness undeservedly. Devlin's lack of cooperation only made her more determined to help him survive his imprisonment, an incarceration for which she still felt blame.

"'Tis my righteous fury speaking and nothing less," Devlin all but snarled. "If you value your safety, you'll leave now and never return."

"Fie, sir! I am weary of your threats!" Alyssa exclaimed with an unconsciously insolent sway of her hips. "I have told you from the beginning, you don't frighten me one jot! You saved my life."

"That was naught but folly, a softhearted, dull-witted impulse that I've lived to regret, and never more than at this moment. Certainly it is an error I would never repeat."

"Say what you will, but I know that in spite of your fierce glowering there is a kind heart within your warrior's body. And so, Devlin Fitzhugh, you will be seeing me often. Now you can continue to rail or you can save your strength and accept the fact. It makes no difference to me."

With that, Alyssa withdrew something from her pocket and shoved it through the bars. It was a hunk of bread wrapped in a scrap of cloth. Devlin glared at it, and then at the girl.

"I'll see you on the morrow," Alyssa whispered softly, and then both she and the weak light of the candle were gone.

Devlin remained where he was, allowing his eyes a chance to adjust to the darkness. This time, unlike yesterday, he'd be damned if he ate the girl's largesse, he swore to himself. Hungry as he might be, it would stay where it was until the wench returned the next day. She could add whatever she brought to the pile, which would continue to grow until she finally realized that he would have none of her ill-conceived generosity. That was the only way to deal with such a headstrong lass.

But a high-pitched squeak and a pair of small, red eyes glowing in the darkness caused Devlin to quickly reconsider his decision. Food strewn on the floor of his cell would only cause it to become more rat infested than it already was. And with not even a few crumbs left behind, the English girl would never believe his assertions that he had ignored her food, that the rats had eaten it. Most likely, the little witch would only laugh in the face of his anger and smile that knowing feminine smile of hers. Lord, but she'd lead some unlucky man a merry chase when she grew older. And in the meantime, she would practice her infuriating behavior on him, Devlin thought in despair, seeing once again the impudent swing of the lass's hips as she argued with him.

Bending down, he swatted at the advancing rat and scooped up the bread, muttering darkly.

Savagely, Devlin bit off a piece, almost choking on it in spite of the honey slathered across its center. But once the last morsel was gone, no sweetness lingered in his mouth.

Dear mother of God but he had dreaded his imprisonment before the girl had made a habit of appearing. How would he ever endure jail and the wench, too? Devlin rested his head against the iron bars and gave a low moan. Surely there was no mercy in heaven.

Then, despite himself, an exasperated smile crossed Devlin's face. A man impressed by bravery, Devlin found he couldn't but admire Alyssa Howett. She was nothing if not a spirited, defiant little soul. Why, not even his blackest look could quell her. And with all that blond hair of hers, and those unusual violet eyes... Perhaps at another time, in another place, she could have tempted him.

But what was he thinking! She was English, one of the oppressors, and he an Irish rebel. She was little more than a girl and he was fast approaching thirty winters. She had an entire lifetime before her, and he, in all likelihood, was a condemned man.

What strange thoughts she wrought within him! They were especially odd when Devlin considered that whether free or imprisoned, he was a warrior, and had little time for women, let alone young girls. And this young girl was intelligent, smart enough to see through his bluster, to know that he bristled not at the small kindnesses she insisted upon showing him, but at being beholden to a female. Yes, she was clever all right, and if he had had his liberty, he would have fled from her immediately.

Within a week, Alyssa discovered, her days in Dublin Castle took on a pattern of their own. As long as she appeared promptly for the midday meal she was expected to share with her father and the governor, her mornings were hers. Then, afterward she was free to embroider or sketch until dinner.

Not once had Cecil Howett questioned her amusements or disturbed her wanderings, apparently pleased that she was keeping out of trouble. Most important, his attitude gave her entry to any manner of place all over the castle grounds.

Flipping through her drawings, Alyssa smiled at her chosen subjects: children playing in the lane outside the jail, alert wardens walking the wall, maids scurrying across the courtyard with laundry, Devlin pacing in his cell, unaware he was being observed. Those of the gallowglass were her favorites, though Devlin Fitzhugh would not be one to indulge an artist's endeavors and pose willingly. In fact, he was not a man accustomed to enforced idleness of any kind.

Naturally, she made certain to include a daily visit to the Irishman's cell, if only to help rectify his foul humor. She hoped her father didn't find out, but even if he did, Alyssa knew that she wouldn't abandon Devlin Fitzhugh. After all, when he'd been in danger for his life, he hadn't hesitated to protect her. He was a hero, despite the absurd interpretation the English put on the event. Traitor, indeed!

Alyssa contemplated her charcoal drawing of the man who had risked everything to save her from those descending swords, and she trembled. She had been such a fool—yet what an acceptable outcome the near tragedy would have, if her father were right. Transported to England, Devlin would spend time in her father's jail where they could be together. It would have been better to live with him in Ireland, but that was out of the question.

Still, Alyssa would be with the man she loved. And love him she did. Studying a sketch of an imaginary scene, Devlin outdoors, she traced the strong line she'd made of his shoulder, the proud angle of his head, and the planes of his chest as he aimed a bow and arrow. His eyes were focused and intense, his lips parted slightly in concentration, his attitude superbly confident as if guaranteed his arrow would find its target. But wasn't that part of why she loved him— his arrogance and total assurance of his position? She doubted another man like Devlin Fitzhugh existed anywhere.

Her beloved aunt had died and Devlin had come into her life within days. Surely, he was the faerie folk's answer to her prayers for an escape from Cecil Howett. Now all she had to do was convince Devlin that fate had brought them together, not her foolishness.

He seemed to have stopped growling as much when she visited him last. In fact, occasionally she thought he was even pleased to see her, not that he admitted it. Like most men, he needed to think he was in control of his destiny, and she'd not deny him that privilege—false though it might be. Closing her eyes, Alyssa imagined his face lowering slowly to hers and tasted his lips on hers, firm, demanding and welcome. If only her dreams could become reality.

Cecil Howett sat at a desk in the outer room of the quarters assigned him. He held his breath as he took the missive from London being proffered him by Newcomb's secretary. Waiting until the man had left the room, Cecil turned the document over in his hands. The seal had been broken and the contents most likely read by Newcomb already. With nervous fingers, Howett unfolded the paper, his eyes quickly scanning the message contained therein. Then his shoulders slumped in disappointment. It was what he had most feared. Devlin Fitzhugh was to be executed at dawn the next day.

Damnation! The report of the rebel jailbreak had emphasized that Fitzhugh had averted Alyssa's murder! Didn't that mean the man should be spared? Apparently not according to Her Majesty. How was he going to inform Alyssa of the decision? And how was he going to explain that his promises had meant nothing? He knew how important the man had become to her, unwise though that was. Hadn't he but recently learned she had been sneaking into the prison every day to see him?

It might be best to delay giving his daughter the news until after Fitzhugh's death sentence had been carried out. Of course, having no advance warning would add to the girl's sorrow, but it would also give her one more day of peace, and her young life had seen upset aplenty as of late.

Resolved, Cecil rose from his desk and walked to his cupboard to fetch some wine when Alyssa burst into the room, her bright presence making the gloom within his heart that much darker.

"Is it true a courier from London has arrived?" she asked breathlessly, only to abruptly cease her question as her eyes fell upon the royal decree open upon the desk, and she saw Devlin's name written in large, bold letters.

"Alyssa, don't!" her father warned, hastening to her side. But it was already too late.

"Dear God in heaven!" The softness of her voice made plain her shock. Slowly, Alyssa sank into her father's chair. "You must do something to stop this," she proclaimed in anguish, catching desperately at Cecil's sleeve.

"Would that I could, sweetling, but I fear your Irishman is beyond hope."

"You gave me your word that Elizabeth would not order his execution," she accused. "You must do something or his death will stand forever between us. Surely, you have simply to—"

"I tell you I can do nothing," Cecil interjected, his guilt shortening his temper. Yet, he spoke the truth. Having discovered his error in extending false hopes to his daughter, Cecil was not of a mind to make the same mistake again. Now that Alyssa knew her Irishman's fate, it was best she quickly realize the futility of the situation.

"'Tis a hard lesson to learn, to accept the things

about which we can do nothing, but impress it upon your heart, girl, and it will serve you well in life. That is all the solace I have to offer.''

"'Tis little enough, but mayhap it is better than your lies,'' Alyssa retorted with bitter resentment. Then her demeanor changed, as horror completely penetrated her anger and denial. "Tell me, does he know?" she whispered weakly.

"Nay. Newcomb and I have only learned of it ourselves.''

"Oh, Father, I beg you—'' She'd act the dutiful daughter for the rest of her life, only Devlin had to be saved!

"I've already told you, there's nothing to be done. Your Irishman is doomed, Alyssa.''

At his words, the girl's sobs rent the air. Yet her father remained steadfast. After tomorrow, Fitzhugh would be executed, and Alyssa could begin to put the ordeal behind her. Thinking it best for his daughter to give way to her emotions, he withdrew quietly from the room, walking the corridors of Dublin Castle until he could no longer hear the girl's distress.

With every step he took, Cecil wondered how he might make this situation easier for Alyssa. The only thing that came to mind was moving the execution forward. If the deed was done, it would be over before she knew it had happened. He'd talk to Newcomb about it right away. Surely the man owed him that much.

Though Alyssa had given herself over to grief with abandon, her tears began to slow and her shoulders began to stop heaving shortly after her father's departure. She knew she had to pull rein on her emotions. Soon, Devlin would be gone, she told herself, sniffling, and she would be the one who would see to it. With her help, he would make good an escape tonight. He had to! Damn her father and his empty words! Cecil Howett was even more charlatan than she had thought.

Rapidly, ideas began to formulate in Alyssa's mind. The overnight guard on duty this week had a reputation for loving gold, and he had been helpful in the past. She still had a good deal of the coinage her aunt had left her. If she had learned anything at Dublin Castle, it was that with money, one could buy almost anything. She only prayed her little fortune was worth the price of a man's life.

Having hope to cling to once again, Alyssa stood, smoothed her gown and banished the anguish from her face. There was much to prepare before darkness fell. After tonight, she might never see Devlin Fitzhugh again, but how much more comforting it would be to know he was alive somewhere in his precious Irish countryside rather than moldering in a pauper's grave on the outskirts of Dublin.

The small pouch of gold coins suspended between Alyssa's breasts weighed heavily around her neck despite the slight bulk of her meager inheritance. Trying to be inconspicuous, she took a roundabout route across the bailey that eventually led her to a door at the base of the prison tower.

When she stepped inside, Alyssa's heart began to beat rapidly at the thought of what lay ahead. It was not the notion that she could soon be an enemy of the crown that caused her skin to turn paler and her breaths to become more shallow. No, it was fear of failure that brought about these physical symptoms. If she did not accomplish the purpose at hand, Devlin Fitzhugh was a doomed man, forever beyond the reach of any help she might wish to render.

Praying that her small cache of coins would be enough to tempt Hawkins, the greediest of the guards, into betraying his duties, Alyssa decided a smile sent in his direction would not be amiss.

Squaring her shoulders and donning a sweetly vapid smile, Alyssa left the patch of sunlight painting the floor of the tower just beyond the open door. She ascended through the gloom to the guards' station, where she hoped to find Hawkins alone. The possibility that he might not be there leaped across her mind along with a thousand other things that could befoul Devlin Fitzhugh's escape. Rather than cause maidenly trepidations and abandonment of her plan, however, the reasons for possible failure were swiftly examined and then put aside. She continued with a dainty yet determined tread, her violet eyes taking on a steely cast.

"Now you're not to worry that pretty head of yours, milady. Just you leave everything in my hands. You'll find them quite capable, I assure you," Hawkins said with a twist of his mouth that was more leer than grin.

"Are you certain?" Alyssa questioned anxiously.

"Didn't I tell you that I'll take care of the guards at the base of the tower? Alls I have to do is unlock the rebel's cell, and lead him along the portion of the outer wall that's always steeped in darkness, no matter how bright the moon, to the kitchens. From there, I takes him down to a little-used storeroom, where chests of grain stacked one upon the other hide a small portal that opens onto the trench. Once he climbs out of there, he'll find a horse tethered behind a clump of trees. The rest is up to him."

"But how will you avoid the other guards?" Alyssa persisted.

"I'll set things in motion just before the guards change at dawn. The ones on duty usually doze for a bit and only waken just before their relief appears. 'Twill be a simple matter to get past them, especially when I shares a jug of wine with them at the beginning of the watch."

"Still, I'm worried," Alyssa insisted, glancing over her shoulder to make certain that no one else was nearby.

"There's no need to fret on old Hawkins's account," the man stated, pretending to misunderstand Alyssa's concern as he sidled closer. "I'll be safe enough. Once I get the Irishman clear, I'll come back, drop a tattered Irish cloak and Celtic dagger along the escape route, lock myself in Fitzhugh's cell and throw the keys out into the corridor. Then, when I'm found, I'll pretend to just be coming to after having been laid low by one of them bloody Irish bastards. Begging your pardon for my bluntness, milady, but that's all them buggers are."

"Your plan could work," Alyssa conceded.

"Aye, with your gold and my brains, Fitzhugh will be clear of Dublin Castle by this time tomorrow," Hawkins said, eyeing the small pouch of coins Alyssa held in her hands.

"So be it," Alyssa pronounced, counting out half of her remaining inheritance into Hawkins's dirty palm. What choice did she have other than to place her trust in this man? God help her, he was all she had! "The rest is yours when Fitzhugh has gone."

"And now, milady, to seal the bargain," the guard said, his eyes raking Alyssa's bosom as he bent low to take her hand. Bringing it to his lips, he placed a clumsy, wet kiss along her knuckles.

"I would think half of my gold would have done that," Alyssa protested, trying to tug her fingers from his grasp.

"Ah, but what's a little intimacy between partners?" asked Hawkins with a lascivious grin as he held on to Alyssa's hand. "And I've a feeling that we're about to become mightily close indeed. You rest easy and just go to sleep tonight dreaming of all Hawkins can do."

Alyssa snatched her fingertips from the guard and turned away. She couldn't chide the man for his impudence until Devlin had seen the last of Dublin Castle. But once that had happened, she'd make certain Hawkins never touched her again.

Walking down the corridor, she considered a visit

to Devlin, as was her wont, but decided against it. He would be able to sense her uneasiness, and she couldn't tell him of his impending execution and her plan for his escape when anyone might come along and overhear. Besides, not one to follow, he would only find some flaw in the scheme she had set in motion and want to take command of things himself. No, it was better to wait until the hour for his release was at hand. Then she would visit his cell one last time.

Of course, Hawkins didn't expect her presence tonight, Alyssa thought as she emerged from the tower. But then, what could he do once she was there? Naive she might be, but she was not such an innocent as to place Devlin's life entirely in Hawkins's grimy hands. Despite Hawkins's inevitable protests, it would be she who led Devlin Fitzhugh to freedom's door, handed him a dagger and wished him godspeed.

Tracing the route she would be taking with Devlin that night, Alyssa entered the kitchens, explaining to the cook that Governor Newcomb had given her permission to browse through the stores for anything she might want to make her upcoming journey to England more bearable. With the cook's blessing, Alyssa descended into the storage room, pragmatically counting each step that might have to be taken in darkness that night. Seeing the chests of grain, she paced off their location from the doorway, and managed to reach behind them, her fingers searching for and finding the small, hidden doorway Hawkins had described. Satisfied, she went back to the kitchens, and asked that some dried fruit be placed upon her father's ship when it docked. Thanking the cook, she accepted a small tart with a smile meant to hide her lack of appetite.

Grateful that her plan to free Devlin was viable, Alyssa slowly made her way back to her chambers. She knew her heart should be singing. If all went well, he would disappear into the night's last mist-shrouded vestiges of darkness. He would live, and her debt to him would be paid. But her elation at saving his neck from the ax was tempered by a sadness that prevented complete joy.

Becoming more dejected with each step she took, Alyssa knew it wasn't the idea of spending her inheritance that upset her, though becoming penniless meant giving up all hope of escaping her father, and forsaking forever the possibility of independence that her aunt's secret gift was meant to promise. No, the money and all it stood for was a trifling price to pay for Devlin Fitzhugh's life. Yet, as each moment that passed brought it closer, there was a forfeiture Alyssa was loath to make, one that burdened her heart. After tonight Devlin would have his liberty, but the price exacted would be a steep one. Never in her life was she likely to see him again.

Surely if her father intruded upon her solitude by coming to her chambers in the intervening hours before Devlin's flight, she would not have to hide her schemes behind false tears. The ones she shed would be real enough.

* * *

Devlin stood with folded arms leaning against the wooden door of his prison. To all appearances, his stance was nonchalant. No one looking at him would think his studied indifference to his surroundings masked an alert watchfulness. Nor would any know his position was carefully chosen to give him the best view of the corridor running outside his cell. The only comment that might have been made would have been one of surprise that he was not stationed at his small prison window, trying to catch any breeze the unusually warm summer evening might surrender.

Yet lost deep in thought as he was, the summer temperatures were of no concern to Devlin Fitzhugh. The heat that began to build in his body was of a different sort altogether. It was bad enough that after three weeks another day had passed and the Mac-Mahon's men had made no attempt to rescue him, he thought irritably, but where the hell was Alyssa Howett? She should have been here already, as she usually was, and then his suffering for the day could have been complete.

Hearing shuffling at the far end of the corridor, Devlin waited, both hoping and fearing that it would be Alyssa come to him once more. The dread of torment and the anticipation of pleasure mingled incoherently. When had it begun to happen? When had never wanting to see her again started to shift to being unwilling to survive in this hellhole without her? Had it been after she had stood her ground in the face of his temper? Before that, when she had first brought

him food and comfort? Or was it the moment he had
set eyes on her?

Devlin shook his head wearily. He tried to tell himself that faced with the prospect of never having a
woman again, any female would appeal to him, but
his excuse held little sway with his traitorous heart.

Perhaps it was no more than prison madness descending upon him. How could it be otherwise? She
was English. She was at least partially the reason for
his imprisonment. And still, God help him, he longed
to see her, though her nearness, in the face of his
inability to touch her, brought him as much pain as
it did joy. Surely such emotions bespoke insanity.
Each day became worse. Mayhap if he spoke to the
girl's father, begged him to keep her away…but no,
he couldn't do that. His pride would never allow him
to admit to anyone how much the English wench
moved him. Nor did he really want her to abandon
him. Imprisonment without her daily company was
unthinkable.

"Newcomb and Howett have been closeted most
of the day. Something's afoot," one guard told another as the two passed by Devlin's cell, dispelling
his hope that Alyssa was nearby. "Have you any idea
as to what it can be?"

"No, but whatever it is, I wager 'twill only result
in these cursed Irish being coddled more."

"Aye, there are some here that seem to have their
own maidservants seeing to their needs," the first
guard replied, jerking his head in Devlin's direction.
"Damn me, but I've never seen the like."

Their conversation faded as the men rounded a corner, but it bothered Devlin not a whit. Whatever had them talking would become plain soon enough if it concerned him. What could bother him more than the torture to which Alyssa Howett gently subjected him?

Once more, Devlin peered into the descending darkness, watching and listening for Cecil Howett's daughter. It was growing unusually late. His heart started to race, and sweat beaded upon his forehead as he strained to see if she was coming. He hoped to God she wouldn't. He prayed to God she would.

Chapter Four

"I don't know why you're here. I thought we'd agreed I would see to everything."

The words crept into Devlin's consciousness, causing him to quickly leave sleep behind and become alert. In his experience, he'd never seen anything other than a lone guard occasionally shuffle down this corridor so late at night. Yet the approaching footsteps were hurried, and the sound of Hawkins's voice told Devlin that the Englishman was not alone. Quickly, the agile gallowglass gained his feet. If someone were to come for him, be it friend or foe, he'd not be found curled up upon the straw like some docile farm animal.

"You decided the matter would be left in your hands," came the reply, in hushed yet determined feminine tones. "But I'm not such a fool as to trust you blindly. That's why I've come to oversee things."

The voice was so soft, the whisper so subtle that Devlin almost thought he imagined it. He had done that often enough of late. But he could sense Alyssa

Howett's nearness and knew that what he had just heard was real.

Sweet Jesu! Couldn't the wench be content that she disturbed his dreams without actually seeking him out in the middle of the night?

Based upon his experiences with Alyssa, Devlin would not argue the premise that the world was totally devoid of justice. After hours of awaiting her arrival, he had finally concluded she wasn't coming. Slowly, the tension associated with her had left him, and he had almost been grateful to have a day without the torture her presence seemed to bring.

Now here she was, when she was least expected, and he was the vulnerable recipient of her surprise attack. He was not at all ready to deal with her at the moment. But then, he was never totally prepared for Alyssa Howett. He had tried ignoring her, bellowing at her, threatening her, stopping just short of throwing himself upon his knees and pleading with her to leave him in peace. Yet when he envisioned himself resorting to such a tactic, his hoarse pleas transformed themselves into urgings of quite a different nature. Shuddering, Devlin tried to push aside the images flooding his mind and steel himself for Alyssa's latest assault.

"Devlin. Wake up, man! It's me, Alyssa."

As if he would have any doubts as to who it could be.

"What is it now?" he asked, his voice as quiet as hers, yet drenched with surliness.

Suddenly the key was in the lock and the door began to swing inward. She had never entered his cell before! Why was Alyssa stealing into his wretched surroundings at this time of night? Sweet Mother of God, was she going to offer herself to him? More important, what was he going to do if she did?

"Begone, lass," he hissed, wanting her out of his path when impulse led him to make a desperate bid for freedom. When else would he find himself with unlocked door while most of the castle slept?

"Aye, I will be in a moment," she answered, "and you'll be right behind me."

"What! Don't mock me, Alyssa," Devlin growled, though a glimmer of doubtful hope lit his blue eyes all the same.

"There's little time to talk, Devlin." Alyssa's lovely face was drawn with anxiety. "You're to be executed this morning. We've got to get you out of here now. The guards on duty have been taken care of, but their replacements will be arriving in an hour. If you've any thought of keeping your head attached, you'll have to be well gone by then."

"And him? What's he doing here?" Devlin asked, nodding in Hawkins's direction as the man followed Alyssa into the cell. The Englishman's presence made the gallowglass wonder if the girl could be leading him into a trap, unwittingly or otherwise.

"Me! I'm the one she paid to see to your escape," the guard grumbled. "The better question is what is she doing here? I'm not about to risk my neck by leading two of you out of the tower and around the castle grounds."

"I'll save you the effort," Alyssa stated matter-of-factly. "You'll be locked in the cell now and the keys dropped on the stairway. 'Twill avert suspicion from you.''

"You're giving me orders? This is what comes of having business dealings with a female," Hawkins muttered, "when what I really prefers is the idea of dealing with you in my bed. And after tonight, don't think I won't have you warming my blanket—"

Hawkins didn't see Devlin Fitzhugh's fist coming, nor did he feel the pain before slumping to the floor unconscious.

Devlin turned to Alyssa. Towering over her, he peered into her guileless visage, pearlescent in the moonlight, and he seemed to come to a decision.

"All right, lass. Let's go. I'll place my trust in you," he said softly.

"And I in you," Alyssa replied, reaching into her cloak and handing him a dagger. "I thought you'd have need of this for the journey home."

A surprised Devlin looked at the weapon and then at Alyssa. Her violet eyes were darker than he had ever seen them. In their depths glistened concern, sincerity and something else, some nebulous element that Devlin wanted neither to identify nor analyze.

"We really must be off, Fitzhugh," Alyssa insisted worriedly, her fear for this man's safety forcing her to wrench her gaze from his.

Scooping up the keys and the threadbare Irish cloak to be dropped along Devlin's escape route, Alyssa disappeared into the dark corridor. Once Devlin joined her, she secured Hawkins with lock and key. Then motioning to Devlin, she led the way, her tread so quiet and light that she appeared to float just above the surface of the cold, stone floor.

Following in her wake, Devlin vowed he had never seen so graceful a creature. Then, realizing the insanity of his absorption in Alyssa Howett's gait, he inured himself against her charms, his warrior's demeanor descending upon him once more.

He didn't know where she was taking him, or if her plan had a prayer of succeeding! Yet what did it matter? he asked himself. She was the only hope he had, and if they were accosted, he was armed.

At worst, he would die the death of a fighting man, a fate more palatable than the one the English had planned for him. Grimacing, Devlin clutched the hilt of the dagger. But, when they descended the staircase, there was no need for it, just as she had promised. There were no proud guards ready to do their duty for queen and country, but only sleeping Englishmen, empty mugs lying beside them.

Suddenly, Alyssa and Devlin were at the door in the base of the tower, the one that led into the bailey. Instinctively, Devlin reached out to thrust Alyssa behind him, but before he could lay hold of her slender frame, she took his hand, and began to tug him along after her.

In truth, her efforts had no more effect upon him than a sparrow attempting to pull a boulder. Still, now that the moment of truth was at hand, Devlin found that he followed the girl willingly enough.

Bending his head to pass through the doorway, Devlin drew fresh air, laden with the promise of freedom, into his lungs. But there was no time to savor the heady feeling it gave him. Alyssa was insistently yanking him forward once more, her small hand all but lost within the confines of his large one.

Though she did not lead him towards one of the gates set into Dublin Castle's thick walls, Devlin put up no resistance, his steps following Alyssa's as she moved along a section of stone cast deep in shadow.

Then suddenly, torches appeared on the far side of the courtyard, borne by a contingent of soldiers marching in the direction of the tower. Devlin heard Alyssa's sharply indrawn breath and felt the pulse in her fingertips quicken within his hand, evidence of her surprise.

"'Tis too early for this sort of thing. Her Majesty owes me another hour or two of sleep," one of the soldiers called to his fellows.

"Aye, but though 'tis earlier, 'tis a pleasant enough way to begin the day," another shouted in reply, "executing an Irishman."

"I hope the bastard was told yesterday and spent a sleepless night," the first rejoined. "'Twill be easier to manage Fitzhugh if he's exhausted."

"They're coming for you, to take you to the block!" Alyssa whispered in horror. "Damn Hawkins for a harlot's son. Why didn't he know about this change in schedule, or did he choose not to tell us?"

Before her Irishman could answer, however, the light of the torches crept into the blackness in which Alyssa and Devlin stood. A cry uttered by one of the soldiers alerted all of them, and directly the queen's men were bearing down on the pair with alarming speed.

"Get out of here, lass," Devlin growled. He had no intention of being taken again trying to save Alyssa Howett's pretty neck. But to his consternation, he found he could not loosen the girl's grasp upon him.

"Devlin, this way! Follow me!" Alyssa yelled above the rising clamor, her soprano tones carrying clearly through the night air. Frantically she pulled at his hand until Devlin's sense of logic surrendered to desperation and he once more permitted himself to be guided by her.

Swiftly they ran, the soldiers efficiently closing the gap between them. Then, Devlin found himself going through a doorway, only to realize that it provided no exit from the castle. It was merely the entrance to the kitchens. The girl had become lost, if ever she had had a viable escape route planned at all.

"Hurry. Help me shut the door and slide home the plank," Alyssa directed, her breath coming in frightened gasps.

"'Twill only buy us a little respite," Devlin said stoically, more inclined to face death in the coming skirmish than to chance being recaptured. He didn't want to spend time alone in this place with Alyssa Howett—time during which a doomed man might do and say many a foolish thing in the last moments of his life.

"You great dolt! I know what I'm doing, but I can't manage alone," Alyssa yelled angrily. "Do as I say!"

Against his better judgment, Devlin gave in to her demands. The door was slammed shut and the

wooden bar hastily put into place just as the first
sword landed against the exterior with a heavy thud.

Devlin's dagger weighed heavily in his hands. He
detested the thought of hiding in the kitchens with a
woman when a battle beckoned just the other side of
the door. He had to make Alyssa see that such behavior was impossible for him, to make her understand what he was about to do.

He turned to her in the eerie glow of the banked
fires. She was a golden maid now. Placing his thumb
beneath her chin, he raised her face to his.

"'Tis not that I'm ungrateful, Alyssa Howett," he
began, his husky voice melodic and almost tender,
"but there's no help for it. We've lost. I must go out
to meet my enemy."

"Wouldn't you rather go out the door that leads to
the trench surrounding the castle and find a horse
awaiting you?" Alyssa asked, her eyes caressing
Devlin's face, every plane, every rugged masculine
contour.

"The devil you say!"

As the banging on the door grew louder and more
insistent, Devlin didn't hesitate to trail Alyssa down
the staircase to the storeroom. He should have been
ecstatic to have the possibility of freedom so near, yet
somewhere in the back of his mind, in the portion
that did not deal with the immediate problems of survival, Devlin knew something was wrong. But things
were happening too quickly, and he ignored the feeling as he easily moved the chests of grain and found
the exit Alyssa had promised. He entirely disregarded
his uneasiness as he put his shoulder to the door and

forced it open, then wriggled through a narrow tunnel hardly wide enough to allow his shoulders room to pass. Whatever it was that was disturbing him could be dealt with once safety had been reached.

And then, he was outside, and he could think of nothing other than the liberty he had so miraculously been granted. Already he envisioned himself riding through the forests and across the mountains, freer than the winds that would play against his face and ruffle his hair.

Crawling to the top of the trench, he saw a slim hand appear from the darkness to lie beside his own.

"The horse should be tethered behind yon stand of trees," Alyssa informed him, scrambling up the deep, earthen walls.

Immediately, Devlin and Alyssa began to run, low to the ground, praying all the while that the swirls of rising mist would keep them safe from detection. Reaching the trees, they found that there was, indeed, a horse waiting.

The castle was coming quickly awake, the sound of running guards ready for battle issuing from behind the walls. Devlin swung himself up into the saddle, and looked down at the woman, little more than a girl, who had saved his life. He would remember her forever, standing here in the moonlight, her skirts lost in the smoky mist. There was so much to say to her, and so little time. He could not seem to find the words, and perhaps it was best that he could not.

Alyssa, however, had no such trouble.

"Give me your hand, Devlin, and help me up. Why

are you looking at me with such shock? There's no time to tarry.''

"What are you doing? You've got to go back to your father. You can say I took you hostage and released you once I cleared the castle."

"Go back!" she echoed, her face a study in dismay and bewilderment. "Fie, I can't do that now! They saw me leading you by the hand and mayhap heard me directing your flight as well. I can't return unless you want me to find my head upon the block. They know I helped you escape."

So they did. Devlin swore softly. The reason for his nagging discomfort finally surfaced, and did so quite forcefully. What was he going to do about Alyssa Howett?

Damnation, he didn't want to take the girl with him. What with Muirne's sudden appearance, he had had enough responsibility foisted upon him recently. And now he was to be saddled with Alyssa Howett, too? His free spirit bridled at yet another obligation. Still, what else could he do? Nothing, not if he wanted to be able to live with himself. The girl had been kind to him, had helped him escape, had risked her life for his.

But she was an Englishwoman! To take her with him would mean he would forever be a hunted man. They would never stop seeking him...never. With Alyssa in his charge, he could forget ever truly being free again. And for more reasons than one, Devlin thought in self-derision as the girl stood regarding him expectantly, her face as sweet as a woodland flower dancing with moonbeams.

As she looked at him, Devlin saw something in Alyssa's eyes that made him wary. God's teeth, couldn't she realize he wasn't the hero she thought him to be? He was simply a man, and a man who had made many mistakes during his turbulent lifetime at that. But Devlin vowed he would not add Alyssa Howett to that list, even as he silently conceded that the girl was indeed his responsibility, at least for the time being.

Heaving a sigh, Devlin reluctantly reached down to help Alyssa up behind him. She smiled at him, as if she thought of this as only the beginning of a grand adventure and not a serious undertaking, not the end of the life she had always known. Yet her enthusiasm was almost contagious. The devil take the girl and her winsome smile!

As Devlin's hand closed over hers, he suddenly found that his freedom, curtailed as it had unexpectedly become, was not so sweet as he had anticipated during the long days of his imprisonment. Damn, but the devil take him, too, he thought angrily, for being so softhearted a fool that he could not leave the girl behind.

Just as Devlin began to believe they might escape the city without further notice, the heavy tones of the castle bell resounded through the predawn quiet. On a MacMahon horse, they would have been at the outskirts of Dublin already, he fumed, but this animal was hard-pressed to meet his urgent demands. Still, the gallowglass urged it forward, determined to get them through the cobblestone streets as quickly as he could. The echoing hoofbeats were just one more signal to their direction, and while no one was on the road yet, nearby residents, when questioned, might recall the sound of early travelers. Then, as he reached the turn onto a broad, dirt path circling the city, the air was rent with church bells ringing in every direction.

"Hell's fire," Devlin cursed, driving the horse forward.

"Hurry, Devlin, you must get us away from here," said Alyssa from behind him.

Wasn't it enough that he had to bear her distractingly rounded, female body pressed enticingly against his back, but she had to whisper in his ear as well? Did the woman know no mercy or was she truly an innocent? Though the words weren't those of love, their breathy murmur reminded him he was far from dead—thanks in part to her. Perhaps, if he leaned forward, he'd be better able to ignore the pressure of her breasts against his back.

"We'll have to be cautious. They're alerting the outlying areas of an escape. Local wardens are expected to take notice of whoever passes by and hold anyone suspicious," Devlin explained. Feeling her begin to shiver, he snorted. "Did you think you were coming on a pleasure jaunt? I'm fleeing from a death sentence."

"Look here, Fitzhugh, it wasn't my intention to come along—"

"Oh, no? You were bloody anxious to join me once the guards saw you. Besides, if your life was so rosy, you wouldn't have visited my cell so often. A

walk across the courtyard would have given you
fresher air than the earthy stench of confined men.
Admit it or not, Alyssa Howett, you're running just
as much as I am—and not just from a possible charge
of helping me escape.''

''How dare you!'' Damn the Irishman. It was her
feeling of responsibility for what happened that kept
her visiting him—that and the undeniable magnetism
of the man himself, Alyssa acknowledged silently, but
what gave him the right to probe her wounds, to act
as if he knew the truths within her soul? She had
saved his life—he owed her some consideration for
that.

''Mayhap I should remind you that if it weren't for
me, your head would be on the execution block right
about now—''

''I wouldn't have been in jail under a sentence of
death if it weren't for you being where you didn't
belong the night we were rescuing Niall—or did you
forget that part of the story?''

''No, but haven't I repaid that debt today? It took
the money my aunt left me. I've nothing else.''

''Except for the pretty little neck which you might
be about to lose,'' Devlin said, his voice suddenly
soft. Slowing their weary horse, he tried to appear
casual as he spotted the soldiers blocking the west-
ward road. He had hoped by traveling away from the
north, they would avoid patrols.

''Oh,'' Alyssa murmured, peering around his
shoulder to see the problem. Quickly taking stock of
the situation, she sat up straight behind him and began

giving instructions. "Keep quiet and let me do the talking."

"What?"

"If all they know is that there was an escape, they won't have any knowledge of me," she reasoned. "We might get by since I'm English, especially if I can make them believe you're taking me to my dying sister's bedside."

"On a single horse?"

"The other went lame. Listen, Fitzhugh, you trusted me in the jail. Do it again. If they hear your accent, they'll suspect the worst."

Devlin turned to look at Alyssa and was immediately sorry he did so. Her soft violet eyes were open wide, her lips parted slightly, and her loose hair framing her face. She appeared intense and woefully committed—in this case, to their safety. The ruse even made a certain odd sense, he supposed.

"All right, but don't give them too many details. That's usually what trips up any lie."

Alyssa looked around carefully as they covered the last yards to where five men in the queen's colors stood purposefully in the road, hands on their scabbards. They'd chosen their spot well. The road narrowed here, heading uphill between a rocky cliff and a water-filled culvert of indeterminate depth. Trying to avoid them would not only be a clear sign of guilt, but doomed to failure. Please God and His saints, her plan would work, prayed Alyssa.

"And where are you two headed so early on one horse?" asked the tallest of the Englishmen as he grabbed hold of the reins.

"Off to find a preacher against her father's will,"
said one of the men with a laugh.

"Nay, he'd still be tasting her wares a while," argued another. As if by chance, the others moved to
stand on either side of the horse, adroitly surrounding
them.

"No, I fear we're traveling all too late, Captain."
Alyssa sighed, her voice sweetly tremulous. "This is
Liam and he came to fetch me from my village. My
dearest sister has been in labor for two days and they
don't think she'll survive. Too small she is and her
babes are always big and ripe. We started out right
away, but his horse went lame and we've had to share
this one. Then, coming through Dublin, there was
cannon fire and bells ringing and this poor nag almost
threw us both in a desperate fright." A single tear
rolled down Alyssa's cheek and her lips trembled as
she finished her story. "Please, whatever the trouble
is, we've no part in it. I just want to be there for
Bess—if it's not too late already."

"You've seen no Irishmen?"

"No, just some English soldiers near the castle."

"Liam, you said? That is an Irish name for certain," said the leader thoughtfully, eyeing the large
man in the saddle. Could one built as he truly be a
servant?

"I'll not deny it," answered Devlin, "but I've
served the Hampsteads for near four years and they're
fair enough, unlike some of you English black-
guards."

"Liam, you know Edward won't tolerate your
mouth," berated Alyssa harshly. Making a small fist,

she cuffed him soundly on the ear, much to the amusement of the Englishmen. "Why he puts up with you at all, I don't know, except for your way with the horses."

"Aye, that's one thing the Irish do know is their animals," agreed the commander. "All right then, go along with you and best wishes to your sister. I hope she makes it through."

"As do I, or I fear I'll have to raise her brood," said Alyssa, with a sad smile. "Thank you for your kindness, Captain. God save the queen."

"God save the queen," echoed the English patrol as Devlin kicked the horse and headed quickly up the hill before they changed their minds.

Devlin and Alyssa skimmed along the road for miles without a word uttered between them. Alyssa, unused to danger, kept reliving their narrow escapes and Devlin, no stranger to peril, was intent on seeing them to safety. Finally, however, the need to see how Alyssa fared prompted him to address her.

"I have to hand it to you, Mistress Howett. That was excellent acting back there, though I didn't need the blow to my head," complained the gallowglass playfully as he rubbed his ear.

"I wasn't at all certain you wouldn't hit back, but I had to take the chance."

"Do you think me that much of a fool or a villain?" He was astounded that she could imagine him so.

"Who knew what you would do or say? I wouldn't want to predict anything about you, except that you're too pigheaded for your own good."

"What's that supposed to mean?"

"Nothing, except that I imagine we're safe enough now. Yet still you drive on. Why can't we stop to rest a while?"

"Not until we're far enough west of Dublin to head north into the mountains. We can't afford to lose our advantage of a few hours' head start. I'll tell you when we can rest."

"Very well, but remember, we are *both* exceedingly weary and if you fall off this horse, I doubt I could lift you up unless I did it in parts."

An explosive guffaw erupted before Devlin could contain himself. Lord, the woman *was* an innocent, he realized, unable to banish the images of her "lifting parts" of him. Hell, she did it without even trying. What she could accomplish with a little effort.

"Are you all right, Fitzhugh?" Sitting behind him prevented her from seeing his face, but something was wrong.

"Ah—yes, it was just a cough, nothing to worry about. Trust me, I'll know when it's safe to rest."

There was no need to answer him, Alyssa realized. Trust him? Of course she did. She trusted him with her life or she wouldn't be headed off into the wild regions of the Irish countryside with him. Only her arms clutched about his trim waist kept her from slipping off their horse. Yet she knew without doubt that if she fell, he would risk his own life once again to save hers. How could she not believe in a man with scruples like that? Sighing, she turned her head and rested her cheek against the muscular planes of his shoulder, comfortable in the knowledge he was taking charge of their journey for now.

Hearing that soft expulsion of breath, Devlin shook his head wearily. Again he had gotten himself into a situation where he couldn't do as he wanted. Alone, he would be far north already, but the horse couldn't travel that fast with two riders and he couldn't abandon her.

Thanks to Alyssa's intervention, he was on his way back to his daughter's side. Once they joined the MacMahon, the problem would be what to do with Alyssa Howett in an Irish camp. Eamon would acknowledge the debt the MacMahons owed her for assisting Devlin and permit her to stay, of course, but would she be happy living with an outlaw band?

Feeling her arms snug about his waist, he suspected he knew the answer to that, but damn it all, he didn't need another complication in his life. Wasn't it enough that he was a father to a babe without being saddled with a woman almost young enough to be another daughter of his, much as his feelings for her were far from fatherly? No, he'd not be responsible for Alyssa Howett, too, not once they'd reached the camp anyway. Kicking his heels against the horse's flanks, Devlin turned north, determined to outrun the demons threatening him.

Chapter Five

The sun was high when Devlin urged the animal off the road and toward the sound of a stream in the distance. Alyssa felt the change in pace and stirred from the peaceful doze she'd been enjoying.

"Is anything wrong?"

"I think it's time to rest our mount a while. There's water and maybe a fish or two for the taking, if we're lucky."

"Where? I don't see it."

"The English won't either, I hope," Devlin said. He guided the horse carefully down a rocky grade away from the road. "But when you're used to living off the land and out of sight, you learn a few tricks. There, right below us, see?"

And, miraculously, Alyssa did. A narrow course of running water gleamed in the sun, offering cool refreshment she hadn't realized she craved. "I never would have guessed it was there," she murmured.

"Actually, it ran along the road a few miles back, but I thought it wiser to wait until it wasn't visible,"

Devlin admitted. Quickly he dismounted, helped Alyssa down and guided their horse to the stream.

"Easy, girl, easy. Don't take too much," he cautioned, stroking the mare's neck. She seemed to understand him and drank softly, backing off the water without complaint as he led her to the nearby grass. "If you watch her, I'll try to catch us some dinner."

"How?" questioned Alyssa, accepting the loose reins and looping them around a nearby tree. Still fascinated by his mesmerizing control of the horse, she almost expected the fish to leap into Devlin's hands voluntarily. After all, she had, hadn't she?

"Watch and see," he admonished. A man unaccustomed to justifying his every action, the gallowglass was weary of explanations. He strode purposefully to a small tree, broke off a narrow branch and whittled one end to a sharp point with the knife she had provided in the escape. A few minutes later he was poised on a rock in the middle of the stream, staring intently into the moving water.

He was only a man, Alyssa told herself, and certainly no one her aunt would have approved of, but it was no use. Perched above the life-giving run with his spear, Devlin appeared a god of old, about to throw a thunderbolt. His muscular legs were bent, his firm thighs straining the cloth of his tunic as his eyes carefully studied the movement beneath the surface of the water. Motionless in his patience, he was supremely intent, his goal at once obvious, his determination absolute. He was a man of deep convictions and a strong soul, Alyssa realized, thankful again that

he had been the one she'd needed to rescue and not
the little Irish weasel who'd first grabbed her.

Then Devlin's arm lunged in a movement almost
too quick to see and he held up the makeshift spear,
a trout wriggling unhappily on its end.

"Is one enough for the two of us or are you hungry?" he called with a laugh as she applauded.

"If it's as easy as you make it appear, you might
catch us a half dozen while I find some kindling for
a fire."

"Sure and I'd have to choose a greedy woman for
my trail mate." He chuckled, finding true amusement
in her arch look.

For the first time since she'd known him, the full
force of Devlin's dimpled grin was turned on Alyssa
and she very nearly swooned. The man *was* a god,
she decided, either that or the devil incarnate. Anyone
else with that fetching a glance only appeared in
dreams. Before she was through, she'd know him as
a woman knows a man and they would build a dream
of their own.

"What's keeping you? Take this fish so I can catch
the others. Even a tot like my daughter would move
faster than you."

"Your daughter!"

"She's the main reason I was so angry at being
captured," he confided. Handing her the first of his
catch, he retreated to the rock and went back to his
task.

"What of the babe's mother?" Alyssa asked trem-
ulously, but there was no response from the silent
hunter. Angry one minute, friendly the next, then so

remote he was gone altogether from human contact, Alyssa couldn't fathom the man, but it didn't change the facts. Like it or not, she had just helped someone else's devilishly handsome husband escape from jail, becoming a fugitive in the process and for what? Not that she probably wouldn't have helped him anyway, Alyssa scolded herself, but she would not have been so personally involved had she known he was wed. What had come over her? Was she as desperate to escape her father's control as Devlin had suggested?

Risking another glance at the Irishman, Alyssa was startled to see he had removed his tunic and was splashing the icy-cold water from the stream over his upper body. Without the dust of the jail, Devlin was even more appealing than he'd been the night he'd rescued her. Given his reddish hair, fair complexion and muscular physique, he could have been a Viking lord out to conquer the world or one of the handsome courtiers Elizabeth was said to favor. How could she have been such a fool as to imagine he might notice her? No wonder her father still considered her a child.

"I hope you're not offended by the sight of a man's body, Alyssa," he said, dropping four more fish at her feet, "but perhaps it wouldn't bother you so if you didn't stare."

"I wasn't staring at you, I was just... daydreaming."

"And I'm Henry Tudor," he muttered, replacing his tunic. "Look, like it or not, I had to rid myself of the jail's stench—even if only a little bit of it. I'll not apologize."

Stomping off to start the fire, he regretted his harsh

tone, but, damn it, when a good-looking woman like Alyssa stared, it did things to him—even if he didn't expect it. And, such a condition was all the worse when he knew he couldn't indulge his desires. She was too attractive for her own good—or his, fumed the gallowglass, and it would be at least two days till they reached the MacMahon's camp.

"Devlin, you never answered my question before," began Alyssa, as he gutted the fish. Determined to know the worst, she wasted no time. "Who is missing you at the MacMahon camp?"

"Other than Niall, who tends to follow me around like a puppy, probably no one much," he replied, surprised at her interest. Why would she care, unless she was getting nervous about her own welcome among Eamon's people?

"What about the daughter you mentioned?"

"I fear she's too young and recently come into my life to even know me, let alone understand that I'm the reason she exists." Holding the fish carefully over the fire, he glanced over at Alyssa, surprised that the meager heat of the fire was putting color in her cheeks.

"But what of your wife? Wouldn't she explain to the child? Won't she be worried about you—and your capture? If it were me, I'd be out of my mind for the fear."

"Aye, but we both know you'd do something about it," said Devlin, reaching over to pat her shoulder, before he thought about what he was doing. "Otherwise I wouldn't still be breathing. No, I've no wife to care about my comings or goings. Indeed, it will be just me to worry about Muirne's. I knew her mother a while back, but never realized I had a tyke until the day Niall was taken.''

"How could she have borne your child and not told you? For that matter, how could you not have noticed?'' Alyssa was enthralled by the unusual tale and the look of sadness in Devlin's eyes.

"Muirne's mother was a Macguire, not a Mac-Mahon. I visited their clan almost four years ago,'' he explained awkwardly. Handing Alyssa a piece of fish, he continued. "It wasn't anything more than two lonely people seeking comfort. After a few weeks, I went home and only when she died did her clan bring the child to me. They needed every bit of grain for themselves and couldn't afford to keep an extra mouth, not even so little a one. Muirne became mine.

"I'd never thought about passing on my blood to another, but now that it's happened, I have to admit it's awfully important to raise her right.''

Reaching her small hand up to his unshaved cheek, Alyssa stroked the fine reddish hair, a soft smile on her lips, a tear in her eyes. He was indeed the man she had imagined. How could she have doubted him?

"Aye, Devlin Fitzhugh, I understand and I only wish my own father had been as devoted as you,'' she confided.

"I think we'd better get back on the road,'' Devlin announced curtly, horrified by the intimacy that had sprung up between them so easily. "We've been here a good part of the afternoon.''

As he reached down to help her to her feet, Devlin was struck again by Alyssa's beauty. If only he had anything to offer her, he'd be tempted, very tempted to pursue her. But he was merely a gallowglass to Eamon MacMahon and a father to Muirne Fitzhugh. That wasn't much to offer to a woman like Alyssa Howett, he feared, and besides, he didn't need another responsibility. He was already choking trying to reconcile his duty to Eamon and Muirne without taking on a third concern. No, he'd find her a niche at Eamon's camp, some way she could be herself and not complicate his life. Much as he might enjoy such a complication once in a while, Alyssa deserved more and he meant to see she had it.

It was pitch-dark when they stopped again, and while Alyssa was glad of the respite from riding, she couldn't imagine what Devlin was up to when he helped her dismount and led the way down to a small farm. Motioning her to silence, he unsaddled their horse and headed toward the paddock. She watched in amazement as he led their mare into the enclosure and led another animal out. Within minutes he had the new horse saddled and they were on their way again.

"Devlin, what is going on? Why didn't we just take that horse and keep the other?" she whispered urgently in his ear.

"I couldn't take that farmer's only horse."

"But you did steal this one. That makes no sense."

"Why not? It wasn't stealing, it was an exchange," he said with a survivor's logic and sense of honor.

"Without asking the owner's permission, I still think theft is a valid description," she argued. "This horse is bigger than ours was and probably worth more. Besides that, what will your farmer say in the morning when he discovers the switch? Won't he report it to the authorities?''

''The run-down look of his holdings tell me he's an Irishman. He wouldn't talk to Her Majesty's representative, let alone ask their help. Besides, the farmer got the better part of the deal, Alyssa, and our horse couldn't have gone much farther.''

''What makes you say that?''

''The mare was utterly exhausted with the two of us on her back and a wee foal in her belly.''

''What?''

''The guard you bribed gave you a breeding horse. In due time, that farmer will have two horses to work his land,'' confirmed Devlin. ''He'll think the faerie folk have blessed him and that's the tale he'll tell for years to come.''

''As long as they bless us with smooth roads,'' murmured Alyssa wearily, ''I'll not complain again.''

As she drifted off to sleep against the firm support of Devlin's back, Alyssa thought she heard the sound of laughter, but she couldn't be certain. All she knew was that she was safe, Devlin was looking out for her, and he *wasn't* married. God was good.

By the next evening, however, Alyssa was not quite so satisfied with her lot. Devlin had pushed them all last night and today as well, following barely noticeable trails through green meadows and hillsides ideal for camping, but he'd not hear of stopping except for two brief respites to water the poor animal. Finally,

the weary blonde decided she had to object. After all,
if she had intended to die on the trail, she could have
stayed behind and let the soldiers kill her.

"Devlin, I'm sorry, but we must call a halt to this
mad flight—at least temporarily—"

"That's not your decision," he answered absently.

"I've not made any complaint, but—"

"And now is not the time to start, Alyssa."

"Can't we call a halt, at least for a few hours?"

"Not until we're back at Eamon's camp." Devlin's
tone was becoming curt. Unused to having his actions
questioned by anyone, let alone a woman to whom,
on some level, he was indebted, Devlin was too tired
to attempt to be polite.

"Well, I won't make it that far," insisted Alyssa.

"What?"

"I wasn't born to the saddle the way you apparently were. My legs are so numb, I'm not even certain
they'll support me, but I'd like to give them a chance
to try before I fall off this horse and die in the road."

Devlin slowed their mount and turned to look at
his passenger. Was it possible she was as uncomfortable as she said? Many was the time he had traveled
three or four days without rest and been none the
worse for it. Were women usually so fainthearted or
was it the strain of fleeing capture and the sentence
of death that were defeating Alyssa's spirit?

As he glanced at her, he saw her eyes seemed more
deeply set than he'd noticed before and faint bluish
circles emphasized their violet hue. Now that he was
paying attention, he realized even her arm about his
waist was less firmly embracing than earlier in the

day. Perhaps a few hours' respite wouldn't hurt. They were safely beyond the pale.

"All right, we'll stop to water the horse and stretch our legs too," he agreed gruffly. "Perhaps I should have been a bit more considerate, but I just wanted us to be safely out of Dublin's jurisdiction."

"I'd think that happened sometime yesterday."

"When you're running for your life, it doesn't pay to take chances," Devlin defended, helping Alyssa down. "Besides, there are blueberry bushes over there. You can eat to your heart's content."

When Alyssa didn't respond, he turned from where he'd led the horse to drink. Surprised not to see the blonde where he'd left her, he was startled to see her collapsed on the ground, massaging her left calf.

In an instant he was back at her side.

"Are you all right? What happened?"

"I told you I couldn't feel my legs. I imagine the sensation will return soon enough."

Without giving her a chance to object, Devlin knelt down, took her leg in his large hands and gently began to rub it, bringing feeling back all too quickly.

"Oh, oh, that's enough. It hurts," Alyssa objected. "It's as if a thousand needles are sticking me. Stop!"

"That will pass soon enough. It's only the flesh coming back to life. Now, where else might I rub?"

"No—nowhere. I'm fine everywhere else," she said quickly, already uncomfortably warm from his touch. True, his hands had never strayed above her knee, but the image of Devlin's soothing her sore derriere was too deliciously embarrassing to be wise. "I think I'll just nap a while, right here."

Rising to his feet, Devlin nodded and moved back
toward the stream. She was much too attractive for
an Englishwoman, for any woman, he frowned. Her
shapely legs, even through her stockings, were too
tempting to make him regret her dismissal of his attention. His desire for her had been sorely tested just
now, but he'd managed to maintain control. He had
no choice but to remain aloof, he reminded himself,
looking over his shoulder at the unmoving woman.

Alyssa Howett was a pretty picture to contemplate,
however, no matter what the circumstances. Her hair
caught the sun and seemed to sparkle, even as untamed as it was after the last two days. Its soft curls
framed her heart-shaped face with bright light, giving
her a warm glow of unexpected sincerity, a trait he
didn't usually associate with the English. Still, she
was not a part of his future, the gallowglass warned
himself once more. The only female he could afford
in his life now was Muirne; she would be more than
enough to keep him busy. Of that he was certain.

Alyssa lay still in the late-afternoon sunlight. She
had been so very stiff and exhausted, she should be
sleeping. Yet, every time she closed her eyes, she saw
Devlin hurrying to her side, concern sketched upon
the rugged planes of his face. He might deny it. He
might be rough and rude ofttimes, but he did care for
her and that knowledge had set her atingle as much
as his touch. Now, all she had to do was convince
him of his feelings. She had no other life available to
her. She had chosen Devlin Fitzhugh as deliberately
as he'd traded horses with the farmer. In fact, she
realized suddenly, she probably would have insisted

on accompanying the Irishman even if the guards hadn't spied her. After all, what was there in England for her, except a father who had never kept his word?

"Alyssa, eat something. The berries are sweet and here's a bit of remaining fish," he urged some time later. "We still have almost a day's journey ahead of us, but then you can sleep as long as you like."

"Are you sure I'll be welcome in an Irish camp?"

"You helped me escape. There'll be no question of your welcome," Devlin assured her. "In fact, I warrant there'll be fighting over who gets to sit beside you at the celebration Eamon's sure to order."

"As long as you're on one side of me, I won't worry," she said softly, "but my Gaelic is barely understandable."

"Most of the MacMahons speak English, and those that don't will learn soon enough if it means speaking with such a pretty lass as yourself."

Now why had he said that? he wondered, appalled. Hadn't he convinced himself the girl was to be left alone?

"Ah, there's the famous smooth-talking you Irish are known for," Alyssa said. She smiled and her eyes sparkled with pleasure. "I'd wondered if the English jail had destroyed your sense of humor or if you were atypical."

"Atypical I may be, but I swear true that you are a lovely English rose, clearly meant to bloom in Irish soil."

There he went again! He didn't know what had come over him, Devlin realized with a start. It was as if the faerie folk had cast a spell on his tongue, forcing unwise truths from his heart. Maybe it was because she'd seemed so forlorn sitting alone staring out at the stream as though she hadn't a friend in the world, but he'd said too much. There was no purpose in it and no future. And now she stared at him as if he were some mythic hero.

"Come, we must be on our way," he urged. Extending his hand, he pulled her to her feet and guided her to their horse.

"Whatever you say, Devlin." In all her seventeen years no one had ever complimented her so wonderfully, Alyssa reflected, her physical discomfort forgotten in the splendor of his words. It was just one more sign that he was the man for her and, maybe, he even suspected it too.

They rode through the settling darkness, only the stars overhead shedding light on the primitive tracks Devlin followed. Once a shooting star burst unexpectedly out of the east and Alyssa wished quickly that the Irishman would one day be hers. But, the star had fallen beyond view before she'd finished her wish. Still, she'd completed most of it; surely it would count, the girl assured herself. Snuggling against Devlin's powerful back, she nestled comfortably into his strength and closed her eyes. Like it or not, tomorrow they'd be with other people who would probably frown on her touching him so. She'd best enjoy it while she could, Alyssa thought, drifting easily off to sleep. Tomorrow, she'd be home.

Chapter Six

Alyssa had known from the manner in which Devlin was urging their horse forward that they must be nearing the encampment. The fact had been reinforced when the hint of cook fires was carried towards them on capricious breezes. And now their mount was thundering into a clearing ringed by ramshackle huts, the animal's last burst of speed coerced by its forceful rider.

Tightening her grip around Devlin's waist, Alyssa pressed her cheek against his broad back. It was a simple, spontaneous act, but she hoped it conveyed her surging apprehension. If it did, Devlin gave her no sign, merely loosening her hands in order to dismount.

The moment he sprang from the horse, he seemed to forget her as he was surrounded by the inhabitants of the camp, men clapping him on the shoulder or cuffing him playfully. But their smiles and joy at his appearance made them seem no less fierce to Alyssa. They were a noisy, rough-and-tumble lot, all talking at once without bothering to listen to either Devlin or

one another. Certainly, they were not at all the sort
of subservient Irish who had been permitted to tenant
her aunt and uncle's plantation. Even the women
made her uneasy. Dressed in coarse, tattered clothing,
they divided their time between gushing over Devlin
and casting angry, suspicious glances in her direction.

From Alyssa's vantage point it was obvious that
these people valued Devlin Fitzhugh as both a warrior
and a friend, just as it was obvious that she was regarded with distrust. Not that she had had much
choice, but what had she been thinking when she had
demanded Devlin take her with him?

Alyssa thought about taking the horse's reins in
hand and bolting from the camp, surely no more than
a den of cutthroats. But the animal was spent and she
had nowhere to go.

Wearily, Alyssa looked to Devlin to help her dismount, to introduce her to this raucous throng. But he
was too busy reveling in his reception, demonstrating
the swagger of a returning warrior tempered by a boyish smile that displayed his single dimple in the most
raffish manner. It was impossible to be annoyed with
him. Especially when all he was interested in at present was asking after his daughter. Surely Alyssa
couldn't fault him for that, not when she had spent
so much of her own childhood dreaming that Cecil
Howett would one day appear, just like this, to claim
her.

"Where is Muirne?" Devlin was inquiring as he
grabbed the hands of an old woman. His dark blue
eyes were alive with anticipation, and his smile was
enough to take any woman's breath away, no matter

what her age. "I have to see her now, Sinead, if only to prove to myself that my sparse memory of the lass is actually more than some dream visited upon me by the faerie folk. Take me to her."

"You've always been the domineering sort," the elderly Sinead responded with a sad smile. "As if your bullying would have any effect on me!"

"Must I resort to charming you into doing my bidding, old woman?" Devlin asked, his melodic voice resonant with mock seduction.

"I fear that won't work, either, you rascal. Your daughter is safe enough, Devlin Fitzhugh, though you will have to learn a bit of patience before you see her. The little one is not here, but back with her mother's people."

"What?" Devlin asked incredulously, disappointment washing across the clean, sculptured planes of his face, effectively erasing all signs of his dimple. His expression tore at Alyssa's soft heart, but if she gave any sign of his effect upon her, the Irishman never noticed.

"Now, now, lad, nothing is amiss," Sinead was reassuring him. "'Tis merely that the Macguires returned when they heard about your capture, claiming that under the circumstances, it was their duty to raise the child. Since you're not related to our clan by blood, Eamon had no grounds for denying them, much as he wanted to do so. But stop acting so bleak. Now that you're free, you'll soon set things to rights. You've simply to ride to Macguire lands and fetch Muirne back."

"Then I'll have a horse saddled and leave immediately."

"Ah, Devlin, you've always been an impulsive soul, never happy until you make things the way you think they should be. I suppose it comes from being a warrior living in a land under siege. But this is different, after all. The child is in no danger, and you've yet to make your report to the MacMahon. Wouldn't it be best to deal with the matter of the little one after your duty is done and you've had some rest?" Sinead inquired, the mild reproof in her ancient voice making her words seem more command than question.

Before a rankled Devlin could reply, he was beset by the others once more as they resumed their clamor to learn about his recent adventures. Men jostled each other to hear what the gallowglass had to say, and the women behaved no more demurely. In the midst of such a commotion, it was small wonder Devlin paid her no mind, Alyssa thought with a quiet sigh. With no other option, and feeling absurdly conspicuous still sitting above the crowd, she swallowed her misgivings and slid from the horse, descending into she knew not what.

The moment she landed with a soft thud beside him, Devlin seemed to remember Alyssa's existence. But before he could acknowledge her, a hush fell upon the crowd and the mob parted, allowing a silver-haired man using a crutch to come forward, two younger men in attendance.

"Devlin!" yelled the youngest of the three, barely

able to restrain himself from rushing forward to greet his friend.

Devlin grinned and nodded in Niall's direction, then bowed low and solemnly addressed the man upon the crutch. Despite his infirmity, the older outlaw's noble bearing told Alyssa that this was none other than the rebel chieftain, the MacMahon. She wondered if he was as fierce as her father had claimed, and almost cringed when she pictured herself living under MacMahon's rule.

"I have returned, Eamon, and once more place myself in your service."

"Devlin, I was uncertain that we would ever see you again," the MacMahon said, hobbling forward to engulf his gallowglass in a rough embrace.

"Uncle, I did the best I could to rescue him," the third arrival asserted hurriedly.

"Aye, Cashel, so you said," the MacMahon replied.

Alyssa immediately recognized Devlin's ineffectual rescuer as the same man who had sought to use her as a shield to make good his own escape during the raid on Dublin Castle. She detested him for his cowardice and doubted that he had made much of an attempt to free Devlin Fitzhugh, but Alyssa held her tongue. She was the stranger here, and he was the nephew of the MacMahon. It would do her no good to voice her true sentiments. At best, she could do no more than endure Cashel MacMahon, and treat him with cold civility when circumstances demanded she deal with him at all.

"After Niall's escape the guard was doubled at the

prison. Our only hope was to try and free Fitzhugh when he was being transported to the ship for the voyage to England," Cashel was explaining to his uncle under Devlin's hard, cold stare. "You know my men and I were scheduled to leave again for Dublin on the morrow."

"He was," the MacMahon admitted.

"But there wouldn't have been a voyage to England," interjected Alyssa. Her words compelled all eyes to focus upon her. She shifted uneasily, but refused to be quelled by the stony silence surrounding her. "Devlin was slated for execution three days ago. Your men would have been too late."

"I knew nothing of a death sentence," protested Cashel, squirming under the MacMahon's scrutiny.

"Nor did I," Devlin conceded in response to Eamon's questioning look. "But 'twas true enough."

"And so you decided to come home," someone yelled good-naturedly from the back of the crowd.

"Aye," Devlin responded with a grin, "but only to keep young Niall in hand."

"And you've brought a prisoner with you," Cashel added with a laugh, affecting a tone of camaraderie as he sought to shift attention from himself to the Englishwoman among them. "You're a sly dog, Devlin. You'd not allow me to take her, but yet you've done so yourself. Still, who can blame you? She's a comely enough wench."

Prisoner! She wasn't a prisoner, Alyssa thought indignantly. But before she could vent her ire, Devlin had taken a protective step towards her. She left the matter in his large, capable hands. It felt good to have him thinking of her once more, even if it was only to deny Cashel's assumption.

"Comely Alyssa Howett might be," Devlin pronounced, uncomfortable in the knowledge of just how true he found that statement. "But captive she is not! She is, with your permission, Eamon, my guest."

"An Englishwoman, living here among us?" the chieftain asked doubtfully, eyeing his gallowglass with reservation.

"'Twas her cleverness and bravery that saw me safely out of Dublin Castle," Devlin proclaimed doggedly. "But she was discovered helping me escape. Without her, my head would be gracing the top of a pike. Would you have had me leave her behind to be branded a traitor by her own people and to suffer the consequences?"

"Nay," the MacMahon answered slowly, his reply made after deliberation.

"How do we know it isn't a ploy? That the girl wasn't allowed to take Fitzhugh from the castle so that she could spy upon us and destroy our entire clan?" Cashel murmured softly. As much as he disliked the notion of being under English surveillance, he was not brave enough to raise the possibility to Fitzhugh. Eamon's nephew was gratified, therefore, when the man next to him overheard and agreed, voicing the suspicion loud enough for all to take note.

"Because I say she can be trusted. I'll be responsible for her," Devlin shouted, putting an end to the mutterings of the crowd. Though many had questions concerning the English girl, none wanted to anger the fierce warrior who had just returned to them, especially when he placed his hand possessively on the stranger's shoulder.

"That's all well and good," the MacMahon said, "but tell me, Devlin, what will you do with her?"

"Do? Why, I've not had time enough to consider that exactly," Devlin answered, being less than truthful. Damnation, but that was almost *all* he had thought about. Yet ponder the matter as he might, he could not discover a solution to his liking. Even now, the hand that still rested upon her slender frame burned until he thought it might burst into flames. Would Alyssa Howett never cease being a problem to him?

"She will be welcome at our fires, at least for the time being," Eamon finally pronounced, hoping this would put an end to the undercurrents of resentment he felt simmering among his kinsmen. "But for now, there are more important things to tend to. Have you heard about Muirne?"

"Aye. I'm leaving as soon as I can to bring her back."

"I tried to keep the lass here, Devlin, but the Macguires would have none of it and I had no right to insist—they are her mother's people."

"I understand, Eamon. You did what you thought best. 'Tis but a small matter to have to wait a bit to see her again. After all, a few days ago, I thought she was forever beyond me."

"Well said! You'll leave for Macguire lands soon enough, but first we must raise a glass in celebration of your homecoming. Come along, Devlin. There will be whiskey and song for us all."

Devlin was weary, and covered with the grime of many hours of riding. More important, he wanted to set out on his journey as soon as possible. But the hour was late, and he could not deny his lord's hospitality, especially after Eamon had accepted Alyssa's presence among his people. Flashing a grin that illuminated his features despite the falling dusk, Devlin nodded in acquiescence and followed the MacMahon, finally breaking his hold on his young English charge but keeping her close by his side all the same.

When the clan had settled near the main fire, a small keg of whiskey was brought forth, and after a goblet was pressed into his hand, Devlin was encouraged to relate the particulars of his escape. He did so, giving Alyssa her due, his story earning the girl a few reluctant grunts of approval.

After he concluded his tale, the whiskey began to flow in earnest. Tensions eased and laughter began to dominate. For the time being, anger towards the English was forgotten, and warm Irish memories recollected. Tales of clansmen long dead were recounted with mingled affection, amusement and pride. Even Alyssa was forced to give way to a laugh or two, eliciting a sense of satisfaction deep within Devlin's heart.

Soon, however, he noted that he was not the only one content to watch the glow of the fire create ripples of molten gold along the length of Alyssa's unbound hair, or to lose himself in the beauty of her rare, delicate laugh and occasional smile. Other men, too, were taken by her dark, violet eyes fringed by sooty lashes, or the full, sensuous curve of her lips. Yet what had he expected? Eamon's warriors were not blind. They might curse Alyssa's origins and consider her an enemy, but before they were anything, they were men. Mother of God, if the expressions of his fellows were any indication, the girl would bear careful watching in order to reside in Eamon's camp without incident. With a frown, Devlin threw back his head and tossed down a healthy amount of liquor, wishing his attraction to Alyssa Howett could be as easily numbed as his throat.

"You'll have your hands full with that one," Sinead whispered to Devlin with a nod in Alyssa's direction when the old woman refilled his cup.

"Why do you say that?" Devlin asked. Surely the hoarse quality of his voice was a result of the whiskey.

"Because I doubt you can keep your hands off her." Sinead laughed, fearlessly nudging the gigantic warrior with her scrawny elbow.

"You don't know what you're talking about, old woman."

"We'll see," Sinead replied with a chuckle. Then she padded away wearing an amused smile.

Alyssa chanced a peek in Devlin's direction as she had many times since sitting down beside him. The light of the campfire outlined his handsome profile and cast shadows across his wide chest and down his muscular arms, landing in a rather erotic dance upon the hardened thighs that jutted from beneath his tunic. And when he smiled, as he had been wont to do so freely and easily this past hour or two, Alyssa's heart all but melted. Heaven help her, but he was the most beautiful male she had ever seen. To her ire, however, most of the MacMahon females apparently shared her opinion. They all but surrounded Devlin, bestowing flirtatious smiles and beckoning glances.

One bold, dark-haired wench, Roisin, Devlin had called her, had blatantly asked him to share her blanket. Though he had ignored the invitation, Alyssa had been hard put to ignore the fingertips Roisin had trailed across the bottom edge of his tunic as he sat cross-legged, cup in hand. Had Devlin answered the seductive gesture with a scowl or a smile as he had carelessly swept the woman's hand away? In the dim light, Alyssa couldn't be sure and her uncertainty all but drove her mad. What claim, if any, did Roisin MacMahon have upon Devlin Fitzhugh? And how long before this impromptu festivity ended and she could get him alone to find out?

After a while, the lively songs sung around the campfire gave way to sadder melodies, mournful tunes that commemorated fallen heroes or else grieved over the fate of doomed lovers. Sweet, melancholy notes hung in the air as laughter abated and conversations became hushed, the stillness interrupted only by an occasional stifled yawn.

At last, whiskey and exhaustion sent many of the MacMahon's people to their beds, even young Niall, who, in his exuberance, had perhaps drunk too deeply from his father's cup. Finally the chieftain himself bade his newly returned gallowglass good-night, and took his leave. Devlin watched him go, glad that he had come home to serve so worthy a lord.

Glancing to his left, the warrior saw Roisin still awake and studying him intently, her smile echoing her brazen offer of a few hours before. To his right several men were staring at a drowsy Alyssa in much the same manner. That settled it, an angry Devlin thought with a scowl. The girl would sleep by his side tonight, and they would afford each other protection.

He briefly debated the wisdom of taking the girl to his hut, knowing that this would proclaim Alyssa his woman, something that would keep the other men at a distance. However, he quickly discarded the idea. He might have assumed responsibility for Alyssa Howett, but he had no wish to forge a more tangible commitment to her. Being alone with her, away from prying eyes, would likely lead to just that. He had resisted her youthful temptation for two nights already and three days as well. He had spent hours in the saddle with her lithe arms around his waist and her breasts crushed against his back. Then there had been her sweetly parted thighs hugging the sides of his posterior.

Dear Mother of God, how much more could he endure? Very little, now that he was weary and the whiskey had weakened his inhibitions. He knew well once they entered his shelter, it would be far too easy to share his pallet with Alyssa and allow his hands and mouth to do all the things they had been demanding to do to her for days.

No! Regardless of the message taking her to his hut would send, and in spite of the slight chill of the night air, it was much wiser to sleep in the open, along with many of the others, in the center of the compound. There, he could guard Alyssa without having the opportunity to set his mark upon her. If luck was with him, he might even be able to steal a few hours of sleep.

"Come," Devlin said gruffly, rising and grabbing Alyssa's arm before he could change his mind. "We'll move closer to the fire where you can take comfort from its warmth during the night."

"We're going to sleep out here?" Alyssa asked in surprise. How could she question Devlin about Roisin with so many people around them? "Surely one of those tiny houses would shelter us better."

"I said we are spending the night by the fire," Devlin directed none too gently, causing Roisin to send a smirk in Alyssa's direction.

"No, I'm not!" the pretty Englishwoman protested, stung by Devlin's tone and the embarrassment it caused her.

Her lips drew together in the most delectable manner, urging Devlin to take her in his arms and kiss away her pout. Instead, he merely grimaced and stood his ground.

"Oh, yes, you are!" he commanded in quiet earnest. The girl certainly didn't make resisting temptation easy.

"I thought I wasn't your prisoner. Have you changed your mind?"

"Damnation, lass! You know I didn't take you captive. If you'll remember, I didn't want to take you with me at all," an exasperated Devlin replied, as Roisin hugged herself and laughed softly, the smug sound barely audible to anyone except Alyssa. "But be that as it may, you're here now. And if you go off by yourself, I won't be there in the middle of the night to protect you should one of these dolts decide to ignore the fact that you are more girl than woman.''

"I *am* a woman!"

"Are you telling me you favor one of them and want your privacy?" Devlin asked, his jaw clenching despite himself.

"And if I am?" Alyssa asked, stepping up to him and raising her comely face to his thunderous one. She was furious with him for shaming her so in front of the others, especially the despicable Roisin.

Devlin stood there looking down at her, all sorts of thoughts running through his head. He longed to reach out and crush the loose tendrils of her hair, to feel its silky texture give way to his masculine strength. He wanted to swoop his mouth down upon hers, forget the consequences and carry her off to his tiny hut. He craved all this and more. Yet Devlin Fitzhugh had always been a man of integrity, and desire soon gave way to honor. He ran his tongue across dry lips, finding it took a moment before he could speak.

"Not tonight, Alyssa. For the love of God, don't battle me tonight," he ordered wearily, his voice hoarse and thick. "Can't we settle down and find some rest? Just this once, humor me and surrender to my will. We can deal with the question of your independence and future sleeping arrangements in the morning."

"You're departing camp at first light," Alyssa replied, a catch in her throat.

Was that what this was all about? Devlin silently marveled. Did Alyssa actually think he was going to abandon her at daybreak? Surely she knew him well enough to surmise that he'd not leave her defenseless among so many lusty men. Why, he had even caught Niall looking at her shyly from beneath half-lowered lids. And Cashel! Had that been a sneer or a trace of lechery attaching itself to his impudent mouth? Didn't the girl realize there was no choice to be made in the matter, that she had to go with him?

"Aye, I might be leaving, lass, but you'll be coming, too," Devlin reassured her.

"I will?"

"Aren't you my responsibility?" he asked gently, helping Alyssa find a spot near the fire. He spread two blankets, making certain there was adequate space between them, and waited for her to lower herself on one before he took his place on the other.

"You'll find, Alyssa," Devlin said with just the slightest hint of male arrogance as he made himself comfortable and shut his eyes, "that I take my responsibilities quite seriously."

And you'll find, you stubborn man, that I am nothing if not seriously a woman, Alyssa thought, squirming across the hard ground until her body fit neatly and firmly against Devlin's muscular length. With her back to him, she didn't notice his eyes snap open.

Cashel had watched the outsider and his English whore find a place at the fire. It had bothered Eamon's nephew to see Fitzhugh return. He had thought himself rid of the gallowglass after Fitzhugh had been captured. It had been tricky to make it seem that he was trying to free Devlin without the others discovering that he was creating more obstacles than he found. But he had almost been successful, duping his uncle and the others into believing that Devlin's rescue was nigh unto impossible. At least that was what they thought until Fitzhugh had returned, helped in his escape by a mere English girl!

Cashel ground his teeth in fury. The two of them had made him appear incompetent. It had already been clear that the MacMahon favored the gallowglass over his nephew, no matter that Eamon had fostered Cashel and helped to raise him. And now Devlin and his wench had lowered the MacMahon's opinion of him even more. Cashel hated the two of them. He had to find some way to free himself of Fitzhugh forever. If he didn't, there would never be any hope of his one day ruling the clan. Perhaps the girl was the key.

Though it appeared she was not Fitzhugh's lover, she was his weakness all the same. Hadn't the man defended her against the clan? Mayhap she could be an advantage. An effort to befriend her might yield fruit when and if he decided he could use her, Cashel thought with satisfaction. Aye, that was what he would do, play up to the English wench. With her lush young body and long blond hair, it was a plan that could afford him other benefits along the way. Contented with his decision, Cashel grabbed for one of the women still unspoken for, and made his way to his bed intending to celebrate.

* * *

Alyssa had a difficult time waking the next morning when Devlin shook her shoulder and told her it was time to make ready to depart. She was so sleepy that she wanted nothing more than to cuddle up against him and close her eyes again, and she was not shy about conveying her wishes in a series of soft murmurs. While he found her behavior utterly enchanting, Devlin would not be swayed. He had another obligation to tend to this day and he'd not make his child wait longer than she had to for their reunion.

Bringing Alyssa to alertness with a playful swat across her bottom, Devlin smothered a laugh at the murderous look she sent in his direction. In a good humor, he sought to gain her forgiveness by solicitously bringing her a cup of ale and a slab of meat as she sat upon her blanket. Unusual as it was for a man to serve a woman, Alyssa nevertheless accepted Devlin's attentions as her due, repayment for his churlish behavior. She rewarded him with a half smile, and received a boyish grin in return that completely dispelled any remaining irritation she felt. Could she ever remain angry with so handsome a rogue? she asked herself helplessly.

With a mirthful shake of her head, she rose and left the compound to attend to her needs. When she returned a short while later, only a few people were stirring. But Devlin was waiting for her, two horses saddled and ready. One was a large, muscular stallion, and the other a pretty little mare. Wordlessly, he assisted her in mounting the smaller of the animals, and easily swung himself onto his own steed. Then he led the way out of the camp, ignoring Sinead's mutterings

and looks of warning as she came forward to feed the
fire.

Cashel stood on the outskirts of the campground
and watched the pair disappear into the early-morning
mists. He was surprised to hear a hiss coming from
behind him, a sound that echoed his own hate-filled
thoughts. Glancing over his shoulder, he saw Roisin
MacMahon, her dark hair blowing in the wind, her
eyes riveted on Alyssa Howett's straight, slender
back. If looks were daggers, the English whore would
be spouting a multitude of wounds, Cashel noted with
satisfaction. Though Roisin was a fool to be enam-
ored of Fitzhugh, Eamon's nephew considered, she
might also be dolt enough to be duped into helping
get rid of him.

Chapter Seven

The ride to Macguire lands was far different from the mad flight out of Dublin, Alyssa mused. As she barely concentrated on guiding her small mare through a dense stand of trees, her thoughts were centered on the man who traveled ahead of her. The sight of him as he was meant to be, free and at ease in his homeland, made Alyssa's heart swell with joy. She knew that no matter what the future brought, she would always treasure the memories of these days.

True, there were two horses, and she was no longer seated behind Devlin, wrapping her arms around his impressive masculine frame. But this excursion brought pleasures of a different sort.

She and Devlin were fairly safe here in the forests beyond the pale. Isolated from the rest of Ireland, there was no one to consider them enemies, no Irish to view her with suspicion, no English to brand him rebel. They were only Alyssa and Devlin, two wanderers undertaking a journey together and enjoying each other's company.

Oh, Devlin might have worked to keep her at a

distance these past two days since leaving Eamon's stronghold, but she sensed that gap was somehow rapidly diminishing. Gone was the stony yet desperate male she had known in Dublin, and in his place was another Devlin entirely, a warrior so steeped in confidence that he didn't bother to conceal the playful, almost boyish aspect of his nature. Best of all, her rugged Irishman no longer treated her as a troublesome brat. Instead, it seemed to come naturally to him to treat her with respect and courtesy. If she had thought she loved him when he had been a prisoner in Dublin Castle, she fairly adored the man he was now.

And much as he might deny it, Alyssa suspected that Devlin was aware of her as well. She could have sworn last night she had seen a demanding hunger lurking in the depths of his dark blue eyes when she had caught him studying her across the campfire. When he had realized she was looking at him in return, his expression had become instantly shuttered and he had issued a gruff good-night as he moved farther away from her to bed down for the night.

There had been no more conversation, no more glances sent in her direction, yet Alyssa counted the incident a small victory nonetheless. Surely with time she could make Devlin forget the twelve years that stood between them. Given the chance, she could make him feel as much a lad as he made her feel a woman. If only she were well versed in the arts of flirtation and seduction. But, she was no Roisin. She could do no more than be herself and pray it was enough to entice her Irish warrior.

Devlin turned in his saddle, looking over his shoulder at Alyssa. He liked what he saw as a ray of sunshine infiltrated the leafy canopy overhead to light on the tip of her straight, slender nose. Her hair tumbled about her shoulders in waves of gold, and the corners of her mouth turned up gently in recognition of his attention. Truly, traveling with the girl had not been the burden Devlin had feared, the trial Sinead had predicted. He had rather liked being with Alyssa Howett, enduring minimal torment from the temptation her nearness brought. But then he was man enough to withstand the charms of a wench when the circumstances warranted, he thought smugly, a trace of satisfaction settling across his cleanly chiseled features.

With that the case, surely there was no reason to press on until they were both overcome by exhaustion as he had done the day before. No, it would be safe to make camp early. After all, hadn't he behaved himself admirably on this journey? All he had to do was continue to uphold his reserve and all would be well. So much for old Sinead's warnings. She was, in spite of the wisdom of her many years, still but a woman. What would she know about manly behavior in the face of feminine bewitchery?

"We'll soon stop for the evening," Devlin said, pulling up on the reins and waiting for Alyssa to come abreast of him. "There's a small brook not far ahead, and our mounts will be glad for it."

"Aye, and so shall I," Alyssa responded gaily. "I've ridden more in the past few days than I have in recent years."

"You've a talent for horses," Devlin complimented her. His superiority had been demonstrated by his ability to resist her allure, and he felt he could afford to be magnanimous.

Alyssa smiled prettily in return, an action that evoked Devlin's single dimple.

"Still, I'll be happy to dismount, sir. Demure as this mare has been, I've begun to yearn for solid ground beneath my feet. Why, even Eamon's camp seems preferable to any more swaying atop this saddle."

The moment the words were out of her mouth, Alyssa wished she could recall them, as Devlin's good nature abruptly vanished.

"Our clearing may appear a refuge to you, lass, but to us, it is something to be endured. Know that the MacMahon's people long for their true home, land that was stripped away from them by the English crown," Devlin informed her coldly.

"I'm sorry. 'Twas inconsiderate of me," Alyssa said. Would their differences forever stand between them, haunting them even when they were alone?

"Nay, Alyssa, you did no wrong. Mayhap I am overly sensitive concerning the issue," Devlin acknowledged, uneasy at the sadness he saw reflected in her face. Yet for some unknown reason, it suddenly became important to him that she understood the truth of what had happened to the MacMahons and how he felt about it. "'Tis the injustice of it that galls me, seeing men, women and children cast from their homes. And for what? Failing to swear fealty to your monarch? Still, we Irish are a hearty lot, and under

Eamon's leadership, we've managed to survive the past year and a half. Elizabeth probably considers that, in itself, another crime of which we are guilty.''

''You're being modest, Devlin,'' Alyssa responded with a mischievous smile meant to restore their recent lighthearted mood. ''If my father is to be believed, Eamon MacMahon's people have done more to plague Her Majesty than simply survive.''

''That we have,'' Devlin admitted, a shadow of a grin catching his mouth. Despite himself, and his suffering at the hands of the English, he couldn't consider this girl his enemy. When he was able to momentarily forget the responsibility she represented, she was so enchanting and radiant that her presence seemed to light up the darkest corner of the forest. But that was not a thought to dwell on, he told himself adamantly, remembering Sinead's words.

''We'd best move on,'' Devlin ordered suddenly, ''or the sun will be down before ever we near that brook.''

They rode for a while in companionable silence until Alyssa noticed that the melodic sound of water rushing over stone had begun to compete with the song echoing in her heart.

Soon they were on the bank of the stream. Sliding from the back of the mare, Alyssa was pleased to feel masculine hands around her waist, easily lifting her into the air before gently setting her down. She marveled at how natural Devlin's touch felt, and knew a sense of loss when he withdrew and began to see to his steed. Casting a yearning, sidelong glance in his direction, she was aware of little else...certainly not the anxious dancing of her thirsty horse. When Devlin turned to her, she reddened and quickly looked towards the water, completely ignoring the movements of the mare.

Suddenly, the impatient animal sidestepped, and would have knocked Alyssa to the ground had Devlin's strong arms not reached out to save her. While the animal bent her head to drink, Alyssa found herself flat against the masculine expanse of Devlin's hard chest. She tilted back her head to study his reaction, her innocent demeanor in stark contrast to the smoldering desire that set her violet eyes aflame.

Aghast, Devlin would have released her immediately had she not stood on tiptoe and placed a kiss on his mouth. After she finished, he wondered if it was the summer's heat that clung to his lips when their mouths parted, or something else entirely. Bewildered, he could do no more than gaze down into her upturned face. He had vowed he would not touch her, but he had never contemplated what would happen if she kissed him. He, who had withstood the attack of countless English soldiers, would surely not permit himself to surrender to one, young English girl.

"Don't play with me, lass," he growled, his words harsh. "It could lead to serious business."

"But I'm entirely serious," Alyssa countered. Her inviting smile transformed her into the most desirable woman Devlin had ever encountered. She ran splayed fingers along his broad shoulders and was satisfied with the shudder she felt beneath her touch.

"I'll not steal anything that should, by rights, belong to your husband," Devlin ground out, the cords of his neck bulging and prominent as he fought for self restraint.

"You cannot steal what is freely given, Devlin Fitzhugh." The words were a whisper on the wind.

"But there can be no future for us, Alyssa. Surely you understand that."

"All the more reason to enjoy the present," she murmured, her lips seeking his once more.

At the firm pressure of her mouth, Devlin's resolve began to crumble. It disappeared entirely in the groan that escaped his throat.

Reverently, he reached out with callused fingers to caress her trusting face, reveling in the delight she appeared to take in such a simple, yet intimate, gesture.

When she threw back her head in pure abandon to allow him access to her long, slender neck, Devlin knew he was completely undone. He prayed to God to help him because he knew he could no longer help himself. But before he could convince himself that what he was doing was wrong, he buried his face beneath her chin, inhaling the springtime sweetness that clung to her.

Placing tiny, eager kisses against her soft skin, he worked his way back to her lips. Suddenly it was as if a floodgate had opened and a torrent of pent-up longing was released. Unable to hold himself in check a moment longer, his mouth fiercely claimed hers, and his tongue plundered the honeyed recesses within.

Alyssa wriggled farther into the arms that now embraced her, moaning softly. Her response stirred Devlin more, the pressure of her breasts against him a delightful reminder of the treasures still to be explored.

Experienced hands reached up to capture a straining nipple, the breathy purr Alyssa emitted indicative of the pleasure he was giving her.

Slowly, Devlin undid the brooch that held her cloak. Then he was unlacing her gown, the material dropping away to pool at her feet.

Finding herself clad only in her shift, Alyssa reached out with trembling fingers to free Devlin from his forest green tunic. Nervous, she was unequal to the task. In frustration, she slid her hands down Devlin's sides and slim hips, until she found the garment's hem. Then, her fingertips skimmed the bare flesh of his thighs. She moved her hands upward a scarce inch when she heard Devlin rend the air with an impatient oath. Within a moment, he had removed not only his clothing, but what remained of hers as well. They stood clinging to each other with no barrier to absorb the heat of their torrid skin. Instead, the individual fires burning deep inside each of them spread, joining to form a conflagration that could be extinguished in only one way.

Devlin sank to the mossy bank, drawing Alyssa along with him. Settling her comfortably, he began to worship her body with his. He knew exactly how to proceed, having imagined this moment often enough during his incarceration in Dublin Castle. Reaching out, Devlin wrapped strands of Alyssa's golden tresses around his wrists, willingly binding himself to the woman who had but recently been one of his captors.

The reality of having Alyssa beside him, awaiting his lovemaking, caused Devlin's breathing to become ragged. He urgently ravaged her face with kisses, relishing the effect his actions had on both of them. Her youth and beauty was his for the taking, and he meant to have them now.

His hands once more found her breasts and his blunt fingertips captured the hardened buds cresting each white mound. Expertly, he stroked and teased, applying pressure that caused Alyssa to gasp and sway beneath him, begging for more of the blissful punishment he inflicted.

But when he changed position and took one throbbing nub into his mouth, Alyssa cried out in feeble dissent, a crimson blush stealing over her face and spreading down her neck and shoulders.

Devlin raised his head, probing her startled violet eyes with his smoky blue ones.

"You were made for a man's loving, lush as a summer glen and more beautiful than any woman I've ever imagined," he murmured, his words husky and seductive. "What we do here is natural between male and female, lass. There's no shame attached to you."

Quickly relegating his own rumblings of guilt to the darkest recesses of his mind, Devlin once again bent his head to Alyssa's breast. This time, she welcomed him, arching her back to offer him what he desired.

Her response tore a primitive groan from him. To Alyssa's ears, it was an inordinately masculine sound, at once demanding and despairing, as though Devlin was driven to master her and surrender to her all at once.

She felt the power coiled within his hardened warrior's frame, a power he kept leashed as he touched her with great tenderness. Something compelled her to set that energy free, to marvel at the primal strength of it, to glory in being possessed by it.

As Devlin shifted to bring his mouth back to hers, she grew bold and reached out a tentative hand. She brushed her palm across his broad chest, intrigued by the sensation of coarse, masculine hair. When his muscles quivered beneath her loving assault, Alyssa grew more audacious, her hand traveling downwards over his rib cage and across his taut belly. She could feel him tense as he waited to see what she might do next. Before she could decide, her fingertips acted of their own accord, trailing slowly in the direction of Devlin's manhood.

His sharply indrawn breath gave her courage, and she reached out to stroke him. A savage, guttural sound issuing from the very depths of his soul was his only reply, and Alyssa smiled. She knew that at this instant, Devlin Fitzhugh was completely hers, more enslaved now than ever he had been as a prisoner of the crown.

"Sweet Alyssa," he muttered, his hands sweeping her body possessively, his touch igniting every inch of her. The raw energy she had sensed within him began to surface, and with a deftness born of urgency, he slid his hand between her thighs.

His fingers moved rhythmically, bringing her pleasure of a sort she had never dreamed existed. She felt cherished and feminine, and she wanted him to go on like this forever.

But Devlin had other ideas. His supple ministrations grew faster and more intense, replacing the pleasing stimulation Alyssa had been enjoying with something else entirely. It was a sensation that grew wildly, threatening to consume her. When the throbbing, aching need he had created in her core compelled her to whimper for release, he withdrew his hand.

Quieting her sob of protest with hushed assurances, he knelt, his masculinity swollen with proud desire.

"Open to me, Alyssa," Devlin commanded hoarsely. "Let me enter, sweetling."

Alyssa quickly complied, her breathing rapid and shallow as Devlin positioned himself between her legs. She yearned for a release she did not understand, knowing only that he would provide her salvation.

"Trust me, Alyssa," he instructed tenderly. "'Twill hurt for an instant, but after that, we will journey together to paradise."

At her willing nod, he leaned over to kiss her eyelids, and then plunged deep within her secretmost place, his shaft hard and burning.

Smothering Alyssa's cry of pain with his lips, Devlin restrained himself, waiting until she was ready to continue.

"The worst is over," he pledged in a compassionate whisper. "I promise you it is. Allow me to take you further, dearling. Let me lead you to rapture that will erase the pain. Will you come with me, Alyssa?"

"Anywhere," she answered, her response low and throaty.

Gladdened, Devlin ran his hands again over the womanly curves he had once thought too girlish for his tastes. She was perfect, he realized, humbled. And for this one instant in time, she was his.

Muttering her name as though it were a chant too holy to be spoken aloud, he began the ancient rocking motion that would see them to ecstasy. She fitted him perfectly, her hot, satiny sheath encasing him so tightly that each slow thrust brought him to the brink of passionate madness.

Alyssa, lost in the sweet, mindless haze of love, was unaware of Devlin's fight for control. She only knew that every movement he made brought her exquisite sensations, feelings that began to heighten and pulsate with a life of their own. Soon they united to become a coercive force that threatened to sweep her away. She started to whimper and writhe beneath Devlin.

At first, she merely rose to meet his burning demand, but soon, it was she who took charge. Driven, she quickened the pace and intensity of their lovemaking, awed that she could so easily control the raw, masculine energy Devlin possessed. The notion imbued her with a heady rush of power, and made her feel very feminine, indeed.

But soon, Alyssa noted the divisions between male and female disappearing as their union transformed them into one entity. The impetus that had been building deep inside grew until she swore she could contain it no longer, and she called Devlin's name with a needfulness that increased the frenzy of their passion.

Mightier and mightier the nameless compulsion became, drawing its great strength from their very souls, enslaving them and commanding them until Alyssa feared she would perish from its wild onslaught. Her cries became breathless and more frequent, yet still the pulsating throb increased, swelling, expanding, engulfing her with mindless insistence.

Then, when she was at the point where pleasure was about to become misery, she knew release, knew it with a joy and brilliance that made her give herself over to it wildly and wantonly, calling Devlin's name once more. For an instant, the rapid thunder of his heartbeat drowning out the happy song of the brook was his only response. But then, he answered her with a primal roar, filled with exaltation, brimming with passion, tempered by masculine pride as he, too, found completion.

The burning urgency of desire dissipated, replaced by languid serenity. But even then, Devlin appeared reluctant to release her, though their lovemaking had come to an end. Instead, he lay with her in his arms, her head nestled in the crook of his shoulder, his cheek resting against her hair. He murmured Gaelic words to her, strange and melodic. They were no more than syllables to Alyssa, yet she thought she understood them all the same. But she was too spent to respond. She merely heaved a sigh of contentment and nestled more closely into Devlin's protective grasp.

When he reached for his cloak so that he might cover them both, Alyssa finally dared to look at him.

"It was beautiful," she whispered. "Truly it was paradise."

Devlin met Alyssa's gaze. He was moved by her blush and her shyness. Even with her maidenhead gone, there was an air of innocence about her that touched his heart and set free the sense of guilt he had banished during the throes of passion. Delightful though their encounter had been, he swore to himself he would never touch Alyssa again.

"Aye," he replied sadly, "but this paradise doesn't last forever. Still, I suppose ours was all the sweeter because we knew such joy can never be ours again."

He stiffened, waiting for Alyssa's recriminations or her tears. But only silence hung between them. The reasons he had marshaled in his mind remained unspoken when she didn't argue, didn't seek to dissuade him. For an instant, Devlin knew a stab of disappointment. Then he persuaded himself that it was better for both of them that he didn't have to remind her of their disparate backgrounds, or the difference in their ages. That he wasn't being called upon to explain his inability to provide her with the sort of life she deserved, or his reluctance to take on yet another obligation. But she was an intelligent lass, he reasoned, and she had known from the first there was no future for them.

Devlin was thankful for her understanding, and for the trace of a smile, wan though it was, that lit her face as she looked at him. But most of all, he was grateful for the precious gift she had given him, a gift that would be in his mind and heart for the rest of his life.

As Devlin began to stroke her hair, Alyssa's smile grew. No matter what her handsome Irish lover might say, she was certain that this was not an ending for them, but a beginning. From the look in his eyes, she could tell that she was as much in Devlin's blood as he was in hers. It would simply be a matter of helping him to realize it. Stubborn as he was, it might take time. But she could afford to be patient. The question was, could he?

Chapter Eight

"Padraic, he's come, just as I feared. The scouts outside the camp sent word Fitzhugh is on his way in. Lord knows how he escaped the English—but what we heard was true. He's here and he's brought a woman with him," cried the elderly woman. She'd entered the Macguire's hut without leave but, as his former nurse, she always treated him as a perpetual lad up to no good rather than the head of their clan. "What if he wants Muirne back?"

"Rae, I warned you when you suggested reclaiming the girl, if Fitzhugh lived, he was certain to ask after her. Don't let him see you are distressed. Just remember how sorry we are the wee lassie died and he'll go away again," assured Padraic Macguire, hoping it was so. "Allow him and the woman to wander the camp and see for themselves that the child is not to be found. Then I will speak with them. Regardless, Muirne will come to no harm, I assure you of that."

The child of Maeve Macguire and Devlin Fitzhugh held the promise of great fortune for his people. Rae had seen it in one of her visions two nights after they had left the girl with the MacMahons and he could not afford to ignore such a sign.

Even though it had been awkward reclaiming the babe barely a week after giving her to the other clan, he had explained the matter away by saying Fitzhugh's capture meant the MacMahons owed the child no quarter. Besides, he'd said, better she be raised by her mother's blood than by strangers. Had Fitzhugh been there, it would have been different, but this way, they had to do right by the girl.

There had been no purpose in telling the Mac-Mahon of the prophecy that someday she would lead her clan to gold. For certain, he would have refused to let her go. Not only did the Macguires need the fortune in their future more than the MacMahons, but anyone not of Macguire blood could never understand how reliable Rae's words had always been. The girl would be their salvation, and Padraic felt no remorse for the lies he was about to tell. Please God, he would be believed.

"Devlin, are the Macguires so much poorer than the MacMahons?" asked Alyssa. As they'd come into the small encampment, she saw women and children who seemed underfed and slow moving. Even the few chickens scratching at the ground were scarce more than skin and bones. There were no smells of food or welcoming cook fires to be seen in the camp, and the few huts visible in the clearing were little more than mud and thatch hovels. All at once, Alyssa realized how lucky she was to have been accepted by the MacMahons, who saw no difficulty in feeding another mouth. It was no wonder the Macguires had brought Muirne to Eamon's clan, though it was strange they had returned for her after Devlin's capture. "Where are the men?"

"I don't know what's happened recently, but in years past the Macguires fought Elizabeth's plantation system quite vigorously and lost a great deal both in land and lives," explained Devlin. "That's what brought me north those few weeks that saw Muirne's start. But, sad as it may be, Alyssa, the Macguires' problems are not my concern. Muirne is. You can amuse yourself however you like while I fetch my daughter. I won't be long."

Dismounting, he calmed the young boys fighting to care for his horse and helped Alyssa down. Then, turning from her as if she no longer mattered, he called to a white-haired crone who stood watching them closely.

"Woman, will you tell the Macguire that I wish some words with him?"

Though clearly unwanted, Alyssa took no offense. Indeed, had Cecil Howett ever felt her more important than the queen's business, she might not have been in the Macguire camp at all. Devlin was not Alyssa's lover now, he was Muirne's father, and the English-woman wouldn't fault him for that. Keeping an ear on the conversation behind her, she walked toward a flower-strewn meadow to watch a group of children playing games. Scrawny and poorly dressed, they nonetheless played with a rough-and-tumble energy, chasing around the grassy slope with little discernible purpose. The younger ones might have been having a game of tag, Alyssa supposed, and she looked closely but saw none with Devlin's dimple or bright auburn hair. In fact, it appeared all in the group were young boys, she decided in disappointment. It would have been nice to be the one to hand Devlin his daughter, considering all the pleasure he had given her last night.

Moving toward a young lad playing a reed pipe, the blonde scanned the faces of the older Macguire children dancing. Melancholy though the music was, the girls moved with a youthful grace she couldn't help but admire. Indeed, this might not have been such a bad place for Muirne to grow up, she reflected, but only if her father weren't able to care for her, she amended. From behind her, she heard the old woman speak.

"Our chief is busy, sirrah. He has not time for every wandering Irishman who thinks to claim his hospitality." Better Fitzhugh should learn they were not so meek and defenseless as he might think, decided Rae. If she recalled rightly, he would not take denial lightly, and she'd be able to measure his mood when he protested her dismissal.

"I fear, grandmother, your eyes are failing if you do not know me. I spent a fortnight with the Macguires but four summers past," the gallowglass said patiently. Respect for one's elders was never a waste of time. Indeed, this woman might have been one of those caring for Muirne.

The woman squinted as if trying to recognize him, but shook her head uncertainly.

"Never mind, just tell him it's Devlin Fitzhugh,

come from the MacMahon camp to claim his daughter. In thanks for his caring for her, I've brought a sack of flour.'' It had taken a bit of dealing to get Eamon to part with the hoarded meal, but when Niall had argued that Devlin deserved that and more, even Cashel had fallen silent. "Come, come, woman, we haven't all day. Off with you to your chief and we'll be out of camp in the hour.''

But rather than moving away, the shrunken woman came towards him, her arms outstretched and her eyes filling with tears.

"Oh, sir, you haven't heard then?'' she cried, throwing herself into his arms. "We've scarce recovered ourselves, but I thought Padraic had sent word to your people.''

"Heard what?'' asked Devlin suspiciously. Alyssa turned and saw a frown mar his handsome features. Anyone not knowing him would be hard put to remain calm in the face of his glowering.

"'Tis not our fault, I swear, milord. No one could have saved the wee lass,'' babbled Rae.

He had to concentrate to understand her words, coming as they did between great sobs and moans, and to be sure, Devlin suspected he did not really want to understand her. So newly a father, had he lost the privilege so soon?

"Has something happened to Muirne?'' he shouted, unable to bear the woman's cries any longer. "Where's the Macguire? Let him tell me my daughter's fate.''

"'Twon't change the truth of it, Fitzhugh,'' said a

man coming from behind one of the huts. "I fear to tell you she's dead."

"Dead?"

Devlin's echo was more moan than word and Alyssa felt his anguish in the depths of her soul. Though coming to it late, he'd meant to be a good father. What kind of God denied him that chance while allowing Cecil Howett seventeen years of ignoring his offspring? She shook her head at the injustice of it and started to go to Devlin's side as a dark-haired tiny boy passed her, heading, it seemed, for some nearby trees.

"You know she was like her mother, spirited and headstrong," explained Padraic, one arm reaching up to grasp Devlin's shoulder. "On the trip back from the MacMahons, she grew tired of riding and insisted on walking beside the cart. The women saw no harm in it and she merrily danced along the road, her reddish curls bouncing in the sunlight, as happy as we'd ever seen her—" Padraic's voice broke as he painted the vivid picture, leaving no doubt that tragedy lay ahead.

"And what happened?" Devlin's voice was dead. He had no heart to hear the rest, yet he knew he must—just as he knew he would take the child's body from wherever it lay, her mother's as well, and rebury them with the MacMahons. They had been, after all, his responsibility, even if he hadn't known until too late.

The woman took up the tale now, her speech soft and teary.

"Unseen by any of us, she startled a young vixen

from where it was enjoying its prey and jumped back to avoid her snapping teeth, falling right into the path of the horses. By the time we stopped, the angels had stolen her away.''

Devlin had no words. To think of that bright, happy child trampled by horses made him angrier than he'd ever been in his life and, at the same time, lonelier than he ever imagined possible. Even when the woman he'd loved for years had chosen to marry another, he hadn't felt any emptier than now—over a child he'd only seen once.

Rae and Padraic exchanged glances. Could it be this easy? Would he accept their word so quickly?

"That laughing face buried in the cold ground? How could this happen? 'Tis my fault. It comes from my own soft heart,'' Devlin exclaimed, unable to look in Alyssa's direction.

At his words, Alyssa headed for the woods, anxious to escape his self-recrimination and torment. Directed though they were at no one but himself, they dealt with her nonetheless. If she realized the connection between his concern for her safety and his resulting absence from the camp when the Macguires reclaimed Muirne, wouldn't Devlin do so as well? Then he would hate her. How could she defend herself against that kind of loathing? Stumbling blindly through the trees, her tears disturbing her vision, Alyssa almost stepped on the lad she'd seen leaving the others earlier. She quickly glanced away from where he squatted so as not to disturb his privacy as he saw to his needs. Then she looked again. Was it possible?

* * *

"Where is she?" Devlin asked. "I want to take her with me."

"Son, she's dead nearly two weeks. You don't want to—"

"I want her, whatever her condition. Muirne is my daughter and I owe her a proper burial," the gallow-glass said stiffly. It would not be an obligation he enjoyed, but it was nonetheless his duty. "Her soul must have its prayers said."

"We did that," said Rae, noticing that the child was no longer playing with the others in the meadow. "Believe me, we did all we could for her—because we loved her and hated the thought of losing her and because we knew you'd want it so."

"Fitzhugh, I'd give my life if I could give your daughter back to you," claimed the Macguire. "Her death should never have happened, but we must see it as God's will."

"What kind of a God permits such a thing as this?" cried Alyssa, nodding in the direction of the dark-haired tyke she carried in her arms as she approached them. "This child is his."

"What mean you? Shall I take any child because mine is dead? Do I not know the difference?" bellowed Devlin. His grief and pain resounded to the hills in the distance even as Alyssa offered him no argument. Instead she began to tickle the child and suddenly there was Devlin's dimple—on the left cheek of the lad.

"I assure you this child is a little girl, not a boy, no matter how she's dressed," announced Alyssa, "and I presume from the looks of her, she's yours."

In an instant, Devlin swept the child into his arms
and was whispering in her ear even as she played with
his reddish curls.

"Muirne?"

"Yes," she lisped, her soft response loud enough
for all to hear.

His blue eyes hard and his face oddly emotionless,
Devlin passed the babe back to Alyssa and turned on
the Macguire.

"You said you'd give your life if you could only
return my daughter to me, Macguire. Believe me, I'm
going to take it," the gallowglass promised, putting
all his weight into a crushing blow. Padraic collapsed
on the ground, felled as much by remorse as Devlin's
force. Standing over him, Muirne's father pulled his
dagger from its sheath. "But first, tell me why. Why
would you do this to any man, let alone one who'd
considered you a friend? For that matter, why didn't
you just keep the babe in the first place? I would
never have known about her."

The Macguire shrunk away from the thundering
male, knowing full well he'd not escape Fitzhugh's
rightful wrath.

"It was the only hope we had of surviving. After
we left the child with the MacMahons, Rae had a
vision of the babe leading her clan to gold immeasur-
able and I wanted that chance. You'd been captured
and were to be executed. What would you have done?
We never harmed her," pleaded the leader of the
Macguires. "But when word came from Dublin that
you'd escaped, we knew you'd come seeking her."

Women, children and an occasional man stood

around them now, all listening to their chief try to explain the unconscionable.

"We love her, perhaps more than you," argued Rae, running her gnarled fingers over the child's darkened locks. "With a little walnut juice, her hair was hidden and we thought you'd never find her. We have so little—"

"You have so little that you'd take a man's legacy from him for the sake of a dream?" Devlin shook his head and looked over at Muirne, clearly content in Alyssa's arms.

"Rae's visions are truthful," defended the Macguire. "Let us keep the girl and when we get the gold, we'll share it with you."

"I'll let you keep your life, you miserable imitation of a chieftain, and that's all," decided the gallowglass. "I'd hate for one of my daughter's first memories to be of her father's committing murder. Never, ever come after her again or I swear I'll take your life!"

"He won't, Fitzhugh," said a youth in the crowd. "In fact, it's time Grandfather retired as chief. We'll head farther north and see if the O'Neill needs help. I give you my word. We'll not trouble you or your daughter, no matter what my aunt dreams."

Nodding, Devlin reclaimed Muirne from Alyssa's arms and led his women to their horses.

"I apologize for upsetting you, Alyssa. Now, not only do I owe you my life, but I owe you my daughter's. Thank you," he said awkwardly, a man unaccustomed to needing others' assistance.

"Thanks aren't necessary." The blonde got on her

horse and took the child while Devlin mounted. She was amused to see how quickly he opened his arms to take Muirne back once more. "I can't imagine what I'd say if I were told a child of mine had died."

A child of hers? Saints above, remembering their passion of a few hours ago, Devlin hoped that wouldn't be another problem he'd have to face.

"Pray God you never will be told such a thing," he responded gruffly. Then he sent his horse into a quick canter, making his daughter laugh in delight.

The Macguire stronghold was hours behind them when Alyssa glanced at her traveling companions to discover her heart warming at the sight of them. They were an odd pair, the large, rugged warrior and the merry little gamine with her shorn, walnut-stained curls. But unusual a duo as they appeared, it was obvious they belonged together.

Despite her diminutive size, the child exhibited little fear of the massive stranger who had sired her. Muirne was open and curious, suffering no qualms about making demands of her father. Already he had promised her a pony of her own and a green tunic that would match his.

As for Devlin, his anger had been left in Padraic Macguire's camp, and everything his daughter did seemed to delight him. He'd spent the day ruffling her hair and listening attentively to her infant's prattle.

Alyssa's throat constricted as she watched the two of them ride along together, Devlin's coppery head bent to the girl's darkened one. The relationship building between them brought back childhood memories, disturbing recollections of longing for her own father. How many times had she imagined what it would be like when Cecil Howett came for her? It was a dream she had cherished, a dream that had gone unfulfilled until she had no longer wanted the man in her life. But now, she was able to see her youthful fantasy take shape with another child, another sire, and she could have wept for the beauty of it.

It didn't matter to Alyssa that Devlin was currently ignoring her. She loved him all the more for it. This was a special time for him and Muirne. He was merely giving the child the attention she needed. How remarkable he was, able to take a child he didn't know, and had never yearned for, into his life, into his very heart, all because of the blood they shared.

As darkness fell, Alyssa was lost so deeply in her own thoughts that she almost allowed her mare to collide with Devlin's stallion when he came to a halt.

"The child grows weary," he said with an apologetic smile while Muirne stifled a yawn. "We'll bed down here for the night."

Dismounting with his daughter still in his arms, Devlin lost none of his easy, masculine grace. Carefully, he placed the little one on her feet, bemused when her head barely cleared his knee.

"We'll sup on naught but bread and honey," he told the three-year-old. "But there will be fare more to your liking when we reach Eamon's camp."

"I like bread and honey," Muirne informed him amiably, becoming his shadow as he tended to the horses.

After apportioning their simple meal, Alyssa spread her skirts and sat down at the base of a large oak. She had just leaned back against its ancient trunk when Muirne climbed into her lap. The trusting gesture took Alyssa by surprise, and so did her reaction to having the warm, tiny form nestled against her own. Instinctively, the young Englishwoman reached out to push the child's hair off her forehead, and was rewarded by a sweet, tired smile.

"I'm sleepy, Devlin," Muirne announced.

"Father," Alyssa corrected gently.

"Are you my new mother, Lyssa?" the tot asked, her eyelids beginning to droop.

"No!" Devlin answered hastily, delivering his pronouncement in a strangled squawk that bespoke a lack of composure. This was the last subject he wanted to discuss. It had been awkward enough telling Alyssa that there was no place for her in his life yesterevening, without reminding her of it the very next day. "Your mother is in heaven, Muirne," he stated more calmly. Perhaps it would be enough and the child would let the matter drop.

"But, don't I belong to Lyssa, too?"

"No, you are your father's little girl," Alyssa said, giving the wriggling body snuggled against her a very large hug.

"Oh," the child responded dejectedly.

"But that makes you very lucky, indeed. Why, when I was just your age, I used to pray my father would come for me."

"Did he?"

"Well... no," Alyssa answered truthfully.

Muirne's eyes grew large and her face seemed as though it would crumple.

Alyssa didn't know what to do. She noticed Devlin regarding her oddly and feared she had angered him by upsetting his daughter. "But that's of no importance, now," Alyssa hurriedly assured Muirne. "Isn't it a happy thing that your father came to claim you?"

Muirne nodded in drowsy agreement. But her sympathetic young heart had been touched, and she didn't want the pretty lady holding her to be sad.

"Lyssa," she whispered loudly, "I can share my father with you."

"Why...why...thank you," Alyssa stammered. A crimson blush stole across her face as she looked to Devlin for assistance, But stiff and uneasy, he did nothing more than take an exceptionally long time to spread his cloak upon the ground, forming a bed of sorts.

Finally, he walked towards them awkwardly, holding out his hands for the child.

"I need a good-night kiss first," Muirne insisted, clinging tightly to Alyssa.

Devlin hunkered down next to them and did as he was instructed, marveling at the smooth innocence of his youngster's cheek.

"Now give one to Lyssa, too," Muirne commanded. "Her father never came to fetch her."

"But I don't need a good-night kiss, sweetling," Alyssa said with a shaky laugh that did little to hide her embarrassment.

"Oh yes, you do," Muirne insisted, stubbornly folding her short arms across her chest. Her obstinate look was a blatant reminder of just who had fathered her. "I won't go to sleep until you get one. I won't."

"But mayhap Alyssa doesn't *want* to be kissed," Devlin stated, his tone tinged with exasperation.

"I don't mind." Alyssa spoke up, her eyes filled with mirth as she worked to smother a smile. "There will be time enough for discipline later, when Muirne becomes confident of your affection for her. But tonight, it might be best to do as she asks."

Devlin regarded his overtired child and heaved a hearty sigh of surrender. He leaned over to plant a kiss on Alyssa's upturned mouth, not at all happy about breaking a vow he had so recently sworn, the vow never to touch her again. Meaningless as he intended the gesture to be, he was not prepared for the sparks that danced between them. Suddenly he became very grateful for his daughter's presence.

"That didn't hurt, did it?" the satisfied child asked, stretching out her arms towards her father and entwining them about his neck as he lifted her and carried her to the cloak he had prepared.

It hurt much more than she would ever know, Devlin admitted to himself silently. But he held his tongue. Instead he merely chucked his little one under the chin, and put her to bed.

Alyssa watched him settle down next to the child, as if he meant to use her body as a shield. If the delighted Englishwoman hadn't already adored Muirne Fitzhugh, she would have fallen in love with the child that night as evidence of Devlin's restlessness sounded in the darkness.

Chapter Nine

Of all the things in the world to be doing, Devlin thought with self-disgust as he turned off the road and began to ride across the meadow to a crofter's cottage. He'd been back in Eamon's camp but a few days and already he was being torn in two directions. He should be out hunting as his chieftain had ordained, yet instead, here he was riding from tenant farm to tenant farm looking to barter for a length of woven cloth, all because Alyssa wished one for the doorway to his hut.

He owed her the protection of his ramshackle home, and if the lass were in there with only Muirne for company, he wouldn't care that she wanted to install a veil of privacy. But he was spending his nights inside the hut as well, at his daughter's quite vocal insistence. And *he* didn't want to cut himself off from the prying eyes of others, increasing the temptation he felt every time he crawled onto his pallet. Yet Alyssa had merely mentioned she would like something to hang over the doorway, and here he was, rushing off like some fool to do her bidding after

none of the women in the camp would part with the
yield of their looms. Odd but he hadn't realized material was at such a premium.

Heaving a sigh, Devlin dismounted and sheepishly
approached the crofter's home. Alyssa no more
needed the blasted length of rag than Eamon's people
needed a stag to fill their bellies, but he was being
called upon to supply both. He had known that allowing a woman into his life would mean conflict with
duty. But he hadn't realized it would pervade even
the most trivial aspects of his existence.

At least there was no permanent bond with Alyssa;
she was naught but a temporary problem, Devlin con-
soled himself, as he greeted the wife of the house and
made his purpose known. Though what he was going
to do with his English charge, he hadn't yet decided.

A few moments later, he was once more astride his
mount minus one hand-carved cup and in possession
of a mediocre length of gray cloth. That business concluded, Devlin's thoughts should have been with the
stag he now needed to find, but they remained with
Alyssa instead.

He hadn't touched her since that night she had
given him her maidenhead, unless one counted those
bloody good-night kisses Muirne continued to demand he deliver. Devlin grumbled as he eyed the
length of material lying across his saddle. The damnable thing would only mean more difficulty, more
temptation, more discontent in his once acceptable
life. He looked down at the meager gift, and suddenly
felt his face redden with shame. What was this bit of
thread when compared to the gift Alyssa had be-

stowed upon him, those few stolen moments of ecstasy that had left him with guilt enough to last a lifetime?

Perhaps that would subside once he had settled her somewhere, Devlin mused, turning the horse towards the distant forest and thundering off in a burst of reckless speed. A convent? Nay, Alyssa could not waste away behind stone walls. A husband? Aye, he had to find her a husband, one who would be good to her, who would acknowledge and appreciate her soft heart, who would overlook her obstinacy, perhaps even find it amusing. Someone who would treasure the fires that burned deep within her. But where was he to find such a man? And where was he to find a stag so late in the day?

The moon was just starting to rise when Devlin rode into the MacMahon's camp, a string of rabbits slung over his shoulder. Delaying his hunt until afternoon, he had encountered no stag, not even a hind, nothing but the small game he dropped at Eamon's feet as the chieftain sat before his fire.

Sliding gracefully from his horse, Devlin handed the reins to a small boy. Suspended from the warrior's shoulders like a cloak was the grey cloth. Light though it was, it seemed to weigh him down as he turned to face the MacMahon.

"Those are strange-looking stags," Eamon said with a smile. He nodded in the direction of the rabbits.

"'Twas the best I could do," Devlin admitted, loathing the flush of embarrassment that crept over his rugged face. Failing his lord was not something he did often, and he was uncomfortable with the sensation it produced.

"No matter," the MacMahon said charitably. "Niall was more fortunate. I'll have him share his bounty. And, I thank you for your effort. Your kill will not go to waste. Now, get you some supper."

As he crossed the encampment, his makeshift cape hitting the back of his knees, Devlin could see Alyssa in front of his hut. It was for her he had disgraced himself this day. His ambivalence about doing so left him little peace. But she'd not be a problem much longer, he reminded himself, not now that he had decided to find her a mate. Wordlessly, Devlin handed Alyssa the cloth, brushing aside her delighted smile and words of thanks as he turned to scoop up his laughing daughter when the child ran forward to greet him.

With Alyssa's future settled in his mind, Devlin began to relax. Not that the thought of handing the young Englishwoman over to another man did not rankle him, but he felt it his duty to do what was best for her. And there were no other options, he reminded himself sternly. He'd been unwed too long to be able to accustom himself to taking a woman as his own. Besides, he was an outlaw, and a condemned one at that. Being bound to such a husband was no fate for Alyssa. She deserved better.

Taking a trencher of the food Alyssa had cooked over the fire, Devlin sat and ate, grateful it was not venison upon which he dined. He enjoyed, too, the feminine chatter that accompanied his meal as both

Muirne and Alyssa talked of how they had spent their day. Yet still the question haunted him. To whom would he wed Alyssa?

None of the small tenant farms he had visited that day boasted an unmarried son worth considering. His gaze slid around Eamon's camp, but fell upon no one more promising. None of these men could protect Alyssa as well as he could. And they were outlaws, too. If he was not suitable, then certainly neither were they, though many of them would have clamored to take the girl into their beds.

Especially Cashel, Devlin thought, his brow furrowing as the MacMahon's foster son crossed in front of them and sent Alyssa a smile she ignored. That was one bastard who had better stay away from the lass.

When the comely blonde left the fire to follow a frolicking Muirne, Devlin watched intently. He was satisfied that Cashel did not turn to join her, but went about his business.

Leaning back against his hut, Devlin felt content for a moment, his belly full with a meal cooked by a pretty woman, and his child running playfully about. Perhaps it really wasn't that urgent to find Alyssa a spouse. Try as he had, he could not think of a worthy candidate, anyway. And somehow, much as he told himself that he wanted the girl gone, his inability to supply someone to suit her did not depress him. Surely, he would stumble across someone, sooner or later...in the future. But not now. For now, he'd hold on to this sense of peace, false as it might be.

"Devlin, did you hear?" Niall asked, appearing

suddenly to sit beside his mentor, destroying the warrior's illusion of well-being.

"About your stag? Aye, lad, I did," Devlin replied, unable to hide his smile at the boy's obvious pride. "You've the makings of a fine hunter."

"That's because 'twas you who taught me. When I spied the beast, I concentrated on remembering everything you told me. I approached with arrow drawn, slowly and quietly, though I swore my heart was pounding loudly enough to send my quarry running."

"'Twas a fine job you did," Devlin stated, patting the boy approvingly on the shoulder.

"Aye, but I owe it all to you," Niall gushed. "You saw to it that I've learned to hunt and fish. That I know how to ride in a raid and defend myself in battle. Many is the weapon you've taught me to handle—bow and lance, dagger and sword, yet—"

"Yet what?" asked Devlin absently, lifting a cup of honeyed wine and staring at Alyssa over its rim. When Niall remained silent, Devlin turned to regard him curiously. "Out with it."

"Well," the boy began, his face turning a dusky hue, "there's one thing you've neglected to teach me, and so I've come to ask you about one weapon I've yet to learn to wield."

"What's that?"

"Why, the weapon that will...will make me a man...if...if you understand my meaning," Niall stuttered in embarrassment, casting an adoring look in Alyssa's direction all the same.

Devlin almost choked. Niall, even young Niall

wanted Alyssa warming his blanket? The notion was preposterous!

"Listen, and listen well, lad. If you think of your manhood as a weapon, you're not ready to approach any female, least of all that one," Devlin growled, uncertain whether or not to be furious at the pup's request.

"You told me only yesterday she's not really your woman," Niall protested.

"She's under my protection."

"But I mean her no dishonor, Devlin. I want to take her to wife."

"Wife! You're not old enough to know what marriage means, the life-long commitment it demands."

Hadn't he been seeking a husband for Alyssa? Here he was being presented with one. Yet Devlin couldn't take Niall seriously. Married to the MacMahon's son, Alyssa Howett might have the protection of the entire clan, but Devlin had learned only too well that she was a woman, not a mere girl. She needed the love of a man, not the fumblings of a stripling lad.

"Haven't others wed at my age?" Niall was arguing earnestly. The sincerity in his voice dispelled Devlin's anger so that his heart softened toward the boy once again.

"And doesn't a man find it difficult enough to survive in this country without having to see to someone else's survival as well? You're not ready yet for such a task, you young whelp," Devlin said, cuffing Niall affectionately. "Besides, you'll be the next chieftain of the clan. Is it meet you mingle your blood with that of the English?"

"I don't have to be the MacMahon," Niall replied stubbornly.

"You'd give up your birthright and expect that woman to give up hers? You'd disregard your duty to your kinsmen?" Devlin asked softly. "Is that the action of a true man?"

"No, but…"

"But what? I've never told you it was easy to be a man. Sometimes it means walking away from what we want most," Devlin commiserated, raising his eyes at the sound of Alyssa's laughter as she pretended to chase Muirne through the compound.

"So that's the way of it?" Niall asked in hushed amazement, realization dawning when his glance followed Devlin's.

"Aye," Devlin said absently. "It is."

When Alyssa finally grabbed Muirne's hand and turned toward Devlin's hut with the giggling youngster in tow, she saw Niall MacMahon get to his feet and rush away, leaving a ruffled Devlin behind. A smile claimed her mouth. Niall had tried to steal a kiss that afternoon, and she supposed the young devil had come to confess his transgression before she bore the tale to Devlin.

Since their return to the MacMahon stronghold, Devlin Fitzhugh had been far more resistant to her subtle flirtations than she had expected. Mayhap Niall's admission would jolt him to his senses, bringing a near perfect ending to an already enjoyable evening.

She had taken pleasure in cooking for Devlin tonight rather than their supping from the communal pot, and been gratified when he made fast work of her efforts. She enjoyed caring for his daughter, too. And now he was most likely reminded that other males found her attractive. Surely, she was one step further along in making him realize how good things could be between them, one step closer to his declaration of love. With an enigmatic smile, Alyssa guided Muirne into the hut.

Watching the gentle sway of Alyssa's hips as she entered his dwelling, Devlin grimaced. He'd been fool enough to think that he could leave things alone and wait for fate to send the girl a husband. But after his conversation with Niall, Devlin reckoned he couldn't afford to tarry. Niall had been put off easily enough, but assuredly there would be others who would offer for Alyssa's hand. He couldn't turn them all down without starting dissension among Eamon's men. Not if he didn't take her for himself, and that was out of the question. No, Alyssa would have to be wed sooner rather than later. The idea was a dismal one, and the illusion of contentment Devlin had felt but a short while ago was shattered completely.

He entered the hut. Turning with a heavy heart to tie the gray fabric over the doorway, Devlin tried to convince himself that any grief he experienced in losing Alyssa would pass. He had little luck. Something, he knew, would have to change.

Though the inviting smiles of the MacMahon women had meant little to him since his return from the English jail, he concluded that perhaps it was time he returned them. He had to once again become the

Devlin he had been before that fateful night in Dublin. No one, most especially Alyssa, must guess at the sense of grief he would know when she left him for her husband's household. A man could hide behind his own smile, and perhaps eventually lose himself in those of others.

. Since he had made a conscious effort to be more amiable, every unattached woman in the camp, from the widows to those never married, was after Devlin Fitzhugh, determined to make him her husband. They came to him at all hours with appeals for help with labors that needed a man's touch, and their spontaneous gratitude led to offers to care for Muirne or cook tasty dishes for him. But now their pursuit had reached a feverish pitch and he was tired of dealing with it. All he wanted was tranquillity. Yet, as soon as he retreated to his domain, he was greeted by Alyssa's flirtatious smile, and before he knew it, he was annoyed with her.

"Alyssa, I came back to the hut for peace and quiet, not conversation. Surely you have chores somewhere else that need tending," snapped Devlin. After being haunted all day by one female or another, he had had enough of women for a while—even his daughter. "And take Muirne with you."

Looking at the redheaded gallowglass who had so rudely answered her question of how his fishing expedition had gone, Alyssa was tempted to tell him what to do with his chores. But with the child present, she was forced to hold her tongue.

"Come, Muirne, we'll gather berries in the upper

meadow,'' Alyssa suggested, determined not to give Devlin the satisfaction of a reply. When the little girl clapped her hands and ran to the doorway, Alyssa raised the cloth and they left without a farewell.

Females! fumed Devlin. If he didn't know better, he'd swear something poisonous was in the water the way they had been acting lately. He had resolved the issue of Alyssa in his own mind, but this morning even the usually sensible Sinead had been making anxious noises about his taking a wife. Did they think a man couldn't raise a child alone? He had done fine with his life until now, hadn't he? Why did they think he had suddenly become helpless?

Besides, Muirne was enough of a responsibility to inherit so unexpectedly. A wife was a complication he couldn't even begin to contemplate. And then there was Alyssa. What would she say if he told her he had found a wife? Devlin didn't even want to think of that. She seemed to have accepted his distancing of himself from her relatively well. Certainly he did not hear her tossing and turning in frustration every night as he did, knowing she lay only feet from him, promising untold delight if he would but succumb to the temptation she offered, seemingly unconsciously.

"Devlin, come share a cup?" called Eamon from the door of the hut. His leg had improved so much in the past few weeks that he barely used the crutch anymore. Now he held a jug aloft, offering solace and camaraderie.

"Thanks, Eamon, but no."

"You've not been yourself of late. Is something wrong?" inquired the older man as he stepped inside.

Though Devlin was not a MacMahon, he had always considered Fitzhugh a valued member of the clan, almost a younger brother.

"Nothing a bit of solitude won't cure." The gallowglass smiled ruefully at the MacMahon's concern. "I'm not accustomed to sharing my life."

"Aye and from the look of her, I warrant she's one demanding female in private." Eamon chuckled, relieved the problem was so simple.

"When it comes to bedtime, she's beyond belief," groaned the first-time father. "But then most youngsters feel that way, I understand."

"I'd hardly call Alyssa a youngster—"

"Alyssa?" Devlin couldn't believe his ears. Eamon thought he was disturbed by *Alyssa's* demands? "I was talking about my daughter, Muirne," he explained quickly. "I've not set my claim upon Alyssa. She's simply under my protection and helping me with the wee lass."

"I see," said the white-haired elder, who didn't see at all. Given a woman as comely as Alyssa, even if she were English, he would have bedded her by now. Still, it was Devlin's business if he chose not to enjoy her, though perhaps if he availed himself of other women, he'd not be so edgy. "Well, if there's no other difficulty—"

"None, Eamon, thank you." Devlin rose to clasp the other man's hand, pleased at his friend's concern. "Living with females is just taking some adjustment."

"Then you'll join us two nights hence for a feast in honor of Niall's theft of those sheep from the English stronghold? I've sent word for Andrew's clan to join us.''

''Of course,'' agreed Devlin, suddenly considering the eligible men in the smaller MacMahon clan from the west. Surely if they knew Alyssa's part in saving Eamon's son, one of the men might offer for her. If a man had a weakness for blondes, she was attractive enough to make him forget she wasn't Irish.

Picking up his knife and a piece of kindling, Devlin began to whittle, feeling more relaxed than he had in weeks. Once he could trust someone else with Alyssa, his only worry would be Muirne and life could return to normalcy of a sort, these past weeks forgotten.

Examining the soft wood for its inner spirit, Devlin turned it this way and that before striking the first cut. Each stick of wood held as many secrets as a man, he mused. Nick the right vein, cut away the waste and a work of beauty emerged, but move too quickly, slice too deeply and the potential was lost.

''Devlin? The MacMahon said you were out of sorts and that I might be able to help. You don't know how comforting my touch can be,'' offered Roisin. Without waiting for an invitation, she slipped beneath the door cover and entered. In an instant, her hands enfolded his and she grabbed his whittling. ''How can you see anything in the gloom of this hut? Mine has much more light if you'd like to come by—''

''What I'd like is to be left alone,'' Devlin answered firmly. ''No one asked you in, Roisin. Why don't you leave?''

Never one to be ordered about, Roisin examined his work carefully and let out a cry of admiration.

"Why, it's marvelous, Devlin." Still dancing out of range of his hands, the overly forward female began to wheedle. "You are carving it for me, aren't you?"

"'Tis for my daughter, so please return it." Watching the stubborn way Roisin turned her head, he relented, knowing she'd never surrender the piece if he angered her. "If I make another—"

"Oh, Devlin, of course, I wouldn't want to take Moira's—"

"Muirne's," he corrected, removing the small animal from her hands. "Now, if you'll leave me, I can finish it."

"And begin mine," reminded the vixen who had no conscience. Spying Alyssa approaching close to the camp, Roisin turned to call back into the hut. "I've always enjoyed visiting you, Devlin, especially when your nursemaid and her charge are gone."

Nursemaid? Surely that was not the way Devlin spoke of her, thought Alyssa. He had to have some feeling for her, other than that of gratitude—or did he? Since their night of loving, he'd never spoken of a future together, only of Muirne's growing up. Just what had he been talking of with Roisin? Had she been there long enough to do more than converse? Was that why Devlin had asked for privacy?

"Muirne, go to your father. Alyssa will come soon," she instructed, handing the child her basket of berries.

Leaving camp again, Alyssa surveyed the area as she walked. A group of women were down at the stream doing laundry together, one scrubbing while another rinsed, a third laying the clothes out to dry on rocks at the water's edge, and a fourth monitoring the children's play. Yet Alyssa knew all too well, were she to approach them with Devlin's and Muirne's tunics, they would all suddenly fade away, leaving her to wash alone. It had happened too often in the past fortnight for it to be mere coincidence. Clearly the women resented her English presence and were not about to welcome her, despite Eamon's dictates. Of all of them, only Sinead was civil and that was a far cry from friendly.

Alyssa fought back tears. She wondered again, if she could undo what she had done, would she want to be back at Dublin Castle with Cecil Howett—or worse, in England? And, unhappy as she might be, she could not forget the joy of being in Devlin's arms that one night. Foolish as it was, she knew she'd suffer anything to remain with him. As long as they were together, she told herself, he could someday open his eyes and realize they were meant to be one. If she left the MacMahons, not only would there be no hope of Devlin's love, but her own countrymen would brand her a traitor.

No, she had lived for years waiting for her father's love though they lived apart. Surely she could be happy living with Devlin until he recognized their love. One day he would, she told herself, one day he would.

By the time she returned to camp, Alyssa could smell the cook fires burning and hear the laughter from the men and women gathered around them. Not to her surprise, however, the only voice that greeted her as she passed through the throng was Niall's. Devlin and Muirne were nowhere in sight.

"Alyssa, won't you sit with us for dinner?" invited Niall hesitantly, trying to undo his earlier indiscretion. "We've plenty."

"Yes, lass, do," echoed the MacMahon. It was time he learned more of this Englishwoman. "We've cooked up some of the trout Devlin caught this morning and there's more than enough for you."

"But he and Muirne need to eat—"

"Actually, I believe they're supping with one of the other women," said Niall quietly. He still smarted from Devlin's abrupt dismissal of his interest in Alyssa, and couldn't deny himself this chance to see her, especially when Devlin had abandoned her for the evening. "If you don't share our meal, Alyssa, I'll have to recite my lessons and that hampers my appetite. Have pity, won't you?"

Alyssa laughed at his earnest appeal, knowing as everyone did that Eamon was a stern taskmaster who insisted on his son's learning not only English, but Latin, history and philosophy as well. All too assuredly, an incorrect answer to his father's questions would cost Niall second helpings.

"When you put it that way, it will be an act of charity to join you," she agreed. If Devlin were free to come and go without explaining himself, then she was too!

"Are you missing your people, lass?" Eamon asked later as they sat companionably in the deepening twilight. Niall had gone to play dice and Eamon was enjoying a pipe and the company of a pretty woman, not of his clan, for the first time in years. "Devlin told me some of your story." Indeed, the loss of her only family for Devlin's sake was a major part of the reason the MacMahon had allowed the Englishwoman to remain in camp.

"Nay. There's no one to miss me, either. My sire was a father in name only. There was no love grown between us as there is between you and Niall," said Alyssa bitterly. She'd thought she'd put the old anger to rest, but seeing the ease with which father and son interacted had reopened the old wounds. "And then, of course, there's Devlin and Muirne."

"What?"

Alyssa didn't realize she'd spoken aloud. She'd simply caught a glimpse of Devlin carrying his sleeping daughter into their hut and her mind had noted another loving relationship between parent and child, another relationship in which she had no part.

"It seems clear that Devlin would give his life for that little darling, yet by the calendar she's been with him for so short a time. How much stronger can family ties grow?"

"Until your life becomes secondary to seeing to your child's happiness...until there's no joy in your world if he is away from your side," answered the MacMahon, realizing too late how thoughtless his words were. "I'm sorry, Alyssa, I didn't mean to hurt you, but your father's actions, both political and personal, are incomprehensible to me."

"You said what you believe. No man should ever

have to apologize for that,'' replied Alyssa softly. ''However, I will say good-night now.''

Alyssa crossed the camp, Eamon's words echoing in her heart. Was it possible that her father was so unhappy at her absence? Nonsense, she shrugged, refusing to consider such a possibility. She'd had no choice but to leave him under the circumstances—but wasn't that the excuse he'd given her for his absence from her life for seventeen years?

Too weary to battle such demons, Alyssa forced herself to wonder instead who had amused Devlin and his daughter for the evening. Probably the wretch Roisin, she'd warrant. Well, she'd not ask. In fact, after the way he'd acted earlier, she'd not even bid him good-night.

He heard her enter the hut, but he'd be damned if he acknowledged her. She had disappeared all afternoon and evening, apparently without giving *him* a second thought. Sending Muirne into the hut with the berries—a peace offering, he'd thought, only to discover she was gone without a word. How could he protect her from the hovering males in camp if she went off on her own? Unless she wanted to be pursued. That idea was even less conducive to sleep.

Devlin shifted on the rough pallet that had been his bed for years. Never had it seemed more uncomfortable, especially as he heard Alyssa whisper goodnight to Muirne and slip beneath the blankets a mere six feet away. He imagined her slender waist and could feel the small span beneath his hands as he'd helped her dismount. Her body was decidedly female, yet few men would expect the treasure of her breasts to be so rich, the gallowglass mused, recalling with delight the feel of those precious orbs, the sweet taste of her milky skin.

Perdition! He was doing it again. Every evening of late as they retired, he found himself tortured by the memory of their night together and his promise that it would not happen again. Yet he was only a man, a man being tested to his limit sleeping with her so very close but so out of reach.

Alyssa Howett was English, he reminded himself, and much too young for him, he continued, ticking off the reasons why she was not the woman for him, a list that was shrinking with each passing night. It seemed increasingly difficult as he lay alone in his bed to remember all the evidence that had convinced him he'd be better off without her—and still, he knew celibacy was the only way. For once he yielded to the sweet temptation that beckoned even now, his life would never be his own again.

A small sigh escaped Alyssa's lips and Devlin threw his blanket from him and stood up. Better to sleep outside the hut, he decided. At least there he wouldn't have to endure the same degree of torture. Now, who in Andrew's clan might he consider as her future husband? Malcolm was a bit long in the tooth, but he was kind and gentle...

Hearing Devlin leave the hut, Alyssa allowed herself a quiet chuckle. Why should he sleep soundly while she feared for her future? If she couldn't convince him to love her, who would?

Chapter Ten

Word of the MacMahon's feast had spread quickly and the women busied themselves from dawn to dusk, making cheese and butter, bread, stews and soups while the men saw to the butchering and arranging extra huts for the visitors expected. Wherever Alyssa looked, people were hard at work. Yet each time she'd approached the women to offer her help, she'd been rebuffed.

"You don't know our likes and dislikes—or even how to season a stew. I doubt anyone would eat your soup," said Roisin with a sneer as she stirred a kettle over the fire. "On the other hand, once a man has tasted my wares, he's not satisfied with second-rate."

"If you've never made cheese before, now is not the time to start," chided Fiona crossly. "And I've neither the patience nor the hours to teach you. Anyway, our men want good Irish food—not English castoffs."

At each refusal, Alyssa stood a little stiffer and forced her smile a little broader, but in the end, no woman in camp had use for her hands. Wearily she wandered to the meadow outside camp, Muirne following, and sat in the shade of a large oak.

"Lyssa, tell a story," instructed the child.

"I'm afraid I don't know any Irish stories," Alyssa said, weary of apologizing for what wasn't her fault.

"I want your story, not an Irish story," insisted Muirne.

"All right. Once upon a time, a fairy princess—"

"What was her name?"

"Oh, I think it just happened to be Muirne," amended Alyssa, unable to resist the child's dimple so like her father's. "Muirne was a very beautiful princess—"

"Father says the queen is ugly."

"Your father would have lost his head for certain if the queen knew that." Alyssa laughed. "Just the same, Princess Muirne was very, very pretty and kind, too—"

"Like you," the girl said, nodding and snuggling into Alyssa's lap.

"But, she was put under a spell so the man she loved didn't know that she existed—"

"Maybe the handsome prince just didn't know how to get past the ice maiden's guard," suggested Cashel. He came from behind the tree and squatted by Alyssa's side, his eyes fixed on her breasts. "You are a lovely picture without Devlin hanging over you, but then I saw that back in Dublin."

"Go away. Lyssa's telling me a story."

"Can't I listen, too?"

"No—it's my story and I don't like you," declared the girl.

"I fear Muirne's a bit cranky today. Perhaps you'd better go," Alyssa said, brushing the child's curls with a soft hand.

"Promise to save me a dance at the feast tonight, then I'll go," Cashel bargained. Nothing would irritate Devlin more than to see him partnered with Alyssa, so he meant for it to happen even if it took buttering up the brat. "You wouldn't mind if I danced with Alyssa, would you?"

"Only if you go away now," ordered the would-be princess. "I want to hear my story."

"Yes, one dance. Now, this Princess Muirne loved a knight who fought ugly dragons—"

Cashel walked away slowly. Her voice was sweet now, but he'd bet she could scream with the best of them. Some night he'd have to find out for certain, if only to enrage Fitzhugh.

"Did you expect a cloudless moon or tables so crammed with food?" asked Niall. Fully restored to good humor by a few younger girls from Andrew's clan who found him fascinating, he had stopped to speak to Alyssa during a break in the dancing.

"Well, the MacMahon is mighty proud of you and that flock of sheep you *liberated,* I think was the word he used," said Alyssa. "I somehow doubt the English would agree, however."

"Oh, don't worry, there's not an Englishman for miles," the lad assured her.

"Nay, there's one right under your puny nose, or did you forget how treachery smells?" countered Roisin, joining them. "She's the enemy, not one to be harbored in an Irish camp, no matter what your father says."

"Have you forgotten she got Devlin out the morning he was to be executed, a feat Cashel was incapable of accomplishing?" Eamon's voice was hard, his eyes cold, and his anger nearly palpable. "I'll hear no more talk about enemies and Alyssa in the same breath. I have welcomed her to our hearth and I'll not have anyone disputing it."

"Of course not, who would?" asked Devlin. He'd gone for another cup of ale and come back in time to hear Eamon's words.

"No one, Devlin. You know how drink makes men spout nonsense," Roisin said softly. As she spoke she sidled next to the gallowglass and began to rub her shoulder against him as a cat might around its master's ankles. "Come dance with me, Devlin. I've missed our time together now that you're sharing your hut with your daughter—and her."

"Ah—" He knew he should accept her offer if only to distract himself, yet the pain in Alyssa's eyes bothered him.

"I feel so special when I'm with you. No one else exists," whispered Roisin, her tongue tracing his ear.

"Dance with me, first," demanded Muirne. "You promised me first and then Lyssa. Remember?"

"I don't know the steps, sweet." Nor would she attempt them under Roisin's critical eyes, decided Alyssa. "What if you have my dance with your father as well as yours? I'm certain he thinks you are the most beautiful girl here."

"Am I really?"

"You *are*." Devlin smiled, pleased that Alyssa and his daughter got on so well together. "No one could be prettier."

"Of the children, certainly," whispered Roisin, running her hand under the sleeve of his tunic. "But you can't tell me my charms don't attract you a great deal more than hers."

"Behave yourself, Roisin," said the gallowglass, laughing. Playfully smacking her on the rear, he reached for his daughter and lifted her high in the air. "Come, my sweetling, and dance with me."

"I'll be wanting you next, Devlin," reminded Roisin. "We might even dance together."

Alyssa bit her tongue. She wouldn't sink to the wench's level. A lady never had to reply to an impropriety, her aunt had counseled often enough, though Alyssa had never expected to heed her rules of behavior in the forests of Ireland.

Still, as the night grew later and one woman after another approached Devlin with words of promise and suggestive gestures, the urge to disregard proper behavior became stronger. The children were off with Sinead, supposedly preparing for bed, and the tone of the evening had become decidedly bawdy.

"Devlin, I've a cinder in my eye. Can you get it out? You've such magic fingers, strong and gentle at the same time," praised Sheila. From the other branch of the MacMahons, she nonetheless delighted in seeing Devlin again. Catching one of his hands in hers, she brought it to her lips and licked its palm. "Even here you taste like a man—eager and fearless."

"I would suspect my entire body tastes like a

man's.'' The gallowglass chuckled. The night's ale and the women's words of praise had strengthened his resolve to find a distraction from Alyssa. ''Though I'd be hard put to know what 'fearless' tastes like.''

''Bed down with Sheila and Andrew will give you the chance to find out,'' warned Eamon. ''He considers her his own.''

''Well, he's never told me that,'' objected the woman.

''I never thought I had to,'' protested Andrew from across the fire. ''I've never seen you so attracted to any man but me.''

''Ah, but Devlin's not a man—he's a god.'' Deirdre giggled, second only to Roisin in her intimacy with the gallowglass. Draping herself across Devlin's lap, she wriggled to make him uncomfortable. ''And personally, I'd like to sacrifice myself to him to earn his favors. I'm already on fire anyway.''

''Oh, please,'' muttered Alyssa, rising to her feet. ''I'm going to check on Muirne.''

''Surely she is safe with Sinead,'' began Devlin.

''Let her go, Devlin. We won't miss her.'' The seductress was persistent. ''At least I won't, and I can make certain you don't.''

Alyssa didn't wait for the end of the dispute but walked quickly away. As she approached Sinead's hut, however, Roisin stepped out into her path.

''Devlin Fitzhugh is mine. He was before you came,'' Roisin lied, ''and he will be again—after he rids himself of the guilt he feels for making you lose your father. He enjoys a good time too much to ever settle for a little English sparrow like you. Can't you hear him with Deirdre?''

And, through the sounds of the forest, Alyssa did hear him laughing boisterously—having a grand evening though he had never once paid any attention to her.

"Give it up, and leave with Andrew's clan tomorrow. At least you won't spoil any more lives—like those of the soldiers on duty when you helped Devlin escape. There's talk among the men that they were beheaded in his place—I suppose the Irish should thank you for that—''

The soldiers killed because of her? Devlin belonging to Roisin and Deirdre for years? It was too much to comprehend and Alyssa fled Roisin's cruel words, taunted still by the woman's laughter as she ran sobbing through the camp to she knew not where.

"Alyssa? Where are you going?'' In an instant Devlin was on his feet, Deirdre's pleasures forgotten as he looked after the fleeing Englishwoman.

One of the men must have made an untoward advance, reflected Devlin. Damn, he'd have it out with the bastard—but first, he had to see to Alyssa. Without a backward glance, he hurried after her, leaving Roisin and Deirdre scowling.

Alyssa raced from the clearing and into the surrounding woods, the underlying bramble clutching at her feet, tearing at her hem. Roisin's laughter sounded in her ears, but she paid it little mind as she rushed onward, blinded by her tears.

She had come no closer to gaining Devlin's heart,

being shoved aside of late by others who wanted him, too. And Devlin had allowed it, finding distraction in numerous flirtations of a sort he had never shared with her. His last display had been more than she could bear.

What a dolt she had been, what an utter fool. Why had she ever thought that she could lay claim to his love when he was besieged by so many experienced, voluptuous women?

Never had she known such misery, nor had her heart been so near to breaking. All she wanted was to lose herself among the trees and disappear forever. Dropping to her knees, Alyssa buried her face in her hands and poured out her desolation, choking back sobs that originated in the depths of her soul.

What was she to do, where was she to go now that it was obvious Devlin would never fancy her? Back to her father, a man who had not wanted her either? Back to English law and the sentence that most certainly awaited her? Back to the disdain of the MacMahons? Nay, better she hide herself away in the forest and survive as best she could without ever seeing Devlin and Eamon's people again. She didn't need anyone. She didn't!

But Alyssa's vow of self-reliance didn't stop the tears that laced their way through her fingers or put an end to the uncontrollable shaking of her shoulders. And then, with no preamble, there were masculine hands seeking to soothe her, strong hands made gentle by concern as they stroked her head.

"Alyssa." Devlin summoned her attention, his voice tender but forceful. "Alyssa, look at me."

Her crying wrenched his heart until he was beside himself with anxiety. He swore that whoever had upset her would pay. Gently, Devlin raised Alyssa's naked face to his, cupping her chin in the palm of his hand, using his thumb to wipe away a fresh tear.

"Can whatever it is be so terrible that it brings you this much distress?"

Alyssa looked at Devlin sharply, his ignorance causing her to remain mute. Sweet Jesu, he actually had no notion of the reason for her wretchedness! Could she have misread his feeling for her so completely?

"Come, lass. Whatever the source of your unhappiness, you can tell me and I'll set it to rights."

Tell him? Tell him he had captured her heart, stolen her soul, when it was plain he wanted naught from her in return?

"Out with it, Alyssa," Devlin ordered, a sterner tenor creeping into his husky tone. "I'll not grant you peace until I learn what has so unsettled you."

He demanded a reason, but how could she tell him the truth? Alyssa cast about for a plausible response and did not have to search for long. A portion of honesty, no matter how small, was better than none at all.

"I—I cannot deal with being an outcast," she replied, her words breathy with tears still unshed.

"An outcast? But Eamon has accepted you into his camp!"

"Perhaps he has, but his people have not."

"Have they dishonored you?" Devlin pressed. Anger heated his blood when he recalled the lustful stares that followed in Alyssa's wake whenever she walked through the campsite.

"Nay, but neither have I been afforded courtesy. I am a pariah, barely tolerated by Eamon's people."

"I've seen no evidence of this."

"How could you? You are rarely in camp during the day."

"But... but I must carry out my duties to my lord," Devlin tried to explain, stammering for the first time in the presence of a woman.

"Aye, and I don't fault you for that. However, when you are gone, know what I endure." There, Alyssa thought with perverse satisfaction, that ought to put an end to his prying.

"I'll not tolerate your being treated so shabbily!" an indignant Devlin assured her.

"And what will you do? They but follow your example," Alyssa retorted, coming closer to the truth of the matter than she had anticipated.

"Mine?" Devlin repeated in horror. He had something to do with the tears still glistening in her eyes?

"Aye, yours," Alyssa acknowledged, a torrent of emotion bursting forth despite her best intentions. "Since we've returned from Macguire lands, you've barely spoken to me or paid me any attention. It's as though I don't exist. Why should the others treat me any differently?"

"But lass," Devlin said, hedging, desperate to keep secret the reason for the distance he had placed between them, "I've been occupied carrying out the MacMahon's orders."

"You've not been so busy that you haven't found

time for the other women in camp. How often have I seen you spare a word or grin for them?''

"Such trifling exchanges mean nothing to me," Devlin replied truthfully. The hollow flirtations were no more than a ruse to hide his ill-fated yearnings. But what were his emotions when compared with hers? The notion that he had caused her pain made him uncomfortable. "'Tis just my way—it always has been," he added lamely.

"Not with me."

"Nay," Devlin stated, his response slow in coming and his tone grave as he doubted the wisdom of what he was compelled to say, "not with you. But that is because you are special to me, Alyssa. To tease you would be no game."

"Truly?" Her wide violet eyes studied the huge warrior carefully.

"Truly," he echoed.

Helping her to rise, Devlin silently promised to put an end to his empty play with the MacMahon women, grieved that his behavior had prompted others to treat the lass so poorly.

Alyssa's delicate sniffles ceased and her heart took flight as hand in hand they returned to the feast. She knew the admission her Irishman had made had cost him dearly. And though he had not said he loved her, Alyssa sensed she was closer to the day that he would. The wall Devlin had constructed between them had begun to crack. Soon it would tumble.

When they reached the clearing, Devlin stalked with a determined tread through the groups of merrymakers, his hand possessively on Alyssa's waist.

His rigid carriage and the look on his hardened warrior's face caused conversations to cease.

"I've something to say," he announced, the delivery of his words steady and firm. "Alyssa Howett has been under my protection and, by the MacMahon's decree, entitled to a refuge here. Yet I've recently learned that she has not been made to feel welcome. Such news disturbs me mightily."

Devlin's voice had risen to a bellow. Men began to shift uneasily and women to avoid his harsh stare. Never had Alyssa seen him more forceful, and all his efforts were on her behalf. She felt quite happy and very special, indeed, as she stood at Devlin's side.

"There have been men who have not shown my guest the respect a woman deserves, and women who have treated her as an outcast," Devlin continued.

A few of the guilty parties began to sidle away, until the warrior put an end to their flight.

"Stay," he commanded. "I will have no misunderstandings here."

"There's been no misunderstanding, Fitzhugh. The wench is English. She deserves no better than what she's gotten," a man called out. Others agreed, their bravery drained from the bottom of a keg of whiskey.

Devlin's face was marked by rage, yet he resisted the urge to engage the culprits in battle. He could not wage a private war against his lord's retainers no matter how justified, in front of a visiting clan. Yet by all the saints, he'd see to it that Alyssa Howett was treated well.

Quickly his mind sought a solution to his dilemma. He settled on one soon enough, a remedy he was surprisingly ready to accept as the only one available to him, a remedy that blithely ignored all of his previous arguments for leaving her alone.

"English she may be, but she will receive all of the courtesy due my woman."

A murmur swept through the clearing, and Alyssa stared at Devlin in amazement. He was going to make his declaration to her, pledge his undying love, before the entire gathering.

"You claim her?" Eamon asked.

"Aye, I have decided to make the woman mine," Devlin affirmed. Yet he knew his countrymen could conceive of no love springing up between Irish and English. In truth, neither could he until he had met Alyssa. Still, if she was to be his, he would have to provide these people with reasons they could understand.

"I owe it to her. She saved my life, and has no recourse other than me at present. Then, too, there is no harm in that Muirne is fond of her."

"So be it," Eamon pronounced over the approving murmurs of his people.

Alyssa could feel the blood drain from her face. There had been no words of love, no mention of marriage. No question asked of her as to whether or not she would accept him. All Devlin Fitzhugh had done was proclaim to the clan his intention of bedding her. And what was the source of this magnanimous arrangement—a debt unpaid—pity felt—convenience? Well, she would have none of it!

"You misspeak yourself, Devlin. I am no one's woman but my own."

"We'll see if I can't persuade you otherwise, sweetling, once we retire for the evening," Devlin whispered, bending to nuzzle Alyssa's neck, trying to convey to her how he really felt.

Instantly, Alyssa moved away from him.

"I won't be sleeping in your hut tonight."

A few guffaws sounded, and Devlin was tempted to laugh himself. Lord, even when she was in a rare temper, Alyssa was a fine woman.

"That much is true. There will be little drowsing tonight, dearling," he promised indulgently.

"I mean I shall not be spending the night with you."

"Oh, won't you? Then where will you sleep?" he asked, his blue eyes crinkled with benevolent amusement. "Will you bed down by the campfire?"

Alyssa eyed the men awaiting her answer, men with hungry looks, their faces filled with speculation.

"Not at all," she bluffed, projecting more tranquillity than she felt. "I'll find a space in Sinead's hut."

"Mine?" squawked the old woman. She'd share nothing of hers with the English. But the sight of the troubled girl who had been living among them forced Sinead to relent. The lass had a good enough heart, and she carried herself so regally, trying to deal with her wounded pride in front of her enemies. And there stood Devlin, the great oaf, not at all aware of what he had just done to the girl. He needed to be schooled in how to treat a woman.

"Of course you can stay with me," the Irishwoman

declared in the face of Devlin's astonishment. "An extra pair of hands is always a help."

What was the matter with Alyssa? Devlin wondered in distress as he watched her depart the feast with Sinead amid a burst of good-natured laughter. Since he had known her, Alyssa had been toying with him enough to set his body aflame with desire. And now, when he had surrendered to her pursuit, she wanted no part of him? Did women have any sense of logic at all? And did Andrew's clan, clearly enjoying the spectacle, need such damnable entertainment as Alyssa had provided?

"I'll share your pallet," Roisin called with a swish of her broad hips.

"Nay, I will," shouted a wizened grandmother.

"What say you to me?" a masculine voice rang out, provoking laughter all over again.

A seething Devlin, totally confused by Alyssa's reaction, ignored them all. But he could not ignore the tug at the bottom of his tunic. He looked down to see his solemn-eyed daughter escaped from her bed and insisting upon his attention.

"Lyssa is angry with you," the girl stated.

"So it appears," Devlin murmured, his pride sorely bruised.

"You must have been *very* bad," Muirne pronounced, crossing her arms over her chest and regarding her father with an accusing pout, "very bad, indeed!"

Then she turned on her heel and walked across the compound to her pallet. There would be no demands for playtime with her sire before she went to sleep this night.

Bewildered, Devlin shook his head. What had he done other than attempt to see to Alyssa's happiness? Females! They conditioned a man as fire tempered steel. Well, he would become that steel, strong and unyielding. Alyssa would have to come to him after the way she had embarrassed him. And then, perhaps he would forgive her. The sweet form that forgiveness would take evoked enticing images. It took every bit of resolve Devlin possessed to remain where he was and not run after Alyssa to see if he might forgive her that very moment.

Chapter Eleven

A few days later, an odd pair met on the outskirts of the compound. Cashel kept his voice low, for he didn't want to attract attention, but neither did he want Roisin to harbor any doubt as to her task.

"I said, befriend her—or pretend to. Give her counsel on how to behave toward Devlin."

"But why should I help the English wench?" protested Roisin. "Devlin is interested enough in her without my teaching her to be seductive. Remember, you promised I'd have the man to myself if I helped you."

"I told you we'll both have what we want—you'll see the last of Alyssa Howett and I'll be praised for ridding the camp of a spy, but you must be more clever than the girl," warned Cashel. If he could play on Roisin's pride, she'd agree to anything. "You need to advise Alyssa to flirt with other men, convince her that Devlin will come running back if she seems not to care. Of course, we know that is the swiftest way to put him off a woman, to intimate that she's been with a host of others."

"But why are you helping me?" Roisin was too much like Cashel beneath the skin to fully trust him. "Why would Eamon put his faith in you if Devlin loses interest in the girl?"

"You need not know my mind to benefit. For now, understand that Eamon's not too keen on having a possible traitor in camp. If there is enough dissension, I'll be able to convince the MacMahon I'd be a better man to school Niall than Fitzhugh. That would give Devlin more time to spend with you," confided Cashel. Of course, if all went well, Eamon would banish Devlin from camp, but Roisin wouldn't want to hear that part of his scheme. "While you're dealing with Alyssa, I'll be telling Devlin just how flirtatious his little nursemaid is and how other men are enjoying her favors. That should stir the pot."

"Oh, I love a man with a brain." Roisin giggled. Running her fingers across his chest, she offered him her lips to kiss, but instead he hurried her off. "Begone, someone is coming and we don't want our alliance to be suspected."

Quickly he seated himself in the clearing and pulled out his knife, using it to pick at a piece of food caught in his teeth.

"Rather far afield from camp, aren't you, Cashel?" asked Devlin curiously. "I never thought you were too fond of spending time alone."

"I'm glad you chanced upon me, Devlin. It's the answer to a problem I was trying to resolve," confessed Eamon's nephew. "You see, I witnessed a rather surprising scene earlier and wasn't certain what to do about it."

"Take it to Eamon," advised Devlin. Cashel never could be trusted in regards to any matter and, feeling as low as he did, Devlin didn't want to be party to whatever he was plotting.

"I can't do that. The Englishwoman is involved and you know how uneasy Eamon is with having her about."

"Can't this wait, Cashel?" Devlin frowned. The last thing he needed was to be forced to think about Alyssa. "I'm off to filch a pony for Muirne from the English estate north of here. She's been haunting me for a horse of her own and I have need of some physical activity to keep from going mad."

"That is what I saw unexpectedly—physical activity—"

"What?"

"Well, I know you had a soft spot for that English wench, but I think you're better off than you know to be done with her."

"Speak your piece or let me be on my way," Devlin snapped.

"I came upon them not far from here. She and the man appeared to have met by arrangement rather than accident. Her body blocked my view but it seemed they were rather engaged."

"Aye, she had a thorough teacher," murmured Devlin. He was hard put to believe Cashel, but was it fair to disbelieve him so quickly either? Where was the profit in lying about Alyssa? Unless Cashel still harbored resentment for her part in the escape from Dublin Castle, freeing a man it had been his job to liberate.

"What was that you said?" Cashel inquired with a smile.

"Nothing of import—"

"Why, I would give you the man's name except that I don't want the blood of a kinsman on my hands. But, if you don't believe me, watch the girl in the future."

In a foul humor, Devlin turned his back and strode away. Perhaps a small piece of it was true. Alyssa had flirted with *him* often enough. Who was to say it was not in her nature to entice every man?

Damnation, he fumed. Would tonight be like every other night since she'd turned him down? Would he think of nothing but the blond witch even while stealing Muirne's pony? There was no doubt of it, he thought, frowning, no doubt whatsoever. The only question was, what could he do about it?

"Sinead, I'd like to talk to Alyssa awhile. Why don't you take Moira off somewhere?" suggested Roisin.

"My name is Muirne and I won't go without Lyssa. She's my friend, not yours," announced the child.

"A person can have more than one friend," Alyssa said, "though Roisin hasn't been one before today."

"But she is a MacMahon and one who desires some hospitality," announced Sinead. "Come, child, we'll see if we can find some wild onions for the dinner stew. Alyssa will be here when we come back."

As the duo left, Roisin turned to her enemy.

"Maybe I haven't appeared a friend in the past, but I only wanted what was best for you," the redhead claimed. "Devlin is too stubborn and set in his ways for a young girl like you to tame. Believe me, I've been around him for years and it's still an effort for me to control him."

"Seduce him, yes, but control him? Don't flatter yourself," Alyssa countered.

"In the long run, aren't they one and the same?" Roisin laughed. "But there, you see, you're so innocent, you don't understand men like Devlin. You'll never win him back."

"I didn't lose him, Roisin. He lost me. But what concern is it of yours?

"I want to help you."

"Why would *you* help *me?*"

"To tell the truth, Devlin is chasing everything in skirts these days, from the oldest women to the youngest. At least when you were with him, I knew he wasn't being satisfied and that he would turn to me eventually. Now I'm not so sure."

"I don't know if I want him back," lied Alyssa.

"'Tis your choice, but if you decide you do, you'll want him to come crawling to you, no other way, or you're not a woman who would hold him," baited the Irish woman. Alyssa was sniffing the hook and had almost bitten.

"And how would I do that?"

"Make him think you don't want him."

"I think I made that pretty clear at the feast."

"With a few words and by moving in here with Sinead, but now you have to demonstrate you mean it," advised Roisin. She'd show Cashel just how much smarter than Alyssa she was. "Start flirting with other men. Give away the wares you won't let Devlin have."

"I couldn't—" Even to bring him back to her, Alyssa wouldn't trade on the love they'd shared.

"You needn't actually make love but let everyone in camp see you talking with the others and joking with them as if you hadn't a care in the world. You'll see, a man only desires what's out of reach for the moment. He'll be after you, mark my words."

"And you'll still be after him?"

"Aye, that won't change. But if you hope to have Devlin Fitzhugh, you'll have to accept the idea of sharing him. He's too much man for a woman like you."

Her words, half truths, half lies, sounded plausible enough. Hopefully Alyssa thought so, too, prayed Roisin a few minutes later as she headed off to meet Cashel again to plan their next ruse.

Probably, they'd best switch partners for tomorrow's meetings. She would broach Devlin about Alyssa's antics and Cashel could see the Englishwoman. Hopefully he'd keep his mind on business. For Roisin had a feeling they couldn't let down their guard for a minute if they expected to come out winners in the end—and she meant to win!

Devlin sat in front of his hut, a barely tasted trencher of food held idly in his large hands. The camp was alive with normal activity, but his attention was riveted on Sinead's small dwelling. Though he had watched it carefully for nigh on to an hour, there was no stirring there. No blond head appeared in the doorway. No violet eyes stared out from the darkness.

Damnation, wasn't Alyssa the least bit curious about where he was or what he was doing? It had been five days since she had left him standing in the midst of the feast like some muddleheaded fool. And in all that time, whenever she appeared, she never once glanced his way or acknowledged his presence, though according to Roisin, she had time enough for others.

With a scowl, Devlin looked down and remembered his supper. Somehow, the victuals from the communal pot had lost their flavor and no longer satisfied him, though once he had thought them quite savory indeed. Tonight, much like the past few nights, he had dished out a portion of pottage more from habit than appetite. But again, the concoction had done nothing to warm his insides or erase the bitterness residing in his mouth.

He told himself that he was a warrior. That he had to eat to sustain his strength. But it made no difference. The needs of his heart seemed to outweigh those of his war-honed body. The woman he wanted didn't want him. It was that simple. All of his experience in battle had not prepared him to wage war with a woman. He cast the food aside in frustrated anger.

Almost immediately, a smaller trencher followed suit, spilling its untried contents as it landed on top of his own rejected meal. Feeling like a wounded bear to begin with, Devlin almost roared at his little she-cub. But how could he blame the child for feeling miserable when he suffered from the same malaise?

Ignoring the reminder of just how irritable an unhappy child could be, Devlin felt pity for Muirne. The lass was off her feed and behaving abominably because she was missing Alyssa, too. Turning to his daughter, he saw her temper-stained face and experienced a moment of despair. Hurriedly he wondered what method he would use to try and soothe his ruffled offspring this time, not that anything he might try would have the desired effect. Suddenly, he found himself at his wits' end. What sort of dolt was he that he had no idea of how to deal with the woman he didn't have or with the girl child that he did?

The situation had grown intolerable. Action...that's what was needed. Yet, what to do? He didn't know. He thought of asking Eamon or one of the older men for advice and rejected the idea at once. Whatever they had to say would be from a man's point of view, and he was well versed in that already. What he needed was something that was totally beyond him—to understand the mind of a woman. But whom to ask?

Then, from the corner of his eye, he saw Sinead emerge from her home to fetch water from the stream. Surely if anyone could offer sage counsel, it would be the old woman.

Leaving Muirne squabbling with little Liam under his mother's benevolent eye, Devlin followed Sinead as unobtrusively as possible. He overtook her just before she reached her destination.

"Here, allow me to help," he said with what he hoped passed for a casual smile.

"You don't have to win me over, lad," Sinead reprimanded in amusement. "Save your raffish charm for Alyssa."

"'Twould do me no good," Devlin grumbled, taking the pail and filling it to the brim.

"Ah, I see. Then perhaps you should just accept your fate and grant that the girl doesn't care for you," Sinead goaded slyly.

"That's not true, she loves me," Devlin asserted, his tone defying his companion to contradict him.

"Has she told you as much?"

"Nay, but I know it all the same."

"And have you told her you love her?" Sinead inquired, working to hide the smile that threatened to erupt when Devlin began to shift uneasily.

"I haven't. But she should know I do!" he insisted obstinately.

"Devlin Fitzhugh, surely you have sense enough to understand that a woman has to be told these things! Or have you lived among warriors for so long that you've forgotten?"

"I said the words to a woman once, a woman I thought I loved. But after hearing what I had to say, she chose another."

"And Alyssa Howett must pay for this other woman's sins? There is not much fairness or logic in that."

"It has nothing to do with that!" Devlin growled. He couldn't confide to Sinead that he, a seasoned soldier, feared opening his heart to a mere wisp of a girl.

"If you can't tell her, then show her. You mustn't expect the lass to take things for granted."

"What do you mean?"

"Why, you must woo her!" Sinead crowed triumphantly.

"What? Me? Set out to court a seventeen-year-old?" Devlin bristled. "When she wants me, she knows where to find me."

"You think she should be thankful that the great gallowglass wants to take her to his bed? You simpleton, can't you see it's that sort of attitude that angered Alyssa in the first place? She's a beautiful prize and has to be won...that is, if you want to win her. If you don't, there seem to be plenty who do," Sinead added with a sidelong glance.

Devlin remembered Cashel's accusations and wondered if Alyssa had, indeed, given herself to another. Yet he would dishonor neither her nor himself by asking Sinead the truth of the matter.

The old woman, however, must have read the reason for the misery reflected in Devlin's stormy, blue eyes, and she took pity on him.

"That's not to say the lass has looked elsewhere, but you cannot expect her to wait until doomsday for you. If you want her, pursue her."

"I'd feel the imbecile playing the lovesick swain."

"And wouldn't you be appear more the idiot if you allowed some other man to capture her heart?" Sinead retorted impatiently. "Make your choice man, your pride or your heart."

"But—"

"But nothing. Now give me the pail of water and

allow me to get back. I don't want Alyssa to suspect I've been consorting with the enemy.''

''The enemy!'' a wounded Devlin yelled at the old woman's retreating back. ''Have you forgotten? She's the one who's English.''

''Aye, but in the larger scheme of things, you're the one who's the foe,'' Sinead rejoined, her faint words carried on the slight summer breeze.

Devlin stayed behind, feeling surprised and betrayed that in this instance gender had taken precedence over Sinead's loathing for all that was English.

''Woo her!'' Devlin muttered crossly. The notion was unacceptable—at least it was until he envisioned spending the rest of his life without Alyssa Howett.

As Sinead shooed her out of the hut the next morning, Alyssa was aware of some sort of commotion going on in the clearing. Yet the women were flanking the disturbance so that she had to draw closer to satisfy her curiosity.

Squeezing herself through the throng, Alyssa was surprised to see the men practicing at warfare. They never drilled in the middle of the camp, that she knew of, but they were doing so today. And in the thick of it was Devlin Fitzhugh, training like a man possessed.

Clad as he was in only a half tunic made of leather, a thin sheen of perspiration covered his broad, bare chest, making his bronzed skin glisten in the morning light. The muscles of his arms bulged as he parried and thrust, his powerful legs helping him to stand his ground while he took on three opponents all at once.

''The man is beyond help, at least any I can give him,'' Sinead mumbled, coming to stand beside

Alyssa. "You know why Devlin has the men-at-arms here, don't you? 'Tis to gain your notice. The peacock hopes to impress you with his prowess."

"Then he's wasting his time. I already know how well he can fight," Alyssa said, stealing a look at Devlin's magnificent frame in spite of her words.

"Still, he's a fine figure of a man, isn't he?"

"And so are many of the others," Alyssa lied. "Come, let us pick those berries you've been craving."

The young Englishwoman walked away without so much as a backward glance. Sinead followed, shaking her head, while an enraged Devlin immediately began to attack his fellows with such ferocity that they threw down their swords, forsaking him as well.

When Alyssa and Sinead returned to the camp that afternoon, there was no sign of Devlin. He left behind him no more than a few men nursing bruises from the morning's exercise and Muirne, placed in the care of little Liam's family.

Momentarily, Alyssa's heart constricted with fear. Was Devlin gone for good? A yelp of rage from Liam was drowned out by Muirne's laughter. As the elfish sound of it drifted across the clearing, Alyssa knew Devlin could never abandon the child. Still, peace eluded her when another apprehension arose. But a quick survey of the compound assured her Roisin was still there.

Most likely Devlin had done no more than ride off to get over his anger. Perhaps the solitude would do him good, Alyssa thought flippantly. As for her, it would certainly be easier to get through the remainder of the day without having to avoid him, without having to pretend she was completely unaware of his commanding, masculine presence. Yet somehow, an easy day was suddenly a dismal prospect.

"Saints preserve us! Alyssa, come quickly," Sinead called early the next morning.

Alyssa's sleepy eyes snapped open and she scrambled to dress. What had occurred to excite Sinead so? Dear Lord, had something happened to Devlin?

When Alyssa ran from the hut, however, she saw Devlin not ten yards away. His back was to her, but his solid stance, feet planted wide apart, seemed to indicate no harm had befallen him. All at once, as though he sensed her staring, he turned his head and caught her eye. His interest remained fixed upon her, and his expression became smug.

Alyssa wondered what it was he expected of her, until she whirled around and saw just what it was that had made Sinead call out. There, hanging from a large oak near the hut, was a gory sight, the carcass of a huge stag, its dull eyes open and its tongue lolling from its mouth.

"We've been the recipient of someone's largesse," Sinead gushed, trying to make the best of a bad situation. Appreciated though food was among Eamon's band of rebels, did Devlin Fitzhugh really think such a gift would win the heart of a lass?

"I'm certain the others will enjoy it," Alyssa replied with a nonchalant shrug.

"Aye, 'tis meet to share so fine an animal, but we'll savor the taste of this as well," Sinead said hurriedly when she saw Devlin's foot beginning to beat an irritated staccato upon the forest floor.

"Mayhap you shall, but I've had my fill of venison," Alyssa stated a shade louder than was necessary. "Or have you forgotten the meals we've but recently prepared from Niall's stag?"

"Still, this is a magnificent beast. And hasn't it the largest pair of antlers you've ever seen?" Sinead pressed. Was Alyssa a ninny that she couldn't spare one kind word for Devlin's efforts, misguided though they were?

"What of it? Large antlers hold no sway with me," Alyssa countered with a saucy toss of her head. "'Tis what's done with them that matters."

A strangled, outraged snort from Devlin was the only response Alyssa's comments provoked before he stalked away, a murderous look settled upon his rugged face.

Sitting in the gloom of his hut, Devlin was beside himself. He had tried to demonstrate to Alyssa that he could protect her and provide for her, but still the vixen refused to budge. Old Sinead had been wrong. Alyssa Howett didn't want to be courted. She only wanted to be contrary.

What a fool he had made of himself before the entire clan. He had exposed his heart for all to see, fighting to win Alyssa's attention, giving her first rights to game that, by tradition, should have gone to the MacMahon. And had any of it impressed her? Not at all! What more did the woman want of him?

He was a seasoned warrior of almost thirty summers. He should have been hardened by the destruction he had seen. Yet Alyssa had found a way to storm the barricades he had placed around his heart. With naught but a look, she possessed the ability to transform him into an inexperienced youth with no more sophistication than Niall. God's blood, he'd never had trouble with women before. Why was she the exception?

Well, he'd have no more of Alyssa's games, Devlin swore even as his brain frantically sought a way to melt the frost that had sprung up between them. How was he to tell her he loved her when the lass wouldn't talk to him?

Suddenly the material hanging over the doorway was cast aside and a small form darted into the dwelling.

"Good even, Muirne." Devlin greeted his daughter warily. Somehow, he was not quite up to cajoling the child at present. He only hoped playing with the other young ones had sweetened her temperament.

"Hello," she said, sitting down cross-legged beside him, something clutched in her tiny hand.

"What have you been doing?" Devlin asked, tousling her curls.

"Hitting Liam."

"Hitting Liam?"

"Aye. But I won't do it anymore," Muirne assured him, a smile of satisfaction lighting up her face. "Look!" She opened her fist to show her father a crushed wildflower. "Liam gave this to me."

"'Tis lovely."

"It is."

"And this has made you decide to stop battering the lad?"

"Of course! Don't you know that all girls like flowers?" Muirne asked impatiently.

"Do they now?" Devlin inquired slowly, speaking more to himself than to his offspring.

"Aye. All girls like flowers," Muirne repeated solemnly. She was quite unprepared for the joyful hug her father gave her, playfully tossing her into the air before catching her again.

"I do believe you're right, daughter," Devlin said, setting her down. Why hadn't he thought of this sooner? What did practical, everyday things mean to a woman when compared to frivolous beauty? If he wanted to get Alyssa's attention, he had to give her something she'd never expect to receive from him.

"I am right," Muirne agreed, attempting to smell the wilted blossom she still held.

"Well, I think Alyssa would like some flowers, too, don't you? And we shall get her some," Devlin whispered, making his daughter a partner in conspiracy. "Tomorrow, before anyone else is astir, you and I will gather flowers for Alyssa."

"Good," said Muirne, yawning as she undressed for bed. Disappointing Devlin by not applauding his brilliance, she placed her fragile treasure upon her pallet and lay down to go to sleep. "Then will she come home?" the child asked, her eyes half-closed.

"Let us hope so, little one," Devlin said, bending to place a kiss on Muirne's tiny brow. "Let us hope so."

Chapter Twelve

It was morning when Alyssa awoke again, having been awake until well after the rest of the camp had fallen silent. As usual of late, she had slept fitfully, tossing and turning, her rest disrupted by dreams of hide-and-seek with a changing cast of characters.

First, a giggling Muirne teased mercilessly, dawdling and then running away each time Alyssa got close enough to catch her. But, when Alyssa allowed herself to enjoy the child's pleasure at outwitting her, the scene transformed into Cecil Howett's dodging a young Alyssa's attempts to wrap her arms around him and hold him tight. Then, unexpectedly, the tables turned and her father had been trying to catch her. With seemingly little effort, she'd evaded him, weeping as she did so.

Alyssa struggled to find a more comfortable position on her pallet, knowing there was no reason to arise. Sinead was already gone and seemed to have no need of her. Indeed, since Alyssa's refusal of Devlin, she had been more the outcast than ever. There seemed little purpose in any of her days.

True, Devlin had tried to make amends but he was still playing the role of swaggering male. What of that of gentle lover? She didn't need Devlin's arrogant posturing. What she wanted was his heart.

Alyssa shook her head, lost in contemplating the mysterious ways of men, unfathomable creatures as different from one another as Cecil Howett and Devlin. Her father, if he was to be believed, had sacrificed her love for service to the queen. Devlin had risked not returning to his daughter for service to his chieftain. And now, hadn't he lessened his allegiance to Ireland in considering an enemy as his woman, indeed, determining to win her?

How was one to know what the man was thinking? Would she be but a substitute mother to Muirne if she accepted him—or would he one day admit he loved her? Until she knew, Alyssa could not accept his offerings—no matter how tempting they might be.

Still musing upon the dilemmas surrounding her, Alyssa became aware of rustling in the fuchsia outside the hut and heard poorly muffled peals of childish laughter.

"Shush," came a hoarse, masculine bellow. "Sinead said she was still sleeping. Don't wake her."

"But I want to see Lyssa."

"If you wake her, she won't like it," cautioned Devlin. "You know how out of sorts you are when you don't get enough sleep."

"Is that why you are so angry all the time, Father?"

Alyssa choked back her laughter as she struggled to hear Devlin's reply.

"I'm not angry all the time—"

"Yes, you are, especially at night in the hut when you look at where Lyssa slept—"

"Enough nonsense, Muirne, hush. If you want to wait for Alyssa, you'll have to come over here and be very quiet."

"When will she come and live with us again? Today?"

"I hope so, Muirne, but that's for Alyssa to decide, not us."

Devlin's voice was soft and tinged, Alyssa thought, with an unfamiliar, wistful quality. Blast, if he missed her, couldn't he say so? She was weary of these unanswered questions that ran through her mind night and day. The only way to get the truth was to ask the man point-blank what he expected of her. Hopefully, he would give her an answer she could live with.

"Where is she, Father? Should I go see?"

"Hold your tongue, child. She'll be out soon enough."

Rising and quickly dressing, Alyssa moved to the doorway and, sweeping the cloth out of her way, nearly stepped on a huge pile of wildflowers. It might have been a bouquet picked by a giant: daisies, phlox, lady's slippers, buttercups, queen's lace, and oxeye. The variety and quantity of flowers were overwhelming. That man did nothing in a small way.

But the grandeur of his gifts was never the issue. It was the effort to show he cared that made her feel valued. As she turned toward the giggling bushes to tell him so, a smaller group of delicate posies caught her eye. This collection was more selective, each sprig at its freshest, most fragile stage, the colors complementing one another, the lengths of the stems uniform, the arrangement carefully placed to catch her eye.

"Lyssa, Lyssa, do you like my flowers? Father only picked that little bunch, but I got you lots and lots of them so he had to help me carry them. See, we even made you a daisy chain like mine," bubbled Muirne. "Father said I had to be quiet, but now you're awake so I can talk. Aren't you happy to see us?"

Alyssa wiped the tears of laughter from her cheeks and met Devlin's worried glance.

"Of course, I'm happy to see you, angel, and I love your present. I've never seen such beautiful flowers." Alyssa hugged the little girl as Muirne placed the daisy chain around her neck. The temptation to kiss the pink cheek so close to hers was irresistible and Alyssa found herself clutching the child almost as a lifeline. The small collection of flowers had undone her determination to be aloof where all the pomp of Devlin's chivalry and hunting prowess had failed. This was a gift from his heart—a gentle gesture that spoke volumes to hers.

"Will you come home with us?" asked Devlin softly. "Muirne misses you very much—and so do I—"

"Please, please, you forgot to say please, Father," interrupted Muirne. "But he really means it, Lyssa, truly."

"Your father and I need to talk about this alone, Muirne. Do you think you could go find Sinead and ask her to help you take care of these lovely flowers? I wouldn't want them to shrivel in the sun.''

"Will you come back and live with us if I do?"

"Muirne, don't pester Alyssa," objected Devlin. His face was red with embarrassment, though his eyes held the same question his daughter had raised. "We will discuss it, I promise."

"All right," agreed the girl, "but tell Lyssa she *has to* listen, the way you always tell me. And, take your time—Sinead will watch me until you come back. She likes me."

Devlin chuckled ruefully as his daughter skipped off toward the center of the compound.

"There's one young lass who knows her mind," he said. "In fact, she's been a handful of late. You seem to handle her so easily. Perhaps you could give me some counsel."

"We could start by discussing Muirne," Alyssa agreed. Picking up Devlin's smaller floral offering, the blonde fingered its precious petals and led the way out of camp. "What has she been doing that flusters you, a man accustomed to danger untold?"

"She's a female," grumbled Devlin, "and you women are enough to befuddle any male."

Following behind Alyssa, he had all too enticing a view of her nicely rounded derriere and felt his body already growing impatient with the discussion. If he couldn't master himself, he'd lose her again. By all rights, the woman should be flattered at how easily she attracted him, but he suspected now was not the time to bring that up. "I don't understand the first thing about you women, infant or well-grown."

Alyssa was amused by the frustration evident in his voice. At least he'd lost his pompous self-assurance that he knew best, she reasoned, undeniably happy that they were talking, no matter how awkwardly.

"Give me an instance and perhaps I can interpret Muirne's actions," she suggested. Settling herself on a fallen log in the a small clearing in the forest, flowers in hand, she looked up at the still standing Devlin and smiled encouragingly.

"You said on the way back from the Macguires that when Muirne knew I loved her, I could begin to set rules and expect her to obey them. But how can I convince her that I do love her?" asked Devlin in consternation. "I'm as lost about that as I am about convincing *you* of my feelings."

"And what are those?" Alyssa spoke softly, not intending to challenge Devlin, merely to learn his heart.

"What are my feelings? Woman, how can you even ask me that?" Devlin looked astounded. "Haven't I been wearing myself out to impress you? Didn't I kill the finest stag anyone has seen in years? For that matter, didn't I speak my mind to the clan?"

"You said Muirne loved me—not you—"

"Is that what this is all about?" Devlin couldn't believe his ears. She needed words? After so many years alone, he didn't live that way.

"You made it seem as though I was a good helpmate in life—not that it mattered who I was but simply that I would be useful so you'd make me your woman," retorted Alyssa. "Well, I've news for you, Devlin Fitzhugh. I'll be no man's convenience. I'll certainly not be yours. I want to be considered more than just handy."

"Handy? Hell's fire, Roisin is handy. So are Fiona and Deirdre for that matter, but I haven't asked them to share my hut," argued the gallowglass, confounded by Alyssa's objections.

"Why not?"

"I never felt the need—"

"And now?"

"Damn it all, Alyssa, now I want you. I want to be near you and have you near me every minute of every day. I feel half-dead, as if the sun hasn't shone since you've left me. Is that what you want to hear?"

"Only if it's true," murmured Alyssa, afraid to believe and have the miracle disappear. "I don't want you taking me in out of charity or to tend your daughter—but because you love me—"

"Haven't I just said so?" Devlin was flummoxed by her insistence on the words. Maybe showing her would be better. In an instant, he had pulled her to her feet and wrapped her in his arms, relishing the feel of her feminine softness against his body. As she started to protest, he began to lick at her lips, circling his tongue around her rosebud mouth in quick darting movements until finally taking her in a fiery kiss that seemed to have a life of its own. Eventually, when she sighed and leaned against him for support, the Irish warrior drew his head back and looked at her flushed face, her eyes heavy with unspent passion.

"Doesn't that speak of my love for you, Alyssa Howett?" he asked hoarsely. "Can't you taste it in my kiss? Feel it in my heart pumping so unevenly?

Smell it in my scent? What more must I do to convince you?''

"Is it so very hard to say, Devlin? I've a need to hear the words,'' she confessed softly. To her way of thinking, no man could kiss a woman as he had and not love her, but she'd little experience with the ways of men. Abandoning her former life made Alyssa crave reassurance. If she couldn't have marriage banns and a wedding feast, at least let her hear the magic words of heartfelt passion.

"The MacMahons are not a people of many words, Alyssa, and I've become one like them in these past few years, but for you I'll try to change. Alyssa, dearling, I love you to the best a poor man can. I'd die for you or cross a mighty ocean or beard a fierce dragon—anything you could ever want me to do except surrender Muirne.''

"I'd never ask that of you. You've enough love for us both,'' murmured Alyssa. She ran her small hands over his broad chest and, circling his neck, drew his head to meet hers. "And, I've more than enough for both of you.''

"Prove it,'' Devlin challenged, a playful glint in his eye. "It's been weeks since I taught you about loving. Show me what you remember.''

"I was about to do just that,'' Alyssa laughed happily, giving herself over to the pleasure of loving him, a pleasure too long denied, once again theirs to relish.

Alyssa finished stacking the kindling in front of the home she once again shared with Devlin and Muirne, and shook her head in contented amazement. Growing

up, she would have been horrified at the notion of
living in so ramshackle a place, yet she was happy
here, and would not trade her primitive dwelling for
the finest castle in Ireland.

Her days were pleasant, spent seeing to the running
of her little household. Though the work could be
tiring, each task was welcomed because it was per-
formed for those she loved. With the advent of evening, she welcomed a meal and conversation shared
with a man who cherished her and a child she was
beginning to think of as her own. As for the nights,
nothing else under heaven could bring her the ecstasy
she experienced when she lay in Devlin's loving embrace. Life was good, and Alyssa enjoyed every moment of it.

Shaking herself out of her reverie, Alyssa set about
her chores once more. She had no idea when Devlin
might be riding back into camp. The thought of him
caused her body to quiver in greedy remembrance.
She tried to ignore its echoes of love by reminding
herself of the work still stretching before her. There
was bread to bake, the supper to be set asimmer, wild
onions to be gathered, and time to be put aside for
playing with Muirne.

Searching for her small charge across the compound, Alyssa found her easily. A smile crossed the
Englishwoman's face when she was reminded of how
the child was flourishing among Eamon's people. At
the moment, the little imp was merrily playing with
Eamon's wolfhounds, lean vestiges of better days.
Still, they were huge, admirable creatures full of spirit
and animal cunning. Most of the children kept their

distance from the beasts. But not Muirne. Like her sire, she was fearless. She commanded the hounds as casually as she did Devlin.

Considering the man who protected them both, Alyssa couldn't blame Muirne for feeling so secure. She felt that way herself, as though she had left all reason for trepidation somewhere within the pale. Surely with Devlin to watch over her, there was nothing to cause her harm or mar her newfound happiness.

That evening, Alyssa listened to songs from the other huts as she observed Devlin and Muirne at play. Just now, the little girl was trying to inveigle her father into extending her bedtime. Like all youngsters tempted by the lengthening hours of sun, she resented going to bed while the sky was still streaked with color.

"But, Father, this morning you showed me the moon in the sky while the sun was still up too—"

"Yes, I did," agreed Devlin, clearly mystified by the path of this conversation. His daughter's developing powers of reasoning were a source of constant fascination to this longtime soldier who had thought he had no softer side.

"Well, if the sun can be out when it's the moon's turn and the moon can be out when the sun shines, they don't go to bed when they're supposed to, either," argued the miniature logician. "Can't I stay up like them?"

"All the time?" asked Devlin in mock horror. "How could anybody stay out that long? Here, I'll show you something else that shouldn't be out at this hour.'' Lifting her unto his lap, he began to tickle the little girl's belly, eliciting loud giggles and raucous demands for more.

The setting sun caught the fiery halo returning to Muirne's hair after its mistreatment by the Macguires and seemed to echo itself in Devlin's coloring. They were clearly father and daughter, mused Alyssa, taken by the real affection shared by the pair. Devlin might be new to fatherhood, but he knew how to love a child.

''Come, Muirne, it's time for bed,'' she announced abruptly, rising to her feet. ''I'll come inside and tell you a story, but playtime is over for tonight.''

''But, Father—'' she began.

''—agrees with Alyssa,'' finished the gallowglass. ''Good night, Muirne. Give me my kiss.''

''Only if you give one to Lyssa, too,'' reminded the little girl. Their nightly ritual begun on the trail was one she enjoyed and neither Alyssa nor Devlin objected to it any longer.

Devlin sat contentedly before the fire when the others went in, relishing the path his life had taken. Four months ago, he'd been a free man, committed only to Eamon MacMahon. But now, though Alyssa had liberated him from Dublin Castle, she had apprehended him anew—seizing his heart and holding it captive within her own. Still, he'd not change a thing, not a single thing, Devlin reflected. Overall, his life was good.

''You look mighty pleased with yourself,'' observed Cashel a short while later. Squatting by the fire, he poured himself a cup of ale and looked around. "That woman of yours busy?"

"She's seeing to Muirne. Did you want her?"

"I'd say every man who sees her wants her." Cashel guffawed. "But then we're not as lucky as you. You know, I don't think you ever rightly thanked me for bringing her to your attention that night in Dublin."

"You bloody oaf. If you hadn't tried to take her with you, I would have escaped with the rest of you—"

"And you'd have missed having her by your side and in your bed? These days, there's many a man, Irish and English, looking for a piece of her. 'Tis said there's money in it—"

Devlin glanced at Eamon's nephew, weighing his words carefully. As usual, whatever news he had, he'd drag out for the temporary power it gave him, knowing something the others didn't. Ordinarily, Devlin didn't let Cashel's maneuvers annoy him, but if this concerned Alyssa, he wanted to hear it at once. His patience wouldn't allow for delay.

"Alyssa is being hunted?"

"Aye, by Irish and English, but then you've convinced her you're the best man to protect her. What are you worried about? Or isn't Devlin Fitzhugh as brave as he'd like everyone to think?"

"Don't belabor me with nonsense," grumbled Devlin. "If you've information about Alyssa, share it or begone. I've better ways to spend my time than to squabble with you."

Cashel rose to his feet and looked down at the

seated Devlin, one of the few times the younger man
was physically at an advantage, and smirked at him.

"My sources tell me Cecil Howett never went
home to England and he's up in Ballynon—"

"With a warrant for my arrest? It fazes me not.
What concerns me is your allusion to Alyssa. How
many soldiers are with him?"

"He has a dozen or so, but he claims not be hunting Irishmen. He's promising a reward for news of
his daughter, so a lot of the clans are listening hard.
It may all be nothing but a ruse to find you," spec-
ulated Cashel. "It's commonly known that she left
the castle with you—"

"Why didn't Howett go back to England?"

"Perhaps because his daughter was supposed to
help you escape for the purpose of leading her father
to Eamon's camp so that he could decimate the entire
clan."

"Don't be absurd. I'd trust Alyssa with my life.
There isn't a duplicitous bone in her body." Devlin
scoffed at Cashel's attempt to throw suspicion on the
Englishwoman. "Still, from what she's told me about
her relationship with Howett, it's strange he wouldn't
want to go home."

"From what the stories say, Elizabeth had to send
someone else to fetch the Irish prisoners and Howett's
been hying up and down the coast, worried that his
daughter is being held against her will or is no longer
even alive. 'Tis said he won't go back to England
until he knows for certain that she is safe and happy.
To boot, he's trying to find evidence that she might
not be guilty of the treason the governor claims, but
he hasn't had any success."

"And if she is guilty?"

"That English bastard would probably apologize as he put the noose around her neck, but do it nonetheless," mocked Eamon's nephew. "Didn't Niall tell me Howett had left her for nigh onto eighteen years?"

"Aye, but things aren't always so clear when you've a child to consider," mused Devlin. Since he'd taken on the responsibility of raising Muirne, he'd often wondered at Alyssa's refusal to understand her father's dilemma. Indeed, if Devlin believed Muirne's safety were at stake, wouldn't he trust someone else to raise his flesh and blood rather than endanger her? "Does Howett know she's here?"

"They know you're a gallowglass for the Mac-Mahon. Still, Eamon doesn't make our location public knowledge."

"We have to protect Alyssa. She mustn't venture from camp," planned Devlin as Cashel rose to his feet, more seeds of trouble scattered.

"Are you worried about her safety or your own, Fitzhugh? You know damn well no one gets into this camp without the scouts alerting Eamon or one of us. She won't be taken from here, though truth be told, I wouldn't miss you if you were."

Then he was gone, an ill wind. Devlin frowned even as he wondered about the implications of Howett's being only a day and a half away from Eamon's camp. Should he take Alyssa and head north for a few months or would that put her in greater danger? Or was it truly necessary? Couldn't Cashel have been misled?

Even as he considered that possibility, Devlin knew the answer. However he managed it, the information

Cashel obtained from his informers working for the English overlords was always valid. This would be no different, much as he might wish otherwise.

Alyssa slipped from the hut and settled on the ground beside Devlin, grasping his large hand in her smaller one and looking into his eyes, excitement playing over her face.

"Do you suppose Cashel is telling the truth, Devlin? I've never really trusted him."

Damn, he should have realized that from inside the hut Alyssa would have overheard every word Cashel said. Suddenly a new worry had appeared. Would she still be content here if she could reach her father? Devlin didn't know, but he couldn't deny he was frightened of losing her. Unable to live in doubt, he decided now was the time to end his torment.

"His sources are usually reliable—"

"Then Father refused the queen's command in order to search for me? I can hardly believe such a thing," she murmured, tracing Devlin's palm with a dainty finger. "I thought nothing was more important to Cecil Howett than his duty."

"Maybe once upon a time that was true, Alyssa, but men can change," he advised softly. Taking her hand, he lifted it to his mouth and placed a tender kiss on each finger before stopping himself. "Dearling, if I could arrange it, would you want to go to England with him?"

"What? Of course not," she answered swiftly. "I love you and Muirne. You are my family and I wouldn't give you up."

Her words were spoken from the heart, and true,

yet there was truth still unspoken, Devlin realized. He prodded her to continue.

"But—"

"But nothing. Seventeen years ago, he chose the queen and his infernal loyalty to the crown—"

"So now you want to hurt him by choosing me? That's not fair, Alyssa," cautioned Devlin, his tone cold.

"How could you think such a thing, Devlin Fitzhugh?" Alyssa bounded to her feet, her face flushed, her eyes round with disbelief. "I chose you because I've loved you ever since you rescued me from death in the courtyard of the castle. By all that's holy, Fitzhugh, if the sight of that butchered stag didn't drive me away, nothing will."

"Then I'm stuck with you, am I, Howett?" he asked, a broad smile brightening his face. If they weren't so close to the center of camp, he would have bedded her here and now, the fire in her eyes enticed him so.

"For as long as you'll have me," Alyssa confessed softly. Her anger dissolved in an instant at the sight of that dimple. Dropping down beside him once again, she wrapped her arms around his neck and kissed him passionately, as much to convince him of her conviction as herself.

Never one to ignore so pleasant an invitation, Devlin welcomed Alyssa's advance and returned her kiss with a lingering one of his own. His broad hands stroked her back as his lips trailed sparks across her face and down the slope of her neck. This was his woman, he thought, one with whom he was certainly blessed.

"Alyssa, if I could get word to your father that you were well and happy, would you want me to?" he asked tenderly a short time later. He had seen her wistful glances when he played with Muirne and knew her history with her father disconcerted Alyssa still. Could she set this relationship to rest, there would be nothing to mar her happiness.

Sitting up abruptly, she twisted to look at Devlin.

"Could you do that?"

"I'm not a green youth, Alyssa. I've tracked men for years and lived in the shadow of English patrols more often than I'd care to remember. I'd take precautions not to be followed, don't worry. The question is whether you'd have anything to say to him—"

"I'd tell him of the strong, handsome, kind, and gentle prince who rescued his daughter from the tower and took her to a land of wonder," said the woman in his arms. "I feel I'm living in a fairy tale and if I could let him know how happy I am, I'd never want for anything else for my life to be perfect."

"Fine, tomorrow you will write him a letter and I'll see that it is delivered safely," Devlin agreed

"Tomorrow? What about what's left of tonight?"

"I'm in need of *you* for my life to be perfect," admitted her gallowglass. "Let's go for a walk."

Alyssa's happy laughter echoed amid the sounds of the camp retiring and she followed him gladly toward their meadow, along the path they were fast wearing into the grass.

Chapter Thirteen

By dawn Alyssa had experimented with three different types of berries before settling on walnut stain as an ink that wouldn't disappear as she wrote. Having found a small twig to use as a pen, she was now seeking a suitable writing surface. There was no paper in the camp and the cloth covering the door was too loosely woven for the lettering to remain distinct. Suddenly, she had it.

"Devlin, bring your knife here, would you?" she called. "Good, cut a swatch of material from the back of my shift, the part with the raised lettering, would you?"

"Woman, I've wanted to rip the clothes from your body for weeks, but you know how scarce good cloth is," he said with a chuckle. Suspecting her intent, he had already lifted her gown and was gauging where he would cut when she replied.

"I'm going to use it to write my father. It will be easy for you to carry and conceal if need be, so stop teasing and oblige me, please."

"Anytime, milady, anytime you like, but Muirne is

awake and about at the moment, so it might not be wise,'' he retorted, handing her the material. "What will you say?"

"I thought about it most of the night," she confessed, "when you didn't have me otherwise occupied. Let me write it out and I'll read it to you."

Devlin stood at the door of the hut, watching her fingers move swiftly over the ivory linen, wondering at the words she chose. His heart told him she'd not betray the MacMahons or himself, but there was a seed of misgiving in his gut that he couldn't quite banish. For the past three years, he'd been Eamon's gallowglass, committing his fealty to the MacMahon, but here he was going behind his back to take a message to Howett. Though communicating with the English smacked of disloyalty, Devlin felt he had no choice.

If anything, he was being truly loyal to the woman he'd claimed as his own—and didn't she and Muirne have first call on his life now?

"Listen, I kept it short and pointed.

Dear Father,

I've had word that you fear for my welfare and I want to reassure you that all is well in my life. I am happier than I've ever been and am well loved by a good man and his daughter. Do not worry, but return to England with a clear mind.

Alyssa

Will that make him feel better, do you suppose?"

"Don't you want to send him your love?" asked

Devlin. Pleased as he was by the reference to himself and Muirne, he found it troubling that Alyssa gave no mention of missing her father or loving him. This was her last opportunity for doing so. He'd hope, in similar circumstances, his daughter would behave differently.

"We hadn't found that part of our relationship, Devlin. Remember, we had only three weeks together after seventeen years apart," she reminded him, rolling the cloth and tucking it in Devlin's pouch. "No, I said what is most important, that I am well and he should leave Ireland. When will you return?"

"Hopefully, in two nights. Eamon won't give a thought to my being gone that long. It's happened often enough in the past. Sinead or Niall will give you whatever help you need with Muirne or anything else," assured Devlin. He stroked her soft blond hair and thrilled to the desire in her eyes. Yes, this was his woman, one for whom he'd perform miracles if he could.

"Godspeed, my love," she answered. "We'll be fine."

He steeled himself not to look back at her waving farewell as he left. He'd only feel more unnerved at the sight of her and he wasn't used to this uneasiness that came with caring for others. Mother of mercy, life was complicated when you let love into the picture. As a man alone and unfettered, he had had much less to lose. In his heart, the gallowglass knew he'd not trade the worry for the love that caused it, but acclimatization did not come easily.

* * *

The farmer he sought outside Ballynon was one of
a legion of such hapless souls trying to exist in this
war-torn country, an Irish tenant farmer struggling to
work lands not his own and hampered by the English
demands for crops and taxes. His kind was all over
the hillside, but Devlin looked for a man more alone
than the others. Finally, after watching two farms for
the afternoon and seeing nothing untoward, he'd
made his choice and approached the farmer with his
proposition.

"I just take this letter to the English gentleman at
the inn in Ballynon and collect a reply from the
church graveyard if there is one?" repeated the
farmer.

"Aye, and this haunch of venison is your pay-
ment," agreed Devlin. "A simple task for anyone but
me—"

"Will this anger the English or get me in trouble?"

"It shouldn't, but only the devil knows what angers
the English. One day it could be the sun shining, the
next it's the showers," answered the gallowglass.
"They'd like my head but I doubt they've a use for
yours."

"And if there's no answer, the meat is still mine?"

"The meat is yours, answer or not, but take care
they don't follow you back here," cautioned Devlin.
"I rather like my neck the length it is and wouldn't
want it stretched for being in the wrong place at the
wrong time."

"I'll signal you at daybreak on the morrow if
there's an answer," agreed the farmer. "Otherwise,
it's been a pleasure to help you out. And may you

continue to bedevil the English, Fitzhugh. We've heard much of you in these parts.''

Cecil Howett looked at the dirty piece of cloth in the innkeeper's hands and frowned.

"This is a message for me?" he questioned incredulously. "Other than one of disease and famine, what could it be?"

"There's writing of a kind, sir," offered the publican. "And if there's a message you're to leave it at the church, the grave with angels in flight."

"Yes, yes, give the cloth here," acknowledged Cecil Howett. For weeks he'd been hunting for word of Alyssa, following more false trails and dead ends than he'd ever imagined could exist. What were the chances this was any different?

Yet upon examination, he found that the cloth had initials embroidered on it, *A. H.* Could God have finally heard his prayers? Could it be from Alyssa?

Moments later, Howett reached blindly for the cup of ale on the table and wiped the tears from his eyes, trying to decide what to do. She was alive and he had to be thankful for that. He'd planned to return to the English court once he could be certain of that, but now, how could he be sure she had written the message herself? Someone could easily have forced her to write it—and write it with what? Some sort of stain probably—like barbarians might use. His daughter— his precious Alyssa living with outlaws in the wilds of Ireland, how could he trust in her safety? It was preposterous, of course.

The man who loved her, could that be Fitzhugh?

No, she'd said a good man, Howett reminded himself—but then who knew how she'd been trained to think or what values she had left? No, he couldn't go home yet, not until he was certain she was truly well and happy as she wrote—not until he was certain she had written those words voluntarily. He had to see her himself and know she was well. He could guarantee her safety—she was his daughter. The soldiers weren't after her anyway; they only wanted Fitzhugh.

And, if she agreed to meet him, maybe they could both get what they wanted, he considered, weighing his options.

Devlin finished brushing down his horse and released him into the small paddock near the camp. It was late as he headed toward his hut, fingering the stiff parchment in the pouch at his waist and once again cursed himself for a fool. Alyssa hadn't asked him to get a reply from her father. She had sent what she thought was a one-way farewell. But he, arrogant ass that he was, had decided to surprise her, and now he was the one about to be surprised. He had no notion of what Howett had written.

Whatever the bloody note contained, Devlin wished he'd never set eyes on it. Alyssa didn't know he had, he reminded himself. He *could* simply toss it in one of the campfires, watch it burn and never mention the matter again. Who knew? It could be a plea for Alyssa to come back to him or an angry disavowal of her as a daughter…or even a warning that English soldiers were about to attack.

Running a weary hand through his auburn hair, he

hesitated by a fire and tried to rationalize such dishonorable behavior, but it was no good. He couldn't. There was no getting around it. The message would have to be delivered.

He'd gone to Ballynon to reassure Alyssa's father that she was well, a man who had lost the prize that Devlin had won. It wasn't in him to deny her a last contact from him—and according to the tenant farmer, Howett had played fair, not attempting to follow him or set a watch around the churchyard. Surely such a man wouldn't hurt his daughter with his final message, Devlin told himself, praying desperately his instincts were true.

"Oh, Devlin, I've missed you," Alyssa cried as he entered their hut. Without hesitation, she threw herself into his arms and trailed her slender fingers over his face, her eyes trying to read his expression. "I missed you every minute of every day. It was forever."

"Me, too, Father," called a sleepy voice. "Alyssa had to kiss me twice each night because you weren't here. But you have to give me the kisses you owe me."

"What a greedy little thing you sired." Alyssa laughed, adding in a quiet voice, "but not half so greedy as I am."

"Mayhap you would care to offer evidence of such," Devlin said with a lopsided grin.

"I think it is most definitely warranted," Alyssa teased as Devlin bent down to oblige his daughter.

"Good night, Muirne. I'll see you in the morning."

"You won't leave again tonight?"

"No, dearling, I'm home with you and Alyssa now,
I promise."

"Good." Rewarding her father with a last kiss, the
little girl snuggled back into her blanket and was
asleep in an instant.

Devlin watched her, amazed and thankful for the
unexpected gift of such a child, and then he turned to
Alyssa, also appreciative of the miracle of her presence in his life.

"We've got to talk," he said quietly.

"Did something happen? Didn't you find my father?" Devlin's tone was too serious for Alyssa's liking and she fingered the edge of her apron anxiously.

"Nothing like that. I delivered your message to
him and—and I have one in return." It was best to
get to the issue quickly and be done with it, the gallowglass decided, extending the parchment toward
her.

Worry, excitement and then delight flitted across
her face, but rather than reaching for the letter, Alyssa
stretched up on tiptoes to draw Devlin's head toward
hers.

"I knew I loved you, Fitzhugh," she murmured.
"I'm just finding out how much. Thank you."

Feeling her in his arms again was more than
enough thanks, Devlin told himself, trying to settle
the apprehension in the pit of his stomach. He returned her passion hungrily, anxious perhaps to distract her from Howett's note or maybe just to remind
her what he could give her.

"Devlin, Muirne might awaken," she warned finally, halting his attentions. "Let me read Father's communication and then we'll go for a walk."

"Read it to me," he instructed, determined to know as she did the contents of the letter.

"Of course," she agreed. Taking the parchment from him, she moved to the small table where the candle sat, and felt unexpected tears spring to her eyes at this reminder of the life she'd left behind. Paper to write on, real ink, a parent...

Dearest Daughter—

I hope all truly is as you've said in your letter, but you must forgive a too-long delinquent father if he needs to see with his own eyes that all is well with you. Once I trusted the word of others concerning your welfare. This time I cannot. Please meet me on Saturday at the village church of Kilross so we may say our farewells properly. Should you wish to bring your man (Fitzhugh?), I'll not object, but I shall be alone and unarmed. I trust God will watch over us both,

Your loving father,
Cecil Howett

Silence echoed loudly in the hut as Alyssa finished reading. Devlin was torn by the need to damn Howett for appealing to Alyssa so forlornly and the desire to applaud him for being so fair-minded with regard to his daughter. He doubted he could let Muirne go so easily, even fifteen years from now.

For her part, Alyssa mourned the relationship she might have shared with this man had he but thought about her twice when she was a child instead of waiting until now. Her heart thrilled at the words of love from him and wept at the implication that she would suspect him of treachery. But, could she go without endangering Devlin or infuriating the MacMahon? She sighed deeply and studied the flames of the candle, as though looking for an answer.

"Sweetling, I will take you to meet him if you wish," offered Devlin. He had expected the words to stick in his throat but they hadn't. If this was what she wanted, she would have it.

"But what about Eamon? I doubt he would approve."

"Probably not, but this does not involve Eamon or my duty to him, Alyssa. Our visit to your father is not a meeting of enemies, but one of family," reasoned the gallowglass. "After I ride morning patrol tomorrow, I will discuss it with the MacMahon, but he'll not change my mind. We will leave tomorrow night so as to avoid the English patrols during the day."

"Devlin, thank you," she began. "Our life together will last many years but this is the only time—"

Not wanting to hear her thanks, Devlin silenced her and his worrisome conscience as he knew best, enfolding her in his arms and lowering his lips to hers.

He too had missed her these past two days and he proceeded to demonstrate the fact.

Cashel watched as Devlin mounted his stallion to ride the early patrol. As soon as the gallowglass departed, Eamon's nephew shifted his attention to Alyssa Howett. This morning, the girl was absolutely beaming and Cashel refused to believe that it was for obvious reasons.

Something was afoot! He sensed it. And it could all be traced back to the last discourse he had held with Fitzhugh, informing him of Cecil Howett's continued presence in Ireland. The very next day, Devlin had disappeared. No one else in the camp had thought it strange. The gallowglass often came and went as he pleased if Eamon had no need of him. Yet Cashel, a man of salacious appetite, could not conceive of Fitzhugh leaving his woman if it could be avoided.

He had been pondering the situation when the upstart had returned last night. And now here was the English wench looking inordinately pleased yet fretful, too, as though she were keeping some great secret.

Could Fitzhugh have had the audacity to communicate with the girl's father without seeking the MacMahon's permission, which most assuredly would have been denied? The way the bastard doted on his English whore, such an action was not beyond belief. The possibility made Cashel's blood run cold. It was essential that Devlin Fitzhugh had no contact with the English! Such a thing was far too dangerous.

Aware that he would have no rest until he found

out if such were the case, Cashel kept Alyssa under surveillance as he racked his head for some ruse he could use to discern the truth of the situation.

When Sinead appeared, Cashel noted Fitzhugh's bastard was sent to play with another of the clan's brats, while the two women, wash in hand, turned toward the path to the stream. If there was anyone among the MacMahons in whom Alyssa would confide, it was the old woman. Cashel followed them at a discreet distance, determined to keep hidden and perhaps learn what he wanted to know.

"Out with it, lass," Sinead commanded as she knelt beside the rock she used for laundering.

"I'm certain I don't know what you mean," Alyssa protested with a laugh, submerging Devlin's green tunic beneath the water.

"You can't hide anything from these old eyes, Alyssa Howett. You're as restless as a cat who has spied a fine trout in yonder stream. You want what you want, but you're uneasy about getting your paws wet."

"Is it that obvious?"

"Aye. Now will you take me into your confidence or must I continue my interrogation?"

Secreted behind a nearby bush, Cashel held his breath while he strained to hear their conversation.

"I'll ask you a question instead," Alyssa countered, scrubbing the garment she held in her hands. "How far is it to Kilross?"

"Almost a day's ride. Why do you ask? Are you intending on escaping your man so soon?"

"Nay. I've no desire to ever leave him," Alyssa

admitted with a blush before her excitement over the upcoming journey mounted once more. "'Tis just that Devlin learned my father is still in Ireland. He wants to meet with me in Kilross."

"You contacted him?" Sinead asked sharply. She had no desire to see the English come storming into Eamon's compound.

"Devlin carried my letter and I received one in return."

The arrogant bastard, Cashel fumed. A word in his uncle's ear about Fitzhugh's betrayal would soon set matters right.

"That knave hasn't an ounce of sense where you're concerned," Sinead chided. "The MacMahon will be furious when he learns of it."

Aye, so he shall, Cashel thought gleefully.

"But I'd feel so guilty watching Devlin delight in Muirne, when my own father is worried about me," Alyssa was saying in an attempt to excuse her lover's indiscretion. "Devlin knows that."

"It could be a trap. 'Tis always risky business meeting with the English. Don't look at me that way, Alyssa. I don't care if the man fathered you! Any encounter I've ever had with your countrymen has been less than satisfactory. Eamon will have none of it. You do intend on asking his permission, don't you?"

Cashel listened carefully, ready to scramble back to the campsite and relay his information to the MacMahon before either of the offenders had a chance to make a confession.

"Devlin will talk to him after he completes his patrol."

Cashel relaxed. There was no hurry. A sneer materialized on his face as he imagined the trouble he would make for Fitzhugh.

"And if the MacMahon says no?" Sinead queried.

"I'll not consider that possibility. Devlin will see to it that we go to Kilross," Alyssa insisted stubbornly, wringing out the tunic and laying it on the mossy bank to dry.

Cashel had to agree with the wench's assessment. For her sake, Fitzhugh would go regardless of what Eamon had to say. The realization caused an idea to take hold in the eavesdropper's seething mind, an idea whose potential quickly had him rigid with excitement.

When the talk turned to Sinead's caring for Fitzhugh's byblow when he and his doxy rode forth, Cashel gave his scheme his complete attention.

Mayhap he would keep his counsel and not tell Eamon anything. Informing against Fitzhugh would mean a falling out between the chieftain and his gallowglass. But as fond as Eamon was of the outsider, a reconciliation was bound to take place. Nay, it was far better that Devlin keep his appointment in Kilross without anyone in the compound knowing that Cashel MacMahon had been aware of Fitzhugh's destination.

Then, when the bastard was taken, no connection could be made to the MacMahon's loyal foster son. But connection there would be!

Stealthily, Cashel edged his way back towards the camp. Soon his horse was saddled and he was under

way. Even with the circuitous route he took, Cashel
planned on pulling rein before his English contact's
residence by late afternoon.

The Earl of Knockton should be glad, as always,
to see him. With things already in place, it wouldn't
be too difficult to get word about Fitzhugh's impending arrival to the English forces gathering a mere
twelve miles from Kilross. A contingent could be sent
to capture him while the majority of Her Majesty's
troops set about completing the task they had been
sent to do.

Chapter Fourteen

"Eamon, a word with you privately," Devlin petitioned, catching up with the chieftain and Niall at the edge of the camp. Tired and hungry though he was upon returning from his patrol, the gallowglass had taken no time for himself before going to seek his lord. The matter he had to discuss weighed heavily upon him, and he wanted it done with as quickly as possible.

"Is there a problem?" Eamon probed, taken aback by the serious quality of Devlin's voice and the upset reflected in his steely eyes.

"Aye, of sorts," Devlin spoke truthfully. A twinge of guilt pricked at his heart, knowing that what he had to say would add to the MacMahon's already heavy burdens. Yet there was no help for it. Eamon had to be told.

"If this concerns not the commonweal, then we will adjourn to my quarters. Niall, however, shall join us. It is fitting for him to learn how a chieftain deals with difficulties."

"As you say," Devlin acquiesced. He did not relish confessing what he had done in front of the boy, but he was in no position to demand otherwise.

After entering the hut, Eamon brought out some ale. Devlin took the entire contents of his cup into his mouth and disposed of it in almost one gulp. Hesitating for the briefest instant, he laid the entire story before his chieftain. For a brief moment, a stony silence filled the MacMahon's hut as Devlin waited for Eamon's reaction. Then fury held quarter, Eamon's temper fueled by disappointment.

"I allowed your Englishwoman to live among us despite the fact that Elizabeth's men would be searching for her. Yet in repayment you took it upon yourself to contact this Englishman without my leave?" Eamon asked. The chieftain's mouth was drawn tightly, his displeasure evident. "Didn't it occur to you that your action could have endangered the entire clan—man, woman and child?"

"Know that I would never betray your people," Devlin said quietly. "Had I been taken, I would have died before I provided the English with the location of our camp."

"You have broken fealty with me, Devlin Fitzhugh," Eamon pronounced grimly.

"Nay, Father. Never accuse Devlin of that," Niall interjected, plunking down his cup with an emphatic thud.

"A chieftain cannot rely on sentiment in making judgments, Niall," the MacMahon lectured his son. "When you have taken my place, you cannot afford to allow friendship to eclipse your duty to your people."

"A bond might exist between Devlin and me, but that is not the reason I speak on his behalf," Niall said gravely, brushing aside Devlin's attempts to silence him. "My words are based upon what I have observed of his previous behavior. There is no better warrior in the entire camp, and many is the time Devlin Fitzhugh has put his life in jeopardy to support your cause or carry out your orders. Didn't he rescue me and suffer for it?"

"Aye, he did. Now, however, he places the needs of Alyssa Howett above those of the clan. He makes me question whether or not his first duty is still to me. As grateful as I am to Devlin for what he has done in the past, I must put the future of our people before all else."

"But—" Niall tried to argue.

"There can be no *but*. In addition to his recent transgressions, he prepares another. I know he is committed to this meeting with Cecil Howett regardless of my refusal to sanction it. Is that not right, Devlin?"

"Aye, Eamon. I will not lie to you," Devlin responded simply. The conflict he felt was evident in his face, but his answer made it plain that in this instance he was choosing his woman over his lord no matter how reluctant he was to do so.

"You have served me well for more than three years, Devlin, but mayhap it is time I ask you to quit my fires. Consorting with the English is a thing I cannot tolerate."

"As you say, Eamon, though I will be sorry to leave you."

"I beg you to reconsider, Father," Niall pleaded

as Devlin rose to his feet. "If I were chieftain, Devlin would stay. In all matters except those concerning the welfare of his family, his first loyalty is to you. You cannot realistically ask more from any man. To think otherwise is to open yourself to the possibility of betrayal."

"Well spoken, my son. There is wisdom in what you say, but what if Howett is setting a trap?"

"Then Devlin must be left to suffer his fate," Niall replied solemnly. "There can be no rescue. As for the clan, we will be safe enough. Our men are strong and our sentries many."

"All right, Niall. The decision is yours," Eamon acceded, proud of the maturity the boy had demonstrated. "However, there is still much you have to learn before you will be a fit chieftain. I will grant Devlin this boon. But in return, he will have to prove himself anew by pledging me a favor of my choosing."

"So long as it brings no harm to Alyssa or my daughter, whatever you ask is yours," Devlin agreed.

"Then it is done," the MacMahon pronounced, thinking of the difficult lesson he would be compelled to impress upon Niall in a few short hours. "You leave tonight. But mark me, Devlin, we tell no else in the clan what you are about."

When Devlin stepped out of Eamon's hut, the clearing held no trace of cheerfulness for him. The summer sun beat down upon his muscular frame, but his shame burned hotter still. Imperfection in the service of his lord did not sit well with Devlin Fitzhugh. Nor did the fact that Eamon's anger had been more

than justified. He had earned the MacMahon's wrath
for the sake of Alyssa's happiness, and the fault was
his alone. No one had forced him to pledge himself
to either of them, much less both. It was he who had
made up his mind to do so, and quite willingly, too.

Did that mean, however, that he was doomed to a
lifetime of conflict between his duties to his lord and
his obligations to his woman? God help him if such
was the case, he thought morosely.

Unable to face Alyssa at the moment, incapable of
sharing his disgrace and confusion, Devlin struck out
for the stream. Perhaps the rushing waters would help
cleanse him of his guilt and bring some sense to his
jumbled thoughts. He had not taken more than a few,
determined strides when he was accosted by Cashel
MacMahon.

"Fitzhugh! Wait! I have something to discuss with
you," Eamon's foster son called as he ran to catch
up with Devlin.

"Can't it keep?" Devlin inquired impatiently. "I
am in need of a swim at present."

"Certainly, if your own comfort takes precedence
over your responsibilities to the MacMahon," an unc-
tuous Cashel replied, studying Devlin's countenance
for some clue as to the outcome of the meeting with
Eamon. The troubled set of Devlin's mouth heartened
him mightily.

"Of course it doesn't," Devlin snapped, a self-
condemning blush tinting his cleanly chiseled features. "What demands my attention?"

"I merely wished to consult you about the sentry
assignments for the next two evenings," the cunning

clansman stated, dropping his voice. "I am supposed to stand guard tonight and tomorrow night as well, but in truth, there is a hot and willing woman I feel the need to tumble. Could you set one of the others in my stead? Or perhaps you, yourself, might take my watch."

Devlin's jaw clenched in visible anger. Cashel should know such a request was unthinkable, demonstrating a selfish lack of regard for the clan. Yet how could he chide this cur for thinking the favors of a woman more important than his duty when the same charge could be leveled against him? On the other hand, if he did not rebuke the man, he would be failing Eamon once again by not maintaining discipline among his men.

Were it possible that Cashel knew his situation, Devlin would have struck him a resounding blow for goading him in such an impertinent manner. But as it was, Cashel could have no knowledge of the letters between Alyssa and her father or the confession to the MacMahon. Devlin found his self-abasement increasing as he was forced to reprimand another for a sin, though uncommitted, much like his own.

"Your request is unconscionable, Cashel," he began, working to force the words from his throat. "It is also denied. You should have realized, ere you asked, that I would never assign your task to another so that you might indulge in pleasure."

"Than mayhap you, yourself, might—"

"You miss my point, Cashel. You owe these few hours as sentry to your kinsmen. Even were I to be here tonight, I would not play a part in your being so remiss.''

''Are you going somewhere?'' Cashel queried, accepting the decision of the chief gallowglass with more grace than Devlin anticipated.

''To hell and back,'' Devlin grumbled as he stalked away. He almost envied Cashel's ability to deal so casually with desire for a woman.

Cashel watched Devlin go, content that tomorrow Fitzhugh would be walking into the trap already set in motion. More important, however, Eamon's best warrior would be absent from the camp when he was most needed.

But Cashel's jealous hatred for the man was such that he could not leave well enough alone. He did not see why Devlin's remaining hours should be peaceful ones when the opportunity presented itself to ensure that they were otherwise. Why not arrange things so that all areas of the outsider's life were troublesome before death claimed him? Why not deprive him of his precious Alyssa?

Immediately, Cashel sauntered over to Roisin, busy weaving a fine length of cloth. Bending low, he whispered in her ear.

''You've not had much chance of late to have Fitzhugh to yourself. His whore has kept him that busy. But if you hurry, I happen to know that he is currently bathing in the stream. Surely, with your womanly powers of seduction, you can at last make him your own.''

Without a word of response, Roisin put down her shuttle, rose and left the compound.

Cashel's eyes glittered with sinister intent as he waited a few moments before approaching Alyssa.

"Why, what are you doing here, woman?" he asked in feigned surprise.

"And where should I be?" Alyssa inquired coldly, not bothering to look up from her mending.

"I'd have thought you'd be scurrying to join your man. I saw Devlin not five minutes ago and he told me he was on his way to meet his love at the stream."

"Devlin has finished his discussion with Eamon?" Alyssa asked, dropping the sewing into her lap. Her voice, tinged with anxiety, indicated she would be off in search of Fitzhugh immediately.

"I don't know where he has come from, lass, only where he was going. Am I his keeper?"

"Of course not," she said, wondering why Devlin had chosen to send her such an odd message by an even odder messenger rather than come to her himself when his interview had concluded. Surmising that he wanted to talk with her away from the others, she sent Muirne across the clearing to little Liam's family. Watching that she arrived safely, Alyssa almost laughed aloud as the small boy quickly picked a wild-flower and offered it to Devlin's daughter. Of a certainty, the lad's actions were prompted more by self-defense than affection. But as amusingly wonderful as innocent children were to observe, Alyssa had other things on her mind. She set out to find Devlin.

* * *

Wandering downstream to assure himself of some privacy, Devlin lost no time in doffing his clothes and leaving them in a heap on the bank beside his dagger and sword.

Unsettled though he was, Devlin Fitzhugh nevertheless made a proud, masculine figure standing beside the swiftly flowing water. His well-muscled body was that of a soldier, finely honed by innumerable encounters with the enemy. Wide shoulders gave way to a broad chest, its manly beauty marred only by occasional ridges of scars, the longest of which ran almost entirely across his rib cage and bespoke great valor in battle. But the liberal sprinkling of golden hairs between his taut nipples hid most evidence of these old wounds from view.

As it worked its way down Devlin's body, the fine mat of hair began to diminish until it was naught but a thin strip when it traversed his trim waist and flat abdomen. Lower still, the hair flared out again, wild and unruly as the masculine essence of the man himself. Narrow hips and long, well-muscled legs followed next, making Devlin's lines every bit as graceful as any that had ever been carved in marble.

But there was an evident turbulence within him that no master sculptor could hope to convey in stone. Sorrow, guilt, self-recrimination, all whirled in the darkness shrouding Devlin's soul. He watched for an instant as the water beckoned to him as though it were some ancient balm that would quiet his heart if not heal it.

Wading out into the center of the stream, Devlin was not conscious of its icy sting. All he knew was that he was driven to use the water to rid himself of disgrace.

He began to wash, slowly and thoroughly, as if he were taking part in some primitive purification ritual. Cupping water in his hands, he brought it to his face, allowing his now splayed fingers to follow the course of the droplets as they traveled down his shoulders and chest. Again and again, he repeated the procedure until he no longer felt his cheeks burning with shame.

He might have failed in his attempt to strike a balance between his responsibilities to the MacMahon and those he owed Alyssa, but Devlin vowed he would never allow it to happen again. Resolutely, he set about scrubbing the rest of his body so that he could return to Alyssa and inform her of the permission he had obtained for the meeting with Cecil Howett.

"Would you welcome some help with your task?" a feminine voice rang out.

Surprised, Devlin spun around to see Roisin appear from a clump of trees bordering the stream.

"I'd suppose you have better things to do with your time, lass, than to provide me with a service I can easily take care of myself," Devlin replied brusquely. Dismissing the woman's presence, he made no attempt to hide his nakedness. There were few things sacred in a rebel camp, and the sight of a man bathing was natural enough.

"Either the water is exceeding cold, or you're not very glad I'm here," Roisin commented with a playful pout and a pointed stare at Devlin's manhood.

"If truth be know, Roisin MacMahon, I don't think

I've ever been that glad to see you," Devlin retorted, scrubbing his skin more briskly in his anger. Though it was the woman's way to be openly flirtatious, he had to convey to her that he'd not welcome such behavior since he had claimed Alyssa for his own.

"That can only be because I've never really given you reason to be happy," Roisin stated, her eyes glazed with desire. Hastily, she untied her laces and shrugged her tunic from her shoulders until her large, ripe breasts were bare. Then, with nary a care for Devlin's obvious irritation, she allowed her garment to drop to the ground. Kicking it carelessly aside, she lowered herself into the water. Each second brought her another step closer to a seething Devlin.

"God's teeth, woman! There is nothing for you here!"

"You're much too modest, sweetling," Roisin cooed, lowering her lashes as she looked her fill.

"Be that as it may, I've no interest in the likes of you," Devlin assured Roisin, trying to sidestep her. But she managed to match his movement with one of her own so that they continued to stand face-to-face, chest to chest.

She reached out a palm and wiped it across Devlin's torso, not at all dismayed that he remained impassive as once more he unsuccessfully sought to move away from her.

"Allow me to do as I wish and I'll have you groaning with pleasure right soon," Roisin promised enticingly.

Devlin grabbed her wandering hands and brought his face to within an inch of hers.

"Leave me be, Roisin," he ordered through gritted teeth. "You know I am committed to Alyssa Howett."

"Her! She's too much of a green girl for a man like you. Once you've tired of your young, whey-faced English whore, you'll be wanting a real woman to warm your bed. When that time comes, I intend to be waiting, willing to do anything for you, anything you like, even care for your bastard if need be."

"Get out of my way, you sluttish she-devil," Devlin hissed furiously. He grabbed Roisin's waist and lifted her high to remove her from his path so he could make his way back to the bank unhampered. But before he could set her down to the side, his wet hands, Roisin's slick skin and her delighted squirming caused Devlin to lose his grip. She dropped slowly, her naked body sliding along the length of his own.

"Let us play some more, Devlin," she called as he turned away from her to leave the stream. "I did enjoy it so!"

Alyssa stood, frozen in horror by the scene she had just witnessed. Too far from Devlin and Roisin to hear what they were saying, the girl decided their actions made plain enough just what was going on.

Hadn't Devlin taken the woman's hands within his own, and bent his head to hers? Hadn't he picked her up to run her body along his?

Unable to stand further evidence of Devlin's infidelity, and unwilling to humble herself by making her presence known, Alyssa ran off, undetected.

Leaving the path and striking off into the woods, the heartsick girl stumbled once or twice, blinded by

her tears. She tried to find an excuse for what she had
seen, but could think of none. All that came to her
were memories of Devlin's prior flirtations with almost every unwed female in the clan, and Roisin's
sly warning that any woman who attached herself to
Devlin Fitzhugh would have to reconcile herself to
the idea of sharing him.

Well, she wouldn't share him, she wouldn't! The
others could have him, Alyssa swore vehemently,
finding shelter within a tiny, natural bower. She
wanted naught to do with a man who would betray
her!

Though Devlin might care for her in his own way,
he was obviously incapable of real love or of remaining true. No matter what his intentions, fidelity was
simply not part of his nature.

Yet why would such a man place himself in danger
to bring the letter to her father or agree to take her to
Kilross? The image of Devlin's face, filled with tenderness when they were in the throes of love, almost
convinced Alyssa she was mistaken. But then she
painfully recalled what she had so recently witnessed,
and knew the pangs of misery all over again.

Mayhap Devlin's kindness to her was merely the
result of a rankled conscience. And why would his
conscience plague him if he had not been sleeping
with Roisin all along?

Alyssa didn't want to think about it, but she realized there was one thing she had to consider. What
was she going to do now? Ranting and raving at Devlin would only bring her more false promises and
sweet words. She might even start to believe them

until the lying knave's next lapse. Then her hurt would begin anew. Alyssa couldn't live like that, but what else was she to do? There was no way she could escape the camp and Devlin's watchful eye... unless...unless tomorrow she threw herself on her father's mercy and begged him to take her back. True, the crown considered her as much an outlaw as it did Devlin. But what was a stint in Her Majesty's jail compared to a lifetime spent with a man who didn't love her?

Oh, of a certainty, he had said he did, Alyssa thought angrily, clenching her dainty fists, but only after she had prodded him. Had he been reluctant to say the words because he had not relished lying to her? Had she forced him into insincerity? If she had, she would never do so again. There was no longer anything she wanted from Devlin Fitzhugh other than that he deliver her to her father on the morrow.

Resolving to adhere to her newly devised plan, painful though it was, Alyssa sought to control her wretchedness. If her scheme was to work, nothing could appear to be amiss. When she finally left her hiding place in the forest, there was no evidence of the tears she had shed, the tears she felt like shedding still.

Strolling into the clearing, Alyssa saw Devlin pacing before the home that she, in her disillusionment, had once considered happy.

"Where have you been?" he asked gently. "I was concerned."

"I was nervous about your meeting with Eamon and thought a walk among the trees might soothe me,'' she prevaricated, picking up the mending she had tossed aside when she had gone rushing off to the stream. How she hated Cashel for sending her there. He had to have known what was transpiring, and had likely taken great delight in weaving his mischief. At least her plan to act as if nothing were wrong would deprive the swine of additional amusement.

''Aren't you curious as to the outcome?'' Devlin demanded indulgently while Alyssa bent to add some kindling to her cook fire.

''Aye, most curious, indeed.''

''We have permission to leave tonight, but we must tell no one. Eamon wishes it to remain a private matter.''

''I knew if anyone could charm him into granting us leave, it would be you,'' Alyssa replied with a wan smile.

His only reply was a self-deprecating grunt.

Awkwardly, and against her will, Alyssa reached out to brush away a burnished curl that had fallen across Devlin's forehead. Its dampness was a cruel reminder of his breach of faith, compelling words to tumble out that she would rather have left unspoken.

''You seem caught in some odd mood, Devlin. Are you hiding something from me?''

''Why, no!'' he lied. How could he tell her of the guilt he felt as a result of failing Eamon without asking her to share his burden? She had problems enough without shouldering his, too. As for the incident with Roisin, it was so insignificant to him that he thought it not worth noting, especially when it might only upset Alyssa further.

"Are you certain?" Her violet eyes probed his blue ones.

"There is nothing to tell," he insisted.

Alyssa fell into silence, busying herself with mundane tasks in the hopes that such activity would hide her wounded heart.

She was solemn, Devlin noted, watching Alyssa go about her work for the remainder of the day. He attributed it to her anxiety about meeting with her father and having finally to come to terms with the relationship between them.

But Alyssa's quiet suited him well at present, and so he did not seek to disturb it. He had his own demons to grapple with and possessed no desire for conversation.

They spent the rest of the day without talking. Then Muirne returned to the hut, little Liam in tow, and the pervading silence was shattered as the tiny girl babbled enough for all of them.

It had just grown dark when Alyssa knelt down to place a lingering, wistful kiss on Muirne's cheek.

"Now, don't carry on so," Sinead instructed the saddened Englishwoman. "You'll only upset the little one. Besides, you'll be back before you've had a chance to miss her."

"Aye," Alyssa agreed listlessly while Devlin assisted her in mounting her sturdy mare.

"Where are the pair of you off to?" little Liam's mother inquired of Devlin before he could find his own saddle.

"Another part of the forest for a few days of solitude," Devlin replied with a roguish grin. His ability to lie so smoothly was not lost on Alyssa, and added one more gash to her already injured spirit.

"You devil! And if there's not a babe nine months from now, I'll be sorely disappointed in both you and your legendary prowess, Master Fitzhugh," the woman scolded playfully.

"You'll have to restrain yourself a bit longer, Devlin." The MacMahon's voice sounded in the descending darkness. "I want a word with you before you go."

Leaving Alyssa with the other women, Devlin promptly joined his lord. Accompanied by Niall, the men walked to an isolated portion of the encampment.

"I am calling for my favor, Devlin," the chieftain announced gravely, ignoring Niall's look of surprise.

"As you wish, Eamon. It will be gladly rendered."

"I expect no less. What I want from you is to set up another meeting with Cecil Howett three days hence at Glenderry."

"For what purpose?" a baffled Devlin queried. "He hasn't the authority to restore your lands. And I imagine he is in such disfavor with Elizabeth at present that it would be ill-advised to have him plead your case before her."

"I do not intend to use his voice. I plan to still it." The words were delivered in a quiet but lethal tone.

Horror seeped into Devlin's blood, quickly sending a chill throughout his entire body. He could make no immediate comment, but only stare at the MacMahon in astonishment.

"It cannot be helped," Eamon pronounced, his eyes as frequently upon Niall as they were on Devlin. "Howett has gone looking for his daughter once. He may decide to do so again. We cannot chance his finding our hiding place here in the forest. The safety of the clan requires his death...at least if you wish to keep your woman with you."

"But Father, how can you direct Devlin to kill Alyssa's sire?" Niall questioned, his voice full of outrage.

"I do not command Devlin to plunge the dagger, my son, only to provide the opportunity for us to do so. Remember your imprisonment in Dublin Castle, and Devlin's as well. It was Cecil Howett who meant to transport you to an English jail. Think on that!"

"I told you I would do anything for you, Eamon, that did not cause my loved ones harm. How can you ask me to hurt Alyssa by paving the way for her father's death?"

"How can I not ask you, Devlin Fitzhugh? Such a deed will prove your loyalty to me all over again. Then there can be trust between us as there once was. Besides, your woman need never know. Her ignorance would protect her from pain."

"You demand too much," Niall protested.

"Silence! As chieftain of this clan I would be derelict in my duties to require less. You must understand that I have to ignore my personal relationship with Devlin in order to secure the safety of our people. Were you in my place, Niall, you would be called upon to do the same. Understand that, and understand it well. As for you, Devlin, I expect my orders to be obeyed.''

With that, Eamon turned his back on Devlin and walked off, depriving his gallowglass of the chance to say him nay.

"What will you do, Devlin?" Niall whispered with concern.

"What I must," Devlin growled fiercely before turning on his heel and rejoining his beloved.

"Why did Eamon wish to speak with you?" Alyssa inquired quietly as Devlin mounted his steed.

"Merely to give me advice concerning our journey," Devlin stated, his handsome face emotionless, his eyes staring straight ahead. What else could he say to her? he thought in anguish.

"The MacMahon dared to offer you instruction on so delicate a matter?" Liam's mother laughed. "Fie, Devlin! Surely he knows a rogue like you doesn't need guidance where women are concerned!"

Devlin issued a short laugh which Alyssa found as false as his vows of love. Then they were under way, both lost in their own bitter thoughts.

Chapter Fifteen

Alyssa pulled Sinead's rough woolen cloak closer about her to ward off the chill that had invaded her soul, and concentrated on following Devlin through the dark forest. They'd exchanged few words since leaving the camp hours earlier. Though Devlin had recommended this precaution for reasons of stealth in case of English patrols, he seemed as preoccupied as she. With each mile, Alyssa's uneasiness at leaving the MacMahons' camp was increasing rapidly as they grew farther from the place she'd learned to think of as home. She couldn't bear to think of how this journey would end.

Certainly Cecil Howett would welcome her, Alyssa told herself, trying to avoid the issue foremost in her thoughts, but what would he say at the sight of her?

From what she had seen that morning in spying her reflection in the pool, she looked nothing like the innocent maiden Howett had last seen in Dublin. There was a sauciness and assurance about her that seemed to shout her womanhood, but she supposed that perception might be her own feelings airing themselves.

Still, though she had tried her best, her physical appearance was as bedraggled and impoverished as that of the poorest peasant in Ireland.

Her once upswept hair was completely untamed despite her fervent intentions to master its unruliness. With only a wooden comb to work with, however, it was impossible to keep her blond curls from straying, no matter how she tried.

Only the other night in their meadow, Devlin had said that she appeared a beguiling, wind-spawned goddess of old, favoring him with her graces by wearing his tunic and nothing else. Then, he'd removed even that bit of clothes....

And her present garments—what would Cecil Howett say of those? she thought, forcing her mind away from Devlin. The rose wool gown in which she'd escaped was dirt streaked, and nothing she'd done had removed the grime from its hem. Her stockings were torn and her once dainty slippers were beyond repair. Yet Alyssa suspected this poor semblance of English dress would be more acceptable to her father's standards than the Irish tunic of saffron hue that Devlin had suggested.

Frowning, she shook her head and tried to consider what she would tell Cecil Howett, and just how much she might ask of him. Unbidden, indeed forbidden, her violet eyes kept straying nonetheless to the tall, masculine figure of Devlin Fitzhugh riding ahead of her. The duplicity of the man infuriated her as much as it sickened her and she picked up her horse's pace in reaction.

How could he, to whom she had given her heart,

treat her that way? After loving her so thoroughly and tenderly on his return from Ballynon, convincing her by word and deed that they were as well-suited and permanent a couple as any who ever lived, the knave had shamelessly enjoyed Roisin's wares mere hours later.

Of course, if Roisin's earlier warnings were to be believed, Devlin had always been a man of changeable appetites, but that didn't require her to accept it. No matter what standards Roisin had, Alyssa Howett would share her man with no one—and if Devlin Fitzhugh wasn't satisfied with her, then he could go to hell in Roisin's arms!

"Easy, Alyssa," called Devlin suddenly. Bringing his horse up beside hers, he grabbed the reins and slowed the mare she'd been pushing so hard. "I know you're anxious to see your sire, but we don't have to be at Kilross until midday. There's no need to work your mount like that. What's wrong with you?"

Alyssa was immediately ashamed. She'd been so involved in contemplating her own pain, she hadn't realized that she'd torn past Devlin on the unfamiliar trail or that she'd been riding so recklessly.

"I'm sorry. I guess I was daydreaming," she murmured. "It won't happen again."

"I hope not. Not only don't I want to explain to Eamon that you ruined one of his horses on a journey that displeased him, but if she stumbles or goes lame, we won't make this meeting," he snapped. Unable to avoid releasing some of the pressure building in him, the gallowglass let the harsh words spill out unhindered. "All right, let's get moving—but more carefully if you please. Let me lead the way."

If he led, her small yet seductive figure would not be in front of him constantly, not that he wouldn't see her in his mind's eye anyway, Devlin acknowledged silently. By all that was holy, how had he fallen in love with her, an Englishwoman?

Now, a man of honor for his entire life, he was faced with a terrible choice. In the end, he would have to betray either his chieftain or his woman—and neither was a pleasant prospect. All night long as the miles had flown beneath the horses' hooves, he'd cursed himself up and down for ever encouraging Alyssa to communicate with her father and then again for seeking a reply to her letter.

Contrary to Cashel's dire condemnation of Howett, the man seemed to be genuinely concerned for his daughter's welfare or he wouldn't have asked to see her. Devlin certainly couldn't fault a father for that. Yet, Eamon, a father himself, had condemned the Englishman to death. Bloody damnation, life had been simpler without a woman complicating his existence!

Should he refuse Eamon's bidding and fail to arrange a second meeting, in truth an ambush at which Howett would be executed, Devlin would have to leave the MacMahon camp—if Eamon didn't see him killed. And were it known the MacMahon had exiled him, no other Irish clan would take him or his family in. For that matter, it was doubtful any chieftain would hire a gallowglass in the company of an Englishwoman and a young daughter. Such an entourage did not bespeak courage, ferocity and valor. Yet how could he play false the man who had sired Alyssa?

True, Alyssa need never know who had set the snare to capture and kill her father. The problem, though, was that Devlin would know—and he doubted he could live with himself or Alyssa if he betrayed her blood in such a manner. By all the saints, it seemed as soon as a man thought himself happy and content, he was dealt hard choices that left no easy answers.

Looking over his shoulder to be certain Alyssa was following, Devlin motioned toward a wider path.

"That road will lead us straight into Ballynon within a few hours, but I don't want to be too early. We're best off traveling the rest of the way just after dawn, arriving in town with the farmers going to market. I even have a wheel of cheese from Roisin to trade if we need to explain our presence."

"How generous of her," said Alyssa coldly, as he dismounted and led his horse to drink. "But I suppose you were worth it."

"I didn't hear you," he said, coming back to take her mare to the nearby stream.

"It isn't worth repeating." With that, she slid from her saddle, slipped under his waiting arms and walked away, into the woods.

Devlin looked after her, mystified. He was risking his life by riding to an English rendezvous, his career by insisting on a course of action unpopular with his chieftain and his future livelihood by choosing between his woman and Eamon, and *she* was upset?

Three hours later and she was still being difficult! Devlin didn't want Alyssa to approach the single-storied priest's house until he was certain it truly was abandoned. Since Henry VIII had closed some of the churches, many of their outbuildings had become sanctuaries to homeless clans desperate to defend what little they had to claim. Then, too, there was the possibility that the meeting was an ambush. Trouble could well lie silent within the stone walls that seemed so innocent.

However, neither Devlin's explanation, his natural authority nor his dimpled grin had any effect on the woman who held his heart. She was completely unwilling to listen to reason.

"I will not wait in the shade of cypress trees while you scout the area for signs of deception," she argued, eager to be done with the entire business before another glance at Devlin's handsome face diminished her resolve to leave him.

Devlin sputtered indignantly as she cantered up to the small cottage, desperate to feel her father's reassuring arms about her. She'd had enough of the Irishman's seductive lies. If he didn't want her, she knew another who did.

Besides, anyone could see the place was deserted except for the lone horse tethered out front. The grass leading up to the single door was high and untrampled. For that matter, shutters now incapable of closing tightly hung haphazardly from windows long untended, permitting glimpses of the dark, empty interior. Even the ragged thatching of the roof had become home to a flock of crows, who raucously objected to Alyssa's presence. Clearly, no squad of Elizabeth's soldiers had taken up residence here.

Why was Devlin so worried about treachery? Cecil Howett had never done anything to harm her—she had only suffered from what he had left undone. But after her father had written such a poignant plea for one last meeting, how could anyone think he would expose her? Such a ridiculous notion was all the more evidence that the concept of loyalty was unfathomable to Devlin Fitzhugh, and as such, not part of his nature.

Gritting her teeth against the unpleasant scene ahead, Alyssa thanked God her father had sought to see her again. Had he not suggested it, she would have been trapped in Eamon's camp forever. Now she had merely to make her intentions known to the Englishman waiting inside and her ordeal would be over.

Slipping from the saddle, she turned to enter the desolate priest's house, anxious to put her life with Devlin Fitzhugh behind her.

"Alyssa, wait there," called Devlin, coming up fast and dismounting beside her. His temper was barely in check as a result of her recklessness, but at the moment her safety concerned him most. "Permit me to at least inspect the rear of the building before we go in."

"You don't have to accompany me—stay here if you like."

"Why isn't your father running out the door to sweep you into his arms if all is well?" challenged an angry Devlin, unable to shake his sense of dread.

"Mayhap because he's afraid the Irish would try to trap him or even kill him where he stood if he came out to greet me."

Recalling Eamon's orders, Devlin swallowed hard

at her words and surrendered the argument. Without
speaking, he took her by the arm and moved toward
the closed door.

The gallowglass was still apprehensive, nonetheless. His warrior's instincts engaged, he saw no suspicious signs that would deter Alyssa. He was glad,
however, of his sword at his waist and his dagger
strapped to his leg. If need be, he'd be able to fight
for her.

"I told you, there is no need to take me in."

"I believe in protecting my woman," he replied
softly.

"I trust you mean women," muttered Alyssa.
Shoving open the door to the cottage, she broke from
Devlin's embrace and entered.

"Women?" he echoed blankly, but she was gone.
From inside he could hear her calling.

"Father—it's Alyssa. Where are you?"

"Child! I worried so for your safety," cried Cecil
Howett as he came out of the shadows to embrace his
daughter. A pair of candles stood on a side table in
the small hallway, illuminating the area and making
him appear ten years older than when she had seen
him last. No one could miss the dark circles under his
eyes and the clear loss of weight he had suffered.

"Father, I'm sorry," she said from the comfort of
his arms. Using a small handkerchief, she wiped her
tears before she noticed his cheeks were as wet as
hers. "I didn't realize how much you loved me."

Nodding his understanding, Howett turned to the
entering Devlin and smiled. "Thank you, Fitzhugh,
for bringing her here and for not mistreating her. I

imagined the worst, but I can see she's fared well in your care.''

"Aye, sir, I've—''

"Father, never mind the past. It's what happens now that matters,'' interrupted Alyssa quickly. Taking a deep breath, she stepped back a few paces from Howett, looked at Devlin and then directed her attention to her father. Quietly, but clearly, she spoke the words that had been forming in her mind since the previous day. "Take me home, Father. Whether it's to Dublin or London, I want to leave with you at once.''

"What?'' echoed the men in unison, each eyeing the other suspiciously. She had said she was happy—

"Alyssa, how can you—''

"Daughter, I'll do what you ask, but—''

Even as their voices overrode one another, the shouts of soldiers arriving made it difficult to hear.

"Fitzhugh, you are under arrest by order of Her Majesty, Queen Elizabeth,'' came the cry amid horses' whinnying. "Come out peacefully and the crown will show mercy.''

"But who told them?'' cried Howett, his face a ghastly hue. "I swear this wasn't meant to happen.''

"You're lying,'' scoffed Devlin, grabbing for his sword.

"Lay down your weapon,'' ordered an officer. Crashing the door open against its frame, he and his men entered, blades drawn, giving Devlin no chance to deal with Howett. "No one need be hurt.''

"Only you!'' Devlin bellowed, drawing his dagger with his free hand. Alyssa barely saw the weapon before it was winging through the air, embedding itself in the Englishman's throat. Blood began to spurt, and the gallowglass pulled her out of range as the dying man slumped to the floor. The remainder of the soldiers hesitated briefly, unsure of what to do in the absence of their officer.

"We've got to get out of here," Devlin muttered, knowing this was their only opportunity for escape. Howett was still protesting his innocence, but Devlin couldn't waste time listening.

Another of Her Majesty's men was advancing with weapon drawn. The soldier clearly had no knowledge of either the Irishman's strategy or his skill with a sword.

Devlin began to thrust at this new threat, finding pleasure in making the man retreat, and even greater satisfaction in slicing the fellow's arm, causing him to cry out. Had he leisure, Devlin would have enjoyed the game further. But there was not an instant to be lost.

Realizing they would need a distraction, the gallowglass grabbed the candles and flung them at the desiccated rushes covering the floor. In the space of a breath, flames devoured the dry matting, encircling the soldiers within a fiery snare. Not waiting to see what happened, Devlin shoved Alyssa toward the side window as the enemy began trying to stamp out the growing fire. Smoke clouded the room, obscuring their number, and Devlin knew there could be no more delay.

Quickly, before she realized what he intended, he picked Alyssa up, threw her over his shoulder and climbed through the window. He could not bring himself to leave her behind, no matter her recent declaration that she wished to remain with her father.

Outside the priest's house, the scene was one of chaos. The horses had begun to smell fire and were fighting their tethers to get free, instinct winning out over obedience. Two soldiers came flying out of the door to roll to the earth, trying to extinguish their flaming uniforms, only to further incense the petrified animals, who reared on hind legs and broke their restraints, galloping off into the distance. At their departure, the other horses fought more diligently for safety, and Devlin was hard-pressed to capture his own horse. He had to forsake Alyssa's.

For a brief moment, Alyssa tasted the fear of uncertainty. Perhaps the ambush had been authorized by her father.

No, she told herself. Cecil Howett might be many things, but never a man to risk his daughter's life—not when he'd thrown her away once before and regretted it.

"Up you go," Devlin instructed, boosting her onto his saddle.

"I want to stay here," she protested. Why did he want her with him? Wasn't Roisin enough?

"'Tis a lovely place to be sure, but you're coming along for the ride, nonetheless," he barked. "When we're safe, we have a lot to discuss. And I promise you, we *will* discuss every last thing," he vowed, his lips drawn into a tight grimace as he mounted behind her.

Chapter Sixteen

They rode as though Satan himself were after them. Devlin's heart was thundering in his chest at twice the pace of his horse's pounding hooves. He drove his mount relentlessly, so desperate was he not to be overtaken. His primary fear was not capture or death but that Alyssa would be taken from him.

In the back of his mind, however, lurked another dread—that he had lost her already, no matter that she sat before him, enfolded by his arms. *She had wanted to return to her father!* And while he yearned to know the cause, he was afraid to ask her why, afraid some horrible chasm had opened between them. Yet Devlin knew he must, just as he knew that if he could not deter her, he loved Alyssa too much to keep her with him.

Finally, when Devlin judged them safe and could demand no more of his steed, he pulled rein, stopping in a densely wooded area that would offer cover should the English soldiers have been able to follow their circuitous route. Wearily he slid to the ground and then turned to Alyssa. Without her leave, he placed his strong hands at her waist and lifted her down. Wordlessly, he turned to take care of the horse, unsaddling it and sharing some of the water he carried with the spent beast.

When he finished, there was no other task to claim his attention. What had to be done could be put off no longer. He faced Alyssa, feeling awkward in the presence of her somber stare.

"You wanted to leave me," Devlin said. His face was hard but pained bewilderment was reflected in his deep blue eyes.

"Aye."

"Do you want to do so still?" he asked quietly.

"I don't know."

"Damnation, Alyssa!" Devlin exploded. "No injury I've sustained in battle has ever wounded me so deeply."

"I may never have wielded a sword against a foe, Devlin Fitzhugh, but I've suffered my share of hurts as well," Alyssa cried, tears forming in her eyes and spilling over onto her porcelain cheeks. "Yet none were so terrible as the one inflicted by you."

"Me?" he asked in an astounded whisper. "What did I do that you would not have expected? Did you really think I could leave you there with your father?"

He reached out a tentative hand to wipe away her tears, so concerned with the reason for them that he forgot his own misery.

"That's not what I'm talking about. Your betrayal took place before we ever left Eamon's camp." Alyssa spun around, unwilling to display her heartbreak. "Never have I known so treacherous a man!"

"Mayhap you forget your sire," Devlin retorted, stung by her unfounded accusation.

"My father had nothing to do with that attack," Alyssa protested. "And should you be wondering, Devlin, neither did I."

Devlin reached out and whirled Alyssa about, capturing her in his arms, holding her with gentleness yet unwilling to release her. He brought his face down to hers so there was barely space between them and she felt the caress of his breath on her cheeks.

"I never considered that you did, sweetling. No matter what this trouble is that has sprung up between us, I know you would never do me harm. Can you not afford me the same trust?" Devlin's voice was hoarse, lacking its usual steady confidence. Brave and fierce when confronting his enemies, he nevertheless appeared anxious and uneasy as he awaited the response of this seventeen-year-old girl.

Alyssa could do little more than sniffle.

"You must answer!" Devlin cried.

Nothing but silence greeted him.

"At least tell me what has angered you," Devlin commanded in frustration. "How can we settle this thing when I know not what it is?"

"Have your breaches been so many, that you cannot decide on the one that has upset me?" Alyssa inquired, remaining rigid in the circle of his arms.

Devlin froze for an instant, but immediately discounted Alyssa's knowing about the part he was ordered to play in her father's demise. Even had she been aware of it, she would have realized, as he had discovered himself, that for her sake, he could not have stained his soul with Cecil Howett's blood. At least not if the man had been innocent of treachery. Yet, what could be her reason for wanting to abandon him? To leave him and his daughter and reside among his enemies?

"This is not a time for riddles, Alyssa. I want answers. I swear by all that's holy, I don't know what it is I have done."

"Perhaps you should ask Roisin."

"What has she to do with this?" he entreated, truly baffled.

"It was Roisin who helped you break your vows of love."

"Alyssa, sweetest heart, you must listen to me. I have not touched Roisin or any other woman since we pledged ourselves to each other."

"I saw you, Devlin! I saw you both cavorting naked in the stream." Alyssa tried to break free of his embrace, but Devlin held her fast.

"What you saw was Roisin trying to seduce me."

"And she appeared to be quite successful at it, too."

"From the moment I was aware of her presence, I told her to leave me in peace," Devlin protested.

"Was it pleasurable, Devlin, to run her sleek, lush body along your own?"

"Mother of God, Alyssa! I was trying to move her out of my way so I could leave the stream since she had chosen to stay. But with all of her calculated squirming, I dropped her. That is what you observed. You must believe me."

"Why must I?" she asked coldly, seeing all over again the scenario that had broken her heart.

"Because," Devlin entreated, his voice ripe with agony, "I love you, lass, and you love me."

She merely looked at him, her expression as frosty as a winter's morn.

"You know it's true, Alyssa. Admit it!" Devlin pleaded frantically, staring into the depths of her violet eyes, trying to find some evidence there of her feelings for him. "When you gave me your innocence, I rendered my heart in return, poor an exchange as it might be. But it belongs to you now, to value or not as you choose. I ask only that you do not fling it back to me. If you do, 'twill shatter."

It was unlike Devlin, so proud and independent, to admit vulnerability of any sort. That he should do so where she was concerned had cost him dearly, Alyssa realized. And, if he didn't love her, couldn't he have escaped the ambush at Kilross more easily alone? Her cold resolve wavered, and Devlin, experienced strategist in battle, pressed his advantage. He lowered his head to hers, his mouth seeking her trembling lips. Gently but firmly, he kissed her, pouring all of his devotion, all of his soul into that one act of love.

In his kiss, Alyssa perceived his desperation, sensed his sincerity, and her remaining resistance melted along with her heart. He was telling her the truth.

Her mouth ceased its quivering, receiving strength from his, and she began to return his fevered declaration of love with one of her own.

When their lips finally drew apart, Devlin rested his forehead against Alyssa's.

"Tell me," he murmured, his voice husky and thick. "Tell me that you believe me, that you are staying with me."

"I've just informed you of such," Alyssa replied, lightly running her fingertips along his masculine jawline. "But mayhap you would like me to tell you again."

"Aye. I think it best you repeat it."

This time, it was Alyssa who took possession of Devlin's mouth, eliciting a groan so primitive that it was an eloquent expression of his joy. His response proclaimed he was hers alone; she knew it with a certainty.

"My first and only love," Alyssa uttered with a soft sigh.

"My true love," Devlin whispered in reply. "My only true love...now and always." Then he claimed her, offering his heart, soul and body in ardent proof of his troth.

Sitting beneath the overhanging branches of the willow, Cashel stretched uneasily in the isolated darkness that was his post, hating the tedious routine of sentry duty more than any other aspect of life in camp. Indeed, if Devlin or Eamon knew just how often he had been delinquent from his post in any given fortnight, they would have exiled him from the MacMahon fires months ago. Not that many of his other activities wouldn't cause the same punishment, thought the sentry with a smirk, but that was all about to change. Tomorrow would see a new chieftain for the clan, one who wasn't afraid of making changes or dealing with the English.

How long could Eamon expect them to continue to suffer for the MacMahon heritage? Self-sacrifice might have been noble in Henry's day, but under Elizabeth, it was downright idiocy—and Cashel Mac-Mahon was no one's fool!

The screech of an owl sounded nearby, almost mournful in its cry, and he answered promptly, hard-pressed to keep from whooping with joy. If this plan had borne fruit, the other must have done so as well. Things were finally going as he planned.

About him, shadows began to move, indistinct figures slipping stealthily among the trees, indistinguishable from the dark trunks. Just as arranged, the enemy, unchallenged and undisputed, was attacking in Devlin's absence.

Cashel waited quietly until the English soldiers passed him. Anticipating the first shouts of alarm, he rubbed dirt on his face and hands, took a deep breath and unsheathed his sword. If he intended to be the MacMahon when this was over, he couldn't appear to have missed the fighting. Gritting his teeth, he slashed his arm and waited for blood to run. Then, a wounded soldier, he headed slowly back to camp.

The sun was shining brightly and Alyssa had never been so content. Riding to Eamon's camp, she sat across Devlin's lap, his muscular arms enfolding her as he held the reins of the horse.

After but a few hours sleep, she felt tired, and lazy,

and very much loved. Though the attack at Kilross remained in the back of her mind, and her father's culpability an issue to question, it seemed of little importance when compared to her future with Devlin Fitzhugh. Oh she knew that someday she might feel called upon to send word to her father assuring him that she truly was happy, but not now. Her concern was Devlin and the love they shared.

Wiggling subtly against him, she tilted her head to place a tiny kiss upon his rugged cheek.

"Any more of that, lass, and we'll never get home," he growled with mock sternness.

Home, Alyssa thought, satisfied with the notion. A forest, a crude hut among a people considered her enemy, and yet it was a home, one she relished because she shared it with the seductive, engaging man who held her so protectively.

In playful defiance, she kissed him again and then laid her head back against his chest, content to listen to nothing more than the powerful thud of his loving heart.

When the rise that hid Eamon's camp came into view in the distance, Devlin quickened the pace of his mount. The sudden cantering of the horse made Alyssa squeal her concern that she might fall, but Devlin only laughed and hugged her tighter, swearing he would not allow any harm to befall her. With light, carefree hearts, they continued swiftly forward, the wind at their back.

Devlin, especially, was in high spirits, his one dimple showing as he smiled and teased Alyssa. He had not been given the opportunity to disobey the

MacMahon's directive, and his woman was returning to the campsite with him. His heart spilled over with happiness until he and Alyssa crested the ridge.

There, beneath them in the valley, was what remained of Eamon's compound. The charred remnants of huts marred the primal landscape, a blight upon nature's beauty. What was left of the clan moved about slowly but purposefully, evidently trying to salvage what they could. But nowhere among them did Devlin or Alyssa spy a dear, tiny figure.

With a roar of rage that drowned out Alyssa's gasp of horror at the sight below, Devlin sent the horse into a gallop. The animal flew along the sloping ground, crashing into the ruined settlement. Most of those remaining in the camp were too busy burying their dead, tending to their wounded or scavenging the still smoldering huts to take much notice of Devlin. Everyone, that was, except a surprised Cashel MacMahon, who ground his teeth in hatred at the unexpected sight of the gallowglass and his doxy.

The horse had barely come to a stop before Devlin lowered Alyssa and jumped from its back.

"Muirne!" he thundered. "Did you see my daughter?" he anxiously asked one of the women.

She shook her head numbly, carrying her own dead child in her arms.

"Muirne!" Devlin shouted again in anguish, his deep voice reverberating through the unnatural stillness of the camp only to be echoed by Alyssa's frantic cry. He looked around him. There was death and mayhem everywhere. "Muirne!"

"Here she be. Don't fret," came a familiar, aged

voice, Sinead and Muirne emerging from the trees ringing the clearing. "I was but keeping her safely out of sight in case the English took it into their heads to return."

Devlin and Alyssa ran to the child, the little one filthy and smudged with soot. Lifting his daughter, Devlin clasped her in a fierce embrace, his shoulders shaking in great, silent sobs at finding her still alive.

Quickly gaining control of himself, he turned Muirne over to Alyssa, who covered the girl with an abundance of heartfelt kisses.

"Bad men came," Muirne announced to the adults, her little face grave, her huge eyes solemn. "Sinead and I ran into the woods. We hid until they went away, and then we hid some more."

"I thought it best she didn't see the worst of it," Sinead muttered.

"Thank you, dear friend." Alyssa placed her arms around the old woman and gave her a hug, embarrassing her with its intensity.

"There's no need to be emotional, lass. I've lived through raids enough in my lifetime to know what to do. 'Twas simply a matter of doing it," Sinead reassured her. "But I must say my greatest difficulty was keeping the little one quiet lest we be discovered. If she's to grow to adulthood in a rebel camp, 'tis a lesson she should be taught."

Alyssa nodded and turned to Devlin's daughter.

"Listen to me, and listen well, my little magpie. These are dangerous times, and even when your father is present to protect you, there are instances when you must be absolutely silent."

"How will I know when?" the tired child asked with a yawn.

"When you are told," Devlin said absently, turning to survey the damage to the camp.

"But if I will have to be quiet, then so will you," the child insisted stubbornly, tugging at her father's tunic. "So how will you tell me?"

"Why, we shall have a secret signal. Would you like that?" Alyssa intervened, trying to make a game of it. "Should your father or I run our fingertips across our lips like this, you will know you must be still."

"Fine. As long as I don't have to do it too often. It's hard to be qui—"

The child broke off in midword when Alyssa gave the agreed-upon sign.

"What a clever little squirrel you are," Devlin praised, stroking his daughter's unruly curls.

"Aye, and a tired one as well," Sinead commented. "We were up most of the night. Let me find a place for her to nap while you see to whatever it is that has to be done. That's a fine, good lass," Sinead soothed, leading the child away.

"As much as has been lost, Devlin," Alyssa said, watching Sinead settle Muirne upon a patch of soft grass, "you and I have been quite fortunate."

"I would the others had been so blessed," he replied, his grim eyes dwelling on the surrounding wreckage.

"Aye. I bleed with them for the harm wrought here," Alyssa said sadly, placing her hand in Devlin's to both give and receive comfort.

"Welcome to a rebel camp, milady," Cashel taunted as he approached them, at last able to hide his shock at the pair's return. "Do the efforts of your countrymen quite meet with your approval?"

"Enough of that," ordered Devlin. "What are Eamon's plans?"

"He has none that I know of," the other man sneered.

"Where is he, then?" the gallowglass demanded.

"Beneath yonder tree." With a jerk of his head, Cashel indicated the spot.

"There are naught but fresh graves there," Alyssa noted fretfully.

"Aye, and Eamon lies in one of them."

Devlin's heart constricted with sorrow. Despite their recent differences, Eamon MacMahon had been a man the gallowglass had respected and admired, a man he had also called a friend. Yet when Eamon had most had need of him, he had been absent from camp. Devlin wanted to hang his head in grief and shame, but the present held no time for such personal luxuries.

There was Niall to be seen to, if indeed the boy had been fortunate enough to have survived the attack.

"Where is Eamon's son?" asked Devlin, his gaze searching the camp for him.

"My foster brother has shed his first blood in battle," Cashel replied. "'Tis no serious wound, but I do not want him disturbed."

"I have no choice. The boy will have to be roused. There are decisions to be made," Devlin explained.

"Aye, and I will make them, Fitzhugh." Cashel reached out an arm to stay the warrior when he began to move away.

"You? Eamon had been grooming Niall to succeed him as the MacMahon," Devlin declared, his words ringing loudly as he shook off the other man's hand.

"He's nothing but a stripling lad. The clan needs a man to take charge, and as Eamon's foster son, I claim that privilege." Cashel's voice had escalated to match Devlin's.

Seeing trouble ahead, Devlin sent Alyssa to sit with Muirne and Sinead. Should squabbling break out, he did not want her in the midst of it. Hatred towards the English was running hotly at present, and he would not allow the MacMahons to vent their wrath on her.

For once she obeyed him without comment. Satisfied, Devlin turned back to Cashel and blithely pushed him out of the way to go off in search of young Niall.

The raised voices and the animosity springing up between the two men was enough to garner the attention of the others. They rested from their labors, interested in the goings-on.

Devlin stalked through the camp, going from group to group, an increasingly angry Cashel dodging his footsteps. Soon a crowd assembled in the center of the clearing, aware that something momentous was about to occur.

"Niall," the gallowglass called when he finally saw the boy, his eyes closed and his shoulder swathed in bloody cloth, reclining against a boulder.

"Devlin," he cried with a wan and weary smile.

"I am sorry for your loss," Devlin said softly.

"My father died as he would have wished, in the defense of his people," Niall stated simply. Pain was imprinted on his young face along with a manly attempt to mask it.

A hush grew among those gathered as Devlin drew his sword. Without a word, he knelt in front of Niall, extending the weapon to him in homage.

"I offer you my service, chieftain of the MacMahons, and pledge you my fealty."

Surprise lit Niall's eyes for a brief instant, and murmuring rumbled through the crowd. But before the lad could muster a response, Cashel lashed out.

"Are you daft, Fitzhugh? There's not a man here would place his safety and that of his family in the hands of a mere babe. 'Tis I who shall lead the clan."

"Niall has learned much under his father's tutelage," Devlin proclaimed loudly. "He will learn more from the advice of the older, more experienced men among us. Mark you, he will make a fine chieftain."

"When? A score of years from now?" Cashel inquired in derision.

"I place my trust in him," Devlin announced. He stood once more, but did not return his sword to its scabbard.

"And which of us would trust you?" Cashel mocked. "Listen to him, men! Remember, not only is he an outsider, but 'twas he brought the Englishwoman here, giving her countrymen a reason to butcher us!"

Affirmative mutterings flew through the assembly,

frightening Alyssa. But they died out beneath Devlin's strident voice.

"The woman had nothing to do with this," he cried. "We were a hunted people 'ere ever she joined our band."

"And we were able to conceal ourselves from our foes until she appeared," Cashel appealed to his kin, sensing he had every opportunity to win them over. "Did you know that Fitzhugh and the woman have been communicating with her sire, who is, I remind you, Elizabeth's own representative? Think you that might have something to do with the English suddenly discovering our hiding place?"

Angry shouts arose and several of the men made ready to attack Devlin, but the warrior, proud and brave, held his ground until Niall interjected.

"Hold!" the boy bellowed forcefully, scrambling to his feet, ready to bend the truth to save his friend. "Aye, Devlin and Alyssa contacted Cecil Howett, but it was with my father's knowledge and consent. Devlin has done nothing untoward."

"'Twas done without Eamon's knowledge and you know it!" Cashel shouted at his cousin, furious with the boy for exhibiting some cunning. He hadn't expected it of him.

"And I say that is not the case," Niall challenged, daring the other man to contradict him again. "But you, Cashel, how did you learn of this?"

"Why, Eamon told me, of course."

It was a lie. Both Devlin and Niall knew it, but they could offer the clan no proof, so what would it serve to make the truth of the matter known?

"Did he now?" Devlin asked with deadly softness, his fingers wrapping themselves more tightly around the hilt of his sword.

"He trusted me as he trusted you," Cashel continued. "The difference is I didn't betray him. How was it you were safely out of camp when the English began their slaughter?"

"You common cur! You accuse me?" Devlin longed to throw himself upon Cashel and end his miserable life. But he could not do so when his young friend's future depended on his one advocate remaining calm. With the discipline of a soldier, Devlin stayed where he was, fighting his battle with words rather than weapons.

"Would I leave Muirne here if I had any previous knowledge there was to be bloodshed? How little you know of humanity if you think such to be the case, Cashel MacMahon. Is this the sort of dullard you would choose to safeguard you?" Devlin asked the others.

"No matter what venom this devil's son spews concerning me, you cannot doubt that Eamon wanted Niall to be his successor. Remember that when the English wrenched your lands away and took over your keep, it was Eamon who became the tower of strength you needed for survival. He provided you with shelter and sustenance, and whatever else life demanded. More important, he kept alive your dreams of one day returning to your homes. Do not allow those dreams to die. Do as Eamon wished and accept Niall as your chieftain."

"Very touching," Cashel commented to his kinsmen, "but hardly practical. Are you willing to put yourselves in the hands of this mere boy? Or will you want a man to take control?"

Indecisive murmurs began to surface and drift through the clearing. Devlin looked around him with scorn and once more his voice rose above the others. "You loved and respected Eamon MacMahon. Remember, it is in Niall's veins that his blood runs. Now who will join me in swearing fealty?"

He dropped to his knees once more, his sword held before him. For a moment, there was nothing but silence enshrouding the campsite. Then, one man knelt and then another. One by one they fell to their knees, ready to pledge their service, indeed their lives, to Eamon's son. Finally, only Cashel, of all the warriors, remained on his feet. Seeing himself defeated so soundly by Devlin Fitzhugh, he followed the example of the rest, his heart overflowing with bitter hatred.

"I thank you for your vows of loyalty," Niall proclaimed, his young face serious as he assumed so heavy a mantle of responsibility. "In return, I pledge my life's blood in the service of our people. Rise, kinsmen."

The men complied, and Devlin looked on proudly as the lad was transformed into a man before his eyes.

"We cannot remain here," the new MacMahon informed them, ready to issue his first order. "Though I long to take revenge upon my father's murderers, we must heal and regain our strength before we can attempt such an undertaking. Pack what is left of your belongings. We leave this day for a site at the northwest tip of the Slieve Bloom Mountains. I have seen a place there that will offer us shelter and food aplenty.''

"Surely we do not have to take so drastic an action," Cashel argued. Until such time as he could reach him, the clan's new location would be unknown to his English contact.

"That is my decision," Niall said, silencing his cousin with a fiery glare. "Kevin and Seamus, you are to ride to Andrew's people and the other surrounding clans. Deliver the news of our departure and our new whereabouts to them. We have to keep our alliances strong. Should they need us, or we them, they will know where to find us. Leave now. The rest of you, prepare for our journey.''

The men began to move off to do as they had been directed.

"Devlin, a word," Niall called, sounding very much like his father.

"My lord?"

"I thank you for what you did, and hope I can rely upon you for guidance," Niall said, grasping the gallowglass's shoulder in friendship.

"Aye, my lord," Devlin replied with a smile. "I have pledged all I am to you and yours.''

"'Tis a sad day that has called upon you for such a vow."

"Aye. What was the damage?"

"Seven men slain, two women, three babes. Others are missing, Roisin among them. The bastards came in from the north long before sunrise.''

"From the north, you say?" A suspicion began to

form in Devlin's mind, but he dismissed it. Not even Cashel would fall into league with the English.

"Aye. But we've another matter to discuss. Tell me, did you carry out my father's order concerning Cecil Howett?" the younger man asked, his face filled with concern.

"Nay. We, too, were attacked by English soldiers ere I had a chance to do so. But I must be honest with you, Niall. Had the Englishman presented us with no harm, I could not have done as Eamon commanded."

"'Tis just as well," Niall stated, looking in Alyssa's direction. "But if we ever uncover evidence of Howett's involvement in the raid upon our camp, know I will order his death."

"If such proof surfaces, my lord, I will slit his throat myself," Devlin vowed, his face grim. Then he left to see to the welfare of his women.

Chapter Seventeen

It was a sennight later that Cashel stood by the new enclosure for the horses, securing the last of the posts needed to pen the animals near enough to the lake to make watering them easy. The move from their old site had been an arduous one, with the clan in mourning for their dead and Niall being so obstinate about the requirements of their new camp.

He'd demanded a location on high ground, with ready water, a defensible terrain, and space for individual huts as well as a communal fire. Traveling to such a place hadn't been easy but the MacMahon would settle for nothing less and finally, halfway up one of the Slieve Bloom Mountains, they'd stopped. Then, the real work of setting up camp had begun for man, woman and child alike.

Even the youngest babe had been put to work clearing the central area of weeds and stones or gathering wood while the women helped cut brush and tote unwanted tree limbs and branches out of the way. With Devlin and Niall seemingly watching his every move, and never content unless he was doing the work of three, Cashel especially had been obliged to labor in uncommon ways. He was a warrior, he'd protested, not one who should be set to building fences or setting stones for the campfires. But it had been to no avail, he fumed, recalling Niall's last instructions.

"Fitzhugh's seen more battles than you and he makes no objection, so put a hand to it. And make certain the fence posts are well down into the earth, far enough that the horses won't dislodge them during a storm. After you've finished that, take your mount and ride a half day north of here and circle back around. Take note of the surrounding property and which clans abide there, but say nothing of the MacMahons yet. We've need of information before we give any."

In truth, Niall had taken to the role of the Mac-Mahon much too readily, always quick with a word of criticism or another order to be carried out. Cashel couldn't honestly accuse the boy of being a shirker, since he worked as hard as the rest, but then again, why did everyone have to work so hard, so steadily? It wasn't as if the labor would ever be finished. Any new site always needed improvements, and by the time they were completed, it would be time to move on to avoid the English. At least that was how it *had been* until now. Soon, he'd change the routine, but first he had to get rid of Fitzhugh.

As long as the upstart gallowglass was acting as Niall's adviser, the lad would hold the reins of the MacMahon clan, but once Fitzhugh was gone, Niall could either adhere to Cashel's guidance or suffer a fatal accident. And once the clan was Cashel's, he'd bring them under control and collect the purse the English had guaranteed him. With gold enough in his pocket, being a chieftain would be a pleasant pastime, considered Eamon's nephew.

But how to eliminate Fitzhugh? Only his daughter and the English wench held any sway with him, and the woman avoided Cashel like the plague. The daughter was the key, he mused, turning the idea over in his head. If the brat disappeared, Fitzhugh would move heaven and earth to find her—and if the English had her, the fool would probably walk into Hampton Court to guarantee her safety.

The more the disgruntled Irishman considered his scheme, the more he liked it. He could grab Fitzhugh's bastard when she played around the compound later that morning, tell her he was taking her to her father or Alyssa and deliver her to his contact at Knockton Keep. He'd be back before anyone noticed he was missing. After all, hadn't Niall commanded him to survey the surrounding lands? No one would know he'd left with a small passenger and returned without her.

Yes, it would work, Cashel grinned. Fitzhugh was enough of a doting father to risk anything, to sacrifice everything for the girl and that was exactly what he'd have to do—giving free rein in the camp to Cashel. Without his mentor, Niall would crumple as leader and the others would fall in line, too. Rubbing his hands together, Cashel congratulated himself. If he played it right, he might even get Alyssa as part of the deal. Now that Roisin was gone, he found he missed having a woman around, but money would soon take care of that.

"Liam, are you certain you haven't seen Muirne?" Alyssa asked the child later that same day. Kneeling in front of him, she tried to keep her fear from coloring her voice. "You two wouldn't be playing a trick on me, would you, making me look for Muirne while she's safe and sound somewhere?"

But the boy just shook his head and scurried behind his mother, hiding his face in her skirt. He clearly wasn't going to divulge any secrets, were there any to tell. That was the problem with children, Alyssa mused, one never knew what was a game and what was serious trouble.

She hadn't worried when Muirne didn't return to the hut for the midday meal since the children often played together, fed by whichever woman was closest. Now, though, it was getting toward evening and Alyssa was beginning to feel anxious, especially with Devlin out on patrol and not due back until late.

"Muirne didn't try to follow her father, did she?" Alyssa suddenly remembered the girl's disappointment at not being able to ride with Devlin that morning and wondered if she could have decided to go after him.

"Look here, my lad said he hasn't seen the child," said his mother. "No matter how young, when an Irishman says something, that's the truth of it. She's not been around."

Alyssa didn't know where else to turn unless perhaps Sinead would have an idea of where Muirne was. Hopefully, she headed in the direction of the woman's half-completed hut.

"Sinead, I've got to find her before it gets dark. She doesn't know the lay of the land around here yet and could have fallen into a stream—or be lost and hungry out there alone," she beseeched the old woman. "What can I do that I haven't thought of?"

"Are you sure she's not just asleep in the woods or—"

"I've been searching everywhere for the past few hours and the fact the Liam hasn't seen her really concerns me. You know how she usually torments him. In fact, he must have had ten or twenty flowers ready to give her, but his mother said they hadn't seen her since shortly after we broke fast this morning."

"Her pony?"

"Is still in the pen with the other horses. I've already looked," admitted Alyssa. "I don't know what I'll do if she's hurt or worse—"

"All right, child, calm yourself. I'll speak to the clan and convince everyone to search for her."

"It's almost dark—"

"If we don't find her tonight, she'll turn up in the morning, hungry and dirty, no doubt, but full of stories," Sinead assured the Englishwoman. "Never have a doubt. The faerie folk will watch over her. They've a liking for children."

So have I, admitted Alyssa to herself. *I love her almost as much as I love her father and that love knows no bounds.*

But, try as they might, man and woman alike, no one found a trace of Muirne before night fell. Alyssa

wandered the woods even after everyone else had retired, calling the girl's name in the blackness of the
forest until Niall persuaded her to rest by the fire so
she would be able to search at first light of dawn.

To her amazement, Devlin placed no blame on her
shoulders, but simply held her as she wept, castigating
herself for not watching the girl more closely.

"Alyssa, dearling, except for me, no one cares
more for Muirne than you and I know you'd do anything you could for her. Just say a prayer that she'll
be all right, and trust. That's what I've done in the
rough spots of my life, and it's never turned out too
badly," soothed Devlin. "Besides, the faerie folk like
children."

"That's what Sinead told me," Alyssa admitted.

"Believe her. Get some rest and we'll head out
again at dawn," instructed the gallowglass. Trying to
ignore a sinking feeling, he sat quietly holding Alyssa
until she dozed. But, in his heart, Devlin was aware
that the child knew better than to wander away from
camp alone. All of the youngsters were taught that
from the earliest age. It didn't mean harm had nec-
essarily befallen her, he tried to tell himself, but it
certainly didn't make for an easy night.

Alyssa caught sight of a patch of brown beneath
the fronds of fern and her heart began to hammer.
Maybe—

But no, as she moved toward the patch of greenery,
a large rabbit scooted away, fleeing the intrusive human, and Alyssa let out a deep sigh. It was more than

twenty-four hours since anyone had seen the child and the longer Alyssa looked, the more frightened she was becoming. Devlin might not blame her, but she carried enough guilt of her own not to need his condemnation to feel any worse.

"Muirne," she called. "Everyone is worried about you, dear. Come out or answer me if you can."

That was her biggest fear, that the child was hurt and unable to call for help. A frightened stag or boar could easily maul a little girl.

"Muirne…"

"I didn't think you were supposed to reveal your hiding place in the game," said Cashel. He sat astride his horse on the path behind her. "Or has Fitzhugh's whelp run away?"

"Muirne is missing, as you'd know if you had been in camp," snapped Alyssa.

"I was but obeying my liege's command to survey his lands," defended the Irishman. His eyes narrowed as he considered Alyssa's remarks. Could she suspect him? "Of course I haven't a woman's willing body to survey like Fitzhugh. Maybe the brat was just jealous of you and took off."

Worried as Alyssa was, she couldn't abide Cashel's crude remarks. Still, as she turned away, common sense halted her retreat. Despised or not, the fellow could provide another pair of eyes to search.

"Since you've returned, won't you help us find her?"

"Me? As far as I'm concerned, she can stay lost forever. It will mean one less mouth to feed during the worst of winter," said Eamon's foster son. "Besides, I've been riding since dawn yesterday and Niall is awaiting my report. I'm no child's nursemaid, especially when the brat is Fitzhugh's. Now, step aside and let me pass.''

Alyssa would never be able to explain what made her act so irrationally, but rather than moving, she reached up and took hold of Cashel's reins.

"You must help," she demanded. "Pretend you're a man, for God's sake and have pity on the lost child.''

"Out of my way, you bloody English whore," cursed Cashel, leaning down to remove her hands and reclaim his reins. But, as he bent to do so, his sleeve caught on the ceremonial pin Devlin had placed on her tunic and the material split.

In the instant before he clasped the torn fabric together, Alyssa had seen enough. There, high on the forearm had been clear evidence of a bite—a bite made by a very small mouth.

"You took her, didn't you?" she charged in amazement. "You took Muirne and she didn't want to go with you, so she bit you—"

"And what if I did? You'll never live long enough to tell anyone about it," promised Cashel. Dropping quickly from the saddle, he blocked her path.

"What could you want with an innocent child?" Alyssa was too furious to be afraid. Cashel had caused problems in Dublin Castle during Niall's rescue. Indeed, he'd been the bane of her existence often enough, trying to make trouble between her and Devlin, but to take a babe like Muirne made no sense. "Why?"

She wanted answers as much as she wanted to live, and maybe answers would allow Devlin time enough to join her. He was going to circle this way if he hadn't found Muirne on the other side of the pond, she recalled and from the expression on Cashel's face, that was unlikely.

"Why? Because she was a way to get to your precious Devlin. That's why. Word has been leaked to the other clans and will filter back here that Muirne's a guest of the English at Knockton Keep. If Devlin doesn't surrender himself in exchange for her by the next full moon, she'll be transported to an English jail."

"She's not yet four years old," objected Alyssa. Prison was terrible for Devlin, but for a bright energetic youngster like Muirne? "How could you allow that to happen?"

"Allow it? I caused it. She's Fitzhugh's bastard, that's reason enough."

"And if he does surrender?"

"Then the child will be fostered with some English family, he'll be executed and I'll be chieftain—"

"But Niall—"

"—won't have the power or intelligence to lead for long if Fitzhugh isn't around. You saw for yourself, the men in the clan follow his lead rather than Niall's. With Fitzhugh gone, there'll be no one to oppose me and I'll be the MacMahon, finally."

"And you arranged Eamon's death and the raid on the camp?" asked Alyssa, her voice horrified.

"And the attack at Kilross as well but, unfortunately, you and Fitzhugh escaped. Otherwise I could have blamed the two of you for the raid. Enough talk, Alyssa. It's time you took a final walk in the woods.''

"No, Devlin knows where I am," she claimed, inching away from the villain. She couldn't lose her life without alerting the others to Cashel's crimes. Maybe, if she ran—

"But he doesn't know that I'm here," Cashel countered. "When we find your body, it will be assumed that whoever took Fitzhugh's daughter murdered you.''

He easily outpaced Alyssa and placed his hands on her shoulders, one on either side of her neck, his thumbs in the soft hollow at its base.

"What if Devlin and I were to leave camp and not say anything about your treachery?''

"I fear, Alyssa, you don't know your man very well if you think he could abide that. No, you'll leave camp all right, in death's chariot," promised the warrior.

Moving his hands closer together, he began to squeeze the breath from Alyssa's throat, preparing to crush her windpipe. Even while she scratched at his face, he held firm, exerting all the force he could summon.

She was a bloody whore, deserving of nothing more than death, he told himself, ignoring the accusation in her eyes. Devil's divine, she wouldn't give up, he cursed, shaking her by the neck to speed her demise.

"Alyssa! I've found no sign of her," called Devlin from beyond the trees. "Muirne? Alyssa?''

"Damn you, die," cried Cashel, desperate that

Alyssa should breathe her last before Devlin arrived. "Die, I said!"

But, in the fog enveloping her brain, Alyssa heard Devlin calling to her. She hung on, struggling to remain conscious, fighting Cashel with every ounce of strength that remained. Reaching up, she clawed at the hands doing such damage to her throat, determined to outlive the bastard who held her. Yet, despite her best efforts, everything was fading as she heard Devlin's shout.

"Let her go! Cashel, this is our fight, not hers—"

Then, suddenly, she was free, falling to the ground and gasping for air as a struggle erupted around her. The primitive sounds of men fighting filled the forest. Curses, grunts and the clanging of steel surrounded her, but all Alyssa could do was survive the pain each ragged breath cost her. If she didn't tell Devlin about Muirne, he'd never know. She had to stay alive that long at least, she told herself—Muirne had no one else who could help.

Devlin spared a glance at the spot where Alyssa lay gulping for air, saw her struggle through the simple act of taking a breath and made up his mind. He fought like a man possessed.

"Cashel, you bastard, I'll kill you," he vowed.

"Kill me and you'll still feel my sting." Cashel laughed, half-mad with the disappointment of his dreams gone bad. Slashing his sword wildly at Devlin, he struck only air as the gallowglass put his knife in under Cashel's ribs.

He gave a slight moan and slid to the forest floor

as Devlin stood and looked toward the one woman who meant the world to him.

Alyssa managed to stand and stumble into Devlin's arms. Tears streamed down her face and her breathing was no easier.

Ignoring his own injuries, he tried to soothe her, his hands tenderly sweeping her body. But she would have none of his attentions as she fought to fill her lungs with air enough to tell him of Muirne's fate.

Finally, she was able to relate the story, and she watched Devlin's loving countenance turn grim. The deadly glint in his eyes said that he wished he could resurrect Cashel in order to kill him all over again. Reverting to the fierce warrior who had first stolen her maiden's heart, Devlin was a man to behold. But it was no longer his physical prowess and brute strength that called to Alyssa. Instead, it was the workings of his loyal, selfless heart, a heart she now understood as well as she did her own.

"We should hasten back to camp," Alyssa urged, trying to offer Devlin hope. "You can gather the men and ride off to rescue our little one."

Devlin regarded her with sadness and love reflected in his eyes.

"Nay," he told her gently. "Our warriors have not recovered enough to engage in any battle."

"Then go to Andrew's clan or one of the others," she persisted.

"'Twould take too long to gather forces," he tried to explain. "And in the end 'twould do no good. Knockton Keep is impregnable. Otherwise it would not have stood for so long in our midst under English rule.''

"What will you do?'' she asked, terror clutching at her heart, knowing what he had been trying to tell her before the question ever left her lips.

"What they want,'' he said simply.

"I'm going with you.''

"Nay, sweetling. The danger—''

"Hush. To take me back to camp would add at least a half day to your journey. And I would only follow you. Besides, I may be of help.''

"You could bring Muirne back to Niall, if you think you could manage such,'' Devlin conceded.

The idea of leaving Knockton Keep without him sent dread and despair racing through her blood. But she would not allow her love to face whatever fate held for him standing alone. She would be beside him, whether he liked it or not.

"I can manage,'' Alyssa responded, her voice catching.

"That's my lass.'' Devlin squeezed her hand in reassurance. He was too honest, however, to use words to set her heart at ease.

Gazing into Alyssa's anxious face, there was so much he wanted to say, but he didn't know how. To tell her that he wanted her as his one true wife, that he had meant to seek a priest to say the words if she had agreed to accept him, seemed a bittersweet thing. It was better left unsaid. After all, she was the woman of a rebel outlaw. Perhaps she had known all along it would come to this. Yet of a certainty, neither of them had thought the day of reckoning would arrive so soon.

"Alyssa," Devlin began, his words thick and his throat dry. "Understand that I have no choice. I have to go."

"I know, Devlin Fitzhugh. And for that reason, I will not ask you to stay." The brave smile Alyssa wore was betrayed by the unshed tears glistening in her eyes.

Without further discussion, Devlin helped her onto Cashel's horse and then mounted his own. A wistful look passed between them. It was filled with an awareness of time slipping away, a yearning for days spent together that would not be. Then they rode off, somberly setting themselves to the task at hand.

Alyssa and Devlin stood at the edge of a grove of trees, their horses concealed from sight. A meadow stretched before them, and at its far side rose Knockton Keep, dark and formidable.

"Stay hidden until you see Muirne coming this way. When she reaches you, mount her on your horse and flee," Devlin directed stoically.

"My first and only love," Alyssa murmured, her fingers entwined in his as though she could not bear to let him go.

"You are my one true love, Alyssa Howett. Do not forget that, or me." Devlin bent his head to hers and possessed Alyssa's lips with a savage sweetness that mingled joy at having found her, with despair at bidding her farewell.

"As if I ever could." Alyssa sobbed softly when

he suddenly tore himself away and walked across the meadow with only a single, backward glance.

Coming near to the castle, he called out, announcing his arrival with a defiant roar.

"Usurper of the keep, I understand you have my daughter. Send her forth."

A cultured English voice rang out. "Only when you surrender, you lawless Irish bastard. When I order the portcullis raised, you are to enter unarmed."

"Nay, you will bring the child out to me. Once I see her running free and unharmed to the far side of the meadow, I will throw down my sword and deliver myself to you."

"I'll have none of your tricks. My men and I will meet you halfway. A regiment of soldiers will guarantee you won't escape after the brat's released."

"As you wish," Devlin replied with a curt nod of his head. "But save the lives of your men, and do not attempt any treachery."

The portcullis was raised and the soldiers stepped out, a squirming Muirne carried aloft by the burliest of the Englishmen.

"Father!" she cried from a distance, Elizabeth's troops drawing closer with each instant.

"Muirne!" Devlin drank in the sight of her, impressing her baby features upon his heart, an image he could carry with him to his death. But he was distracted from his purpose by the sound of footsteps, running towards him from behind. He whirled around.

"Stay back, lass," he hissed as Alyssa approached him.

"Don't be angry with me, my love," Alyssa

begged, reaching out to grasp his hand. "I had to know your touch, hear your voice, one last time. When the moment comes that I must leave you, I will do as I have promised. But until then, permit us to be together, savoring each dwindling second left to us."

In answer, Devlin wrapped his arm around Alyssa's waist, rejoicing in the feel of her. It was a sensation he had thought behind him forever. Yet too soon, the English soldiers stood before them, their formation parting to reveal a smug Earl of Knockton. And there, beside him, was Cecil Howett. His face was stern, his demeanor forbidding as he looked with scorn upon the couple standing in the meadow.

The fact that he was alive, and apparently in league with the Earl of Knockton, condemned him in the matter of the attack at Kilross as well. Devlin's arm tightened protectively around Alyssa while her misery at losing her gallowglass grew more bitter still. But before she could voice her anger, Cecil Howett began to rant and rave.

"What is the meaning of this?" he demanded. "This man is not Devlin Fitzhugh!"

Gathering her wits, Alyssa subtly ran her fingertips across dry lips, praying Muirne would remember their pact. To her relief, the child remained silent, though it was obvious she was near to bursting, wanting to refute the matter of her father's identity.

"Are you certain?" Knockton asked in surprise.

"Of course I am. Didn't I have the man under lock and key in Dublin Castle? Didn't the scoundrel take my daughter with him when he escaped? Think you this mere Irish wench is my offspring?'' he demanded contemptuously. "Why, she is no more relation to me than this peasant is Fitzhugh.''

"But the child called him father,'' Knockton argued.

"He probably is,'' Cecil replied unruffled. "But evidently the girl does not belong to Fitzhugh.''

"That's not what Cashel MacMahon said when he delivered the brat to us.''

"That fawning knave! From what you have told me, his schemes rarely work. Did it do any good to ambush the MacMahon's son and hold him captive, a plan hatched and bungled by your Irish toady? Did the raid he orchestrated set him up as the new chieftain making the MacMahons loyal subjects of the queen as he promised? No! Now either Cashel MacMahon has played you false, or else in his haste to ingratiate himself with you, he abducted the wrong child. Whatever the case, you'll have to try something else to bring Fitzhugh to heel. As it is, you are fortunate I chanced to cross your threshold this morning. Had I not, you would have executed the wrong man and been made to appear the fool when Fitzhugh appeared elsewhere.''

"If this is true, why did you pretend to be the outlaw we are seeking?'' Knockton demanded of Devlin.

"I never said who I was, your lordship,'' the gallowglass replied calmly. "I merely asked for the return of my child. 'Twas you who required my surrender, though for what crime, I could not for the life of me imagine.''

"But he has the appearance of a warrior,'' said the

earl, considering Fitzhugh. "Killing one Irish soldier is almost as good as killing another."

"Fie! He has the look of a peasant farmer. From the size of him, I wager he pulls the plow himself."

"Then what are we to do with him?"

"Do with him? Why give him back his brat and send him on his way—unless you want more Irish mouths to feed. But take my word for it, imprison him and there'll be nothing in it for you—no glory, no gratitude from the queen—only added expense."

"Hand them their bastard," Knockton ordered in disgust, "and see to it that they leave my lands at once. I'll not have them poaching my game or picking fruit from my orchards before they depart."

"I give you my word we'll leave immediately," Devlin promised.

"Bah! The word of a peasant farmer—what good is that?"

Alyssa eagerly held out her arms for Muirne, hugging the child as tenderly as if she were her own.

"There, woman! You have what you came for. Now be gone," Cecil Howett directed. But when he turned his back on Alyssa to return to the keep, his daughter boldly reached out a hand to touch his sleeve.

He spun around and Alyssa noted her father's eyes held a misty film to match her own.

"God's blessings on you, kind sir," she said humbly, imitating the melodic cadence of the Mac-Mahons. "I'll hold you dearly in my heart until the day I die."

"And well you should," Cecil muttered pompously after clearing his throat. "Now leave and don't dawdle before we change our minds and take all three of you into custody for trespassing."

As Alyssa watched, the ranks of soldiers closed behind her father, and Cecil Howett disappeared from view.

Devlin, his arm still draped around Alyssa, gently steered his family away from Knockton Keep. They crossed the meadow a tight-knit little group, glad to be together once more.

As Devlin settled Muirne on his horse before swinging himself up into the saddle, the child looked at the adults frantically.

"You can talk now, dearest," Alyssa said, reading the child's mind. Still trying to deal with the poignancy of what had just occurred, she welcomed the distraction of Muirne's innocent chatter.

"I didn't talk to the English," she announced proudly.

"You're a fine, smart lass," Devlin told her.

"But who was that man who said you weren't Devlin Fitzhugh?"

"That, Muirne, is the most decent Englishman I've ever met," Devlin said, picking up his reins and directing his answer as much to Alyssa as to his child. "An Englishman who loves his daughter as much as I love you. Think of him as your grandsire if you will."

Epilogue

The casual song of the birds overhead indicated that the clan had been accepted in their new surroundings by the creatures of the forest, Devlin reflected. The muscles of his bare arms rippled while he worked, his efforts copied by others throughout the developing compound, men also following Niall's orders. It would seem that the young MacMahon had been accepted, too.

Devlin smiled at the thought, his single dimple deepening raffishly while his nimble hands put the finishing touches on his family's dwelling.

"What a fine place it is!" said Alyssa, coming to stand at his side. She slipped her arm lovingly around Devlin's waist, resting her head against him while she admired the construction his love had built.

"'Tis less than you deserve." He placed a kiss at her temple.

"And more than I need to make me happy," she assured him. "It stands so large and sturdy."

"We'll be glad of the room in time to come," Devlin promised, a wicked gleam in his eye. He chuckled when Alyssa reddened. "You wear a blush most becomingly, my love. I am certain that on the morrow the priest Niall has summoned will find you the most fetching bride ever to be wed."

"Only because I will have the handsomest husband in all of Ireland."

"Are my looks the only reason you agreed to be my wife?" he teased, encircling her in his arms.

"Nay. 'Tis whispered around the communal fire that nowhere in this land is there a gallowglass as brave, loyal and gallant as Devlin Fitzhugh. I thought I'd marry you to see if there is any truth to the statement."

"Wench!" Devlin bent his head to hers, but before he could deliver the kiss her lips demanded, Muirne came running to them, calling for their attention.

Dressed in a green tunic that was a miniature copy of her father's, she carried a tiny bow and a quiver of blunt-tipped arrows slung over her arm. It would take a bit of mothering to turn this imp into a lady, Alyssa thought with amusement.

"Lyssa! Lyssa! Liam's mother has told me to tell you she has rabbits to stew for the wedding feast, and she wants you to come by to say how you would like them seasoned."

The kind gesture, one of many the MacMahons had shown her of late, gladdened Alyssa's heart. Love, family, friendship—she truly had found a home.

However, by the look of her daughter, it seemed as if one of its occupants was a bit disturbed at present. Usually talkative and active, Muirne stood regarding her father and Alyssa pensively.

"Out with it, my little hedgehog," Alyssa gently commanded, reaching to ruffle the youngster's hair. "What is it has set you at odds?"

"Liam! He said that if you had a baby he hoped it would be a boy so that he would have someone to help keep me in line. Promise, Lyssa, promise you won't do that!"

"'Twould make no difference, sweetling. There's not a man alive who could tame you," Devlin commented with mock despair.

"And you tell Liam that when there is a babe, it could very well be a girl, and then he'd have two of you to contend with," Alyssa added.

"Poor devil! I know what that's like." A laughing Devlin stood firm in the face of Alyssa's playful nudge. Quite taken with her, he turned to his future bride once more. "Now where was I?" he asked, his mouth descending to hover over hers.

"Father, why are you kissing Lyssa now? 'Tis not time for bed," Muirne protested, shaking her head at his silliness before she ran off to find Liam.

"Oh yes, it is," Devlin murmured in Alyssa's ear, his hands drawing her closer in urgent invitation. "It most definitely is."

* * * * *

Four Bright New Stars!
Harlequin Historical™
launches its **March Madness**
celebration with these four exciting
historical romance debuts:

THE MAIDEN AND THE WARRIOR
By Jacqueline Navin
A fierce warrior is saved by the love of a spirited
maiden bride.

LAST CHANCE BRIDE
By Jillian Hart
A lonely spinster finds hope in the arms of an embittered
widower.

GABRIEL'S HEART
By Madeline George
An ex-sheriff must choose between revenge or the feisty
socialite who has stolen his heart.

A DUKE DECEIVED
By Cheryl Bolen
A handsome duke falls for a penniless noblewoman
whom he must marry in haste.

Look for all four books from four fabulous new authors
wherever Harlequin Historicals are sold.

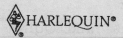

KEY TO MY HEART

Unlock the secrets of romance just in time for the most romantic day of the year— Valentine's Day!

Key to My Heart
features three of your favorite authors,

Kasey Michaels,
Rebecca York
and Muriel Jensen,

to bring you wonderful tales of romance and Valentine's Day dreams come true.

As an added bonus you can receive Harlequin's special Valentine's Day necklace. FREE with the purchase of every *Key to My Heart* collection.

Available in January,
wherever Harlequin books are sold.

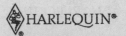

WELCOME TO *Love Inspired* ™

A brand-new series of contemporary inspirational love stories.

Join men and women as they learn valuable lessons about facing the challenges of today's world and about life, love and faith.

Look for the following February 1998
Love Inspired™ titles:

A Groom of Her Own
by Irene Hannon

The Marriage Wish
by Dee Henderson

The Reluctant Bride
by Kathryn Alexander

Available in retail outlets
in January 1998.

LIFT YOUR SPIRITS AND GLADDEN YOUR HEART with *Love Inspired* ™!

Steeple
Hill™

LI298

**Look for these titles—
available at your favorite retail outlet!**

**BORN IN THE USA: Love, marriage—
and the pursuit of family!**

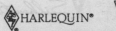 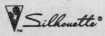

Look us up on-line at: http://www.romance.net

BUSA4

Where were you when the storm blew in?

Snowbound

Three stormy stories about what happens to three snowbound couples, from three of your favorite authors:

SHOTGUN WEDDING by Charlotte Lamb

MURDER BY THE BOOK by Margaret St. George

ON A WING AND A PRAYER by Jackie Weger

Find out if cabin fever can melt the snow this December!

Available wherever Harlequin and Silhouette books are sold.

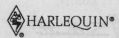 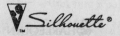